THE DEVIL YOU KNOW

JAMES P. SUMNER

BOTH
barrels
PUBLISHING

THE DEVIL YOU KNOW

First Edition published in 2021 by Both Barrels Publishing Ltd.

Copyright © James P. Sumner 2021

Editing and Cover Design by: bothbarrelsauthorservices.com

ISBNs:
978-1-914191-16-9 (Paperback)

Visit the author's website: jamespsumner.com

Quick, even for me...

THE DEVIL YOU KNOW

ADRIAN HELL: BOOK 9

1

———

There's an old saying about the definition of madness—that it's doing the same thing over and over again, expecting different results. Yet here I am, wondering what the fuck I'm doing for, at minimum, the sixth time in the last two years.

This time will be different, right?

Yeah... *right*.

A little under three weeks ago, I was sitting in a bar in Tokyo, minding my own business and enjoying a nice, cold beer. I tried to do *one* honorable thing and wound up sitting *here*, still finding it painful to take a deep breath.

I guess I'll never learn.

Besides, it's not like I had a choice. It wasn't fate that shaped my journey this time. It was a phone call from a friend in a high place. Well, perhaps *friend* is a bit much. But still... I couldn't exactly say no.

I'm just thankful that Ruby has been so understanding. She nursed me back to health after the yacht explosion. She stood by me without hesitation when I was asked to leave Tokyo. She said as long as she was with me, she didn't care where we were.

She then teased me for the duration of the flight about my fear of heights. I stand by that fear, given my history of things going to shit whenever my feet leave the ground.

Honestly, she's just like Josh—only hot and far more open to sleeping with me.

I smile to myself as my mind wanders off to a memory of my old friend. I forget where we were. Possibly Florida. It was warm. We were checking into a motel on the outskirts of the city. I was there to work a contract. Josh was always in charge of the logistics and the admin. He was usually good at it too. But on this particular occasion, he had booked us into a motel when a gay rights protest was in town. The receptionist saw two guys checking in and assumed, I guess. We got to the room to find one king-sized bed and flowers on the nightstand. I seem to recall a lot of eyerolling on my part. But Josh... oh, he loved it. Camped it up the entire stay, insisting that he would be the big spoon.

I took the floor, which he said was a gentlemanly thing to do. Then he reminded me that I wouldn't stand a chance with him anyway.

After the job was done, we left town. On the way out of the motel lot, he played *It's Raining Men* on the radio.

He was a dick, but he always made situations fun. Never took himself or this life too seriously. Sometimes I think he only did it for my benefit. I was in a dark place then. He knew his job was to keep me from eating a bullet long enough to get through it. I remember when we got back in touch, after The Order had sent me to kill him, thinking how stressed out he looked. How tired he was. Understandable, given he was running GlobaTech at the time, but I remember wondering if that's just how he was without the burden of keeping me entertained.

I miss him. Every goddamn day.

I snap back into the here and now at the sound of a friendly, female voice.

"Sir, you can go in now."

I look over at the secretary, who's sitting behind the desk opposite me.

"Hmm?"

She smiles patiently and points to the dark oak door behind her. "I said you can go through. The president is waiting for you."

I let out a quiet sigh of resignation. No turning back now.

"Right. Thank you."

The chair in the large vestibule outside the Oval Office is a little too comfortable, and I struggle to get out of it. As I stand straight, more things creak and crack on my body than I can identify.

Getting blown up on a boat sucks.

I knock once on the door, then push it open. I pause in the threshold as I take in the Oval Office before me. I liken it to Niagara Falls. It has this mystique about it that never fails to inspire awe.

I glance around at the pictures of former presidents on the wall. At the seal in the middle of the navy carpet. At the Resolute desk and the man sitting behind it.

President Schultz looks over and gestures me inside.

"Come on in, son," he says with that distinctive southern drawl. "You look like a goddamn spare part standing over there."

I smile politely and step inside, closing the door behind

me. He stands as I approach the desk and moves around it to greet me. He extends his hand, which I shake.

"Thanks for coming on such short notice," he says.

I shrug. "Did I really have a choice?"

Schultz smiles. "Not really. But manners cost nothing."

I look around the room again.

"Been a while since I was last here." I nod toward the desk. "I see you managed to get your desk cleaned."

Schultz sighs, frowning. "Yeah. That desk is a hundred and forty years old. A real piece of American history. And you ruined it with a goddamn bloodstain."

"Yeah, but it was a bad guy's bloodstain, so that's okay. Bit of spit shine and varnish and it's as good as new. Besides, that bloodstain helped you get your job." I smile. "You're welcome."

Schultz rolls his eyes. "So you keep reminding me. Not been feeling thankful for it lately."

"Being a politician getting you down, Ryan?"

He points his finger at me. His expression hardens. "Listen to me, you arrogant son'bitch. You get a lot of leeway for reasons still passing my understanding, but in this building, in this room, it's *Mr. President*."

I hold my hands up. "Apologies."

He nods once. "Thank you. I don't give a damn what you think of me personally, but respect the office."

I nod back. "I do... when there's someone inside it worth respecting."

He ignores me and walks over to the sofas in the middle of the room. "Take a seat, son."

I do. He sits opposite.

"I'm gonna cut right to the chase, Adrian. The world's changing. Our way of life is evolving. Many folks still have a long way to go. For others, it's business as usual in unusual

4

times. That's in no small part down to GlobaTech Industries. Their aid, security, and advancements in technology have made recovering from 4/17 achievable in the same lifetime it happened."

I listen intently, waiting for the *but*.

"But..."

There it is.

"...they're also their own worst enemy. Terrorism and warfare are evolving too—and at a rate few people can keep up with. The U.S. military is being left behind. GlobaTech has stopped working its defense contracts. It makes weapons for itself, not for us. Man for man, Buchanan's boys ain't all that far behind our own army. We're losing good men and women to the private sector because they see more action and make more money there.

"On top of that, most of our old enemies are no longer enemies. Hell, some of them are barely even countries anymore. In these unprecedented times of fragile, global peace, I've got more red tape coming out of my ass than ever before. We can't do anything that might offend one of our new allies. Honestly, I don't know if all this is a blessing or a curse."

I shrug. "The fact that we're not at war with anyone is good, surely?"

"You would think. I'm not saying I miss the good ol' days of bombing the Middle East so they don't blow up our buildings, but at least back then, we had an enemy we could fight. Nowadays, GlobaTech do a lot of the fighting. Small time stuff—opportunistic warlords in decimated countries, stolen medical supplies, that kind of thing. The U.N. contract lets them fix those problems without the bullshit I gotta go through to send our troops there."

"And that's a bad thing?"

"In a way. The only battles left to fight are ones our military isn't equipped for. The larger enemies have better weapons and technology, more control over the media, and, therefore, more influence on the public. Hell, son, I could be overthrown by a goddamn Twitter post nowadays."

I sigh. "I feel for you, Ry—Mr. President. I really do. But what does any of this have to do with me?"

"I'm working on an initiative that will give the U.S. government its own version of Buchanan's D.E.A.D. unit. A small team, accountable to no one but me, who can do what needs to be done without the paperwork and the committees. Hidden within an existing system."

I frown. "Why not just borrow Buchanan's? I've heard nothing but good things about them. The big guy hates me, but he's capable. I've spoken to the woman once. She seemed useful. I know Ray. Hell, he's part of the reason I'm able to be here."

Schultz shakes his head. "I can't be seen outsourcing when the going gets tough. It devalues our own military."

I shrug. "You just got through saying our military isn't up to the job anymore. How is that not devaluing them?"

"Our combined forces will once again be seen as the standard in global militia, but it takes time. And honestly, I don't think we have a lot of that. I need a solution now."

I nod. "Okay, but what about all the special forces units you already have? SEALs, Delta, Rangers... countless CIA operatives that no one admits to having. Those guys are elite. Surely, they can do the job?"

Schultz sighs. His expression is strained, probably because he resents the need to have this conversation in the first place. The crow's feet next to his eyes stand out like emblems of a necessary evil.

"Those fellas are the best at a standard of warfare that's

no longer relevant," he says. "The battles being waged are geopolitical. To put it bluntly, we need a smart scalpel, not a dumb hammer."

"Jesus, say what you mean, *sir*."

"I want the best of what we have to be brought together and trained to survive in this new world. I want them to think like our new enemies, to fight them on their terms and win, without anyone knowing we've adapted."

I shift in my seat. "Sounds like a great plan, Mr. President. But I have to ask... why are you telling me?"

Schultz doesn't say anything. He holds my gaze as a long silence falls on the Oval Office.

I look back at him.

Seconds tick by.

...

...

...

Then the penny drops.

He can't mean...

He does, doesn't he?

My shoulders slump forward. I let out a heavy sigh.

"Oh."

2

"You want me to lead this team."

It wasn't a question.

Schultz nods. "I do, son. Your president's calling on you to serve your country."

"But... why? I mean, I'm flattered, but seriously... why? You have SEALs, Marines, those Delta boys... I would think twice about going up against any one of them on my best day, never mind now."

He smiles patiently. "Look, I've always been honest about my opinions on what you do for a living."

"Did."

"Whatever. Whether I like it or agree with it is irrelevant. Fact of the matter is this: on your worst day, you're at least top three in your..." He pauses to clear his throat. "Chosen field. You're perfect for this."

I'm trying hard not to look confused by his logic, but it's difficult.

"That's kind of you to say, Mr. President, but I think you're forgetting that I just got my ass handed to me in front of sixty million people by a girl who isn't old enough to drink. I'm pushing fifty. My worst days aren't as good as they used to be."

He scoffs. "I can't tell if you're trying to be modest, or if you're just plain stupid."

I shrug. "Probably the latter."

"The way you approach things. The way you see situations. It's unique. And it's not just your perspective. It's how you act on what you decide needs to be done. Execution without hesitation—no pun intended."

I let slip a small smile.

"As good as our elite is, they still have limits and restrictions. You don't. That's what I need you to teach these people. That's the only way they will survive long enough in the new world to stop the fight that's coming."

Silence falls. My eyes instinctively narrow at Schultz. This is probably the nicest he's ever been to me. Certainly the most complimentary. He's really giving this the hard sell.

I look closer. He keeps fidgeting with the cuffs of his suit jacket and straightening his stars-and-stripes lapel pin. His smile and friendliness feel forced—not ingenuine but enough to betray his true feelings.

The president's desperate.

"What aren't you telling me?" I ask. "What do you know that I don't?"

Schultz holds my gaze for what feels like an hour.

"Son, the sheer weight of what I know could sink a cruise ship. Unfortunately, a lot of what we have is hearsay and educated guesswork."

I raise an eyebrow. "Educated?"

He pulls a face. "Well, it's NSA intel..."

We exchange a brief smile, sharing a tragic inside joke.

We've both been on the receiving end of the NSA's intelligence gathering in the past. Turns out it wasn't all that accurate. Yes, there were extenuating circumstances, but still... it left a sour taste in our mouths.

He continues. "I'm working closely with Buchanan and GlobaTech to get something more solid. But until we do, we're operating on a worst-case scenario basis. The future of warfare is knocking on our door, Adrian. We need to be able to answer it when the time comes."

"Is it really that bad?"

He shrugs, searching for the words. "If Moses is right, we're looking at a threat to our freedom and security on a scale hitherto unforeseen."

I let out a low whistle and absently scratch the back of my head. "Damn. It must be bad if you're using the word *hitherto*."

Schultz rolls his eyes. "Joke all you want, son. But the storm's a-coming, and we're sailing into it without a lifeboat. We need you."

I have to admit, it's a hell of a pitch. Something definitely has him worried. That isn't enough to make me jump on board, but the fact that Buchanan and GlobaTech are involved and equally spooked gives it more credibility.

But I don't want this. I can still just about walk unaided. After the last few weeks, I want to retire. And not *Tokyo* retire... I mean *actually* retire. Hang up the guns for good and spend my days on a beach, staring at Ruby in a bikini.

Then there's Ruby to consider. She doesn't want the excitement any more than I do. But I also know she would walk through fire if I asked her to.

I need more.

"Tell me about this initiative you mentioned," I say. "And give me the full inside scoop, not your watered-down, redacted bullshit."

Schultz shifts uncomfortably in his seat. "I can't do that unless you agree to come on board. This is beyond top secret."

I shake my head. "I won't agree to anything unless I know everything. I've been down that road with the U.S. government before. Take it or leave it."

He pauses, seemingly weighing up his options.

"Fine," he says with a heavy sigh. "But a word of this leaves this office..."

I hold up a hand, stopping him from making an embarrassing threat we both know he won't—or can't—carry out. "Relax. I'm not going to tell anyone. Chances are I'll be doing all I can to forget this anyway. Just give it to me straight."

He screws his face up in a final moment of indecision, then sighs so hard that he starts coughing. "It's called Project Blackstar. I can count on one hand the people who currently know about it. Including you. There's going to be a committee meeting next week about it. Buchanan's sending someone from GlobaTech to sit in. Someone he trusts."

I nod. "Okay. Well, if you want my opinion, tell him to send Ray Collins. I've worked alongside him a couple of times. There aren't many people in this world I trust, but he's one of them. His input will be valuable."

"Noted," says Schultz.

"What about funding? If Buchanan's D.E.A.D. unit is anything like the CIA one I used to run, the cost of doing that kind of business isn't cheap."

"Money is covered. Don't worry about that."

I raise my eyebrow. "That doesn't sound like full disclosure to me..."

He rolls his eyes. "Jesus Christ. Fine. I'm pulling funding from various military and intelligence projects, both official and otherwise. Internally, there's a lot of reshuffling and downsizing going on within the DoD. We're currently funding things that either aren't needed anymore or don't have as many people as they used to. We've built up a nice little nest egg to play with, so money won't be an issue."

"Don't you have to justify every expense in the budget to the Senate?"

He nods. "We do, and we will. I'm not hiding anything from you, Adrian. That's simply not your problem. You would have an operating budget that would make most countries jealous."

"Okay. And who would I answer to?"

Schultz sits upright in his seat and fixes me with a hard stare.

"Me."

"You and..."

He shakes his head. "Just me. I would seek counsel from the committee and from GlobaTech, but the final word is mine alone. I point you in the direction of the enemy, and you do the job however you want."

My eyes widen involuntarily. "Wow. That's a risky blank check to write me, isn't it? I mean, we've met before, right?"

Schultz shrugs. "Part of the reason you're perfect for this is because you think for yourself. I don't expect you to question any order I give you. But I do know that you would execute that order in the right way. You would do what needed to be done—nothing more, nothing less."

I smile. "That was a compliment, wasn't it? You were just being nice to me."

His expression is like stone. "Don't be an asshole about it, son."

I smile wider. "Sorry. Old habits."

"I might not always agree with what you do, but I must admit... you're a man of unwavering principle. You do what you do because you believe it's right. You don't condone the loss of innocent life. And you certainly don't take issue with putting bullets in people who deserve it. We need you, Adrian. The country needs you. I need you."

I run a hand absently over my beard. It's grown out over the last week or so, thicker than I've ever had it before. It's itchy as hell but oddly comforting. Ruby said she likes it too, which helps.

"How would this work?" I ask. "I mean, I wouldn't know where to start recruiting for something like this. I haven't kept tabs on anyone on this side of things for a long time."

"Glad you asked."

Schultz stands and walks over to his desk. He opens a drawer to the right of his chair and retrieves a small flash drive. He walks back over and holds it out to me. I stand and take it from him.

He points to it in my hand. "That's an encrypted drive with ten classified personnel files on it. Ten of the absolute best this country has to offer, from all branches of the military, official and otherwise. You're to pick three and recruit them. Approach them however you want. Tell them whatever you feel is appropriate and necessary to get them on board."

I stare at the drive in my hand.

I hate these things. Again, nothing good has ever come from me having one.

Schultz points to it again. "Don't access that drive until you're one hundred percent sure you're in. It's programmed to wipe itself twenty-four hours after being opened."

"Huh. Fancy. So, how long do I have to decide?"

He shrugs. "How long do you want?"

I think about it. "Give me a day?"

He nods. "You have one day."

"All right, then." I turn to leave, but another question comes to mind. "Who's your back-up?"

He looks confused. "What do you mean, son?"

"I mean, if I say no, who's your next choice to do this?"

Schultz sits down behind his desk and starts ruffling through some papers in front of him.

"There isn't a second choice," he says without looking up.

"Really?"

He stares at me. "I honestly haven't considered the possibility of you saying no."

"Really?" I say again, chuckling this time. "A little presumptuous, isn't it?"

He shakes his head. "I don't think so. I have a pretty good insight into how you think, son. And I've seen you act on your principles firsthand more times than I care to admit. Something this important... I think we both know you won't say no."

Am I offended by that?

"I'm that predictable, am I?"

He simply smiles at me and nods to the door. "We're done here. I have a meeting with the Portuguese ambassador in five minutes. Call me when you've made your decision."

His abruptness catches me off-guard.

"Right. Well, then... thanks for your time, I guess."

He murmurs something, but I can't make it out. I take

one last look around the room and catch myself reminiscing about the last time I was here.

Those were the days, huh?

I turn and leave, shoving the flash drive into my pocket.

Now to give Ruby that same sales pitch and see what she thinks.

3

The hotel Ruby and I are staying in is on Massachusetts Avenue, just off Dupont Circle. It's a short walk from the White House. I reckon it would usually take around twenty-five minutes at an even pace. It took me a little under twenty because it's mid-November and currently forty-three degrees outside. I didn't think it was possible to be colder and more uncomfortable than I was in Tokyo, but here I am, having the universe prove me wrong yet again.

Can your balls get frostbite?

I open the door to the room. Ruby is lying on the bed, on her front, with her legs bent back in the air, reading a magazine. She's wearing... very little.

I smile.

Her pajama shorts look more like a thong.

She looks over as I close the door and smiles. "Ranulph Fiennes returns."

I roll my eyes and smile a humorless, barely tolerant smile.

She laughs. "So, how did it go? What did Schultz want?"

I shrug my coat off and lie on the bed beside her, hugging my chest and rubbing my arms. I let out a long, painful breath, almost resenting the fact that I have to relay the convoluted explanation Schultz had given me.

"He offered me a job," I say.

Ruby frowns. She pushes herself up so that she's kneeling and sitting back on her heels. "Are you serious?"

I nod. "Sadly, yes."

"I'm guessing he doesn't want you as the new V.P."

"Not quite. He's pretty worried about some big, pending threat. Says he's working with GlobaTech to figure it all out, but he's painfully aware that the U.S. government can't keep up with the advancements in technology and warfare—not like GlobaTech or this apparent new wave of bad guys."

"Okay. So, how can you help with that?"

"He's putting together his own version of Buchanan's D.E.A.D. unit. Y'know, Ray and those guys."

"And he wants you on it?"

I shake my head. "He wants to me to build it."

"You're kidding?"

"Nope. He wants me to recruit three people from a list of the best the DoD and CIA has to offer. Then he wants me to train them and, I think, lead them."

She shifts on the bed so that she's sitting with her legs crossed in front of her. Her expression tells the same story as what's in my head right now—a mix of confusion, concern, excitement, and flattery.

"What did you say?" she asks after a moment.

I shrug. "I said I'd think about it."

"And?"

"And what?"

"What are you thinking?"

I sigh heavily. "I'm thinking we should be on the next plane to anywhere."

She nods patiently. Her eyes search my face, reading me like a book only she can translate.

I raise my eyebrow. "What?"

"Nothing. So, why you specifically? What can you offer this... *super team* that no one else can?"

I sit upright and rest a hand on her leg, absently stroking the soft flesh of her thigh. "Schultz gave me the hard sell. He said the future of warfare is privatized. It's about influence and money, not bullets. He said GlobaTech have been leading the charge for a few years now, leaving most world militaries in the dust. He also said that as we evolve, so do the bad guys. It's at the point now where he genuinely doesn't think his military is equipped to deal with post-4/17 problems. Couple those concerns with whatever he and Buchanan think is brewing, and he's basically running scared."

Ruby stares blankly ahead, processing it all.

"He wants his own D.E.A.D. unit, so the government has at least some skin in the game," I continue. "A small unit answering only to him, which gets to solve problems without politics and bureaucracy getting in the way."

"Just like Ray's team..." she observes. She looks at me with those gorgeous green eyes. "But don't they have countless units like that already? CIA black book-type stuff. SEALs. Deltas. All those people. It's all pretty much limitless counterterrorism, right? What do they need something else for?"

"That's what I said. His argument was that, even though those people have more freedom to do the dirty stuff, they still have limits. They still serve a committee and an agenda. There's no place for that in the new world." I gesture to the TV. "You've seen how the news works nowadays. What use is a ghost with a license to kill when you can topple governments with a fucking tweet?"

Ruby rolls her eyes. "Oh, like *you* know what Twitter is."

"I read about it in a newspaper once." I flip her a one-finger salute and smile. "Schultz has a point. He was... nice to me. It was weird. He complimented me."

"Damn. He must be serious."

"He is. Says I'm the first and only choice to train the limits out of these people. Make them like me."

"And that's a good thing?"

She smiles playfully.

I push her gently away. "Yes, that's a good thing. He said that despite his reservations about the life I lead, he can't ever fault my moral code. He trusts me to make these new people the deadliest threat to terrorism the government has ever had in its arsenal, while keeping them on the right side of the moral debate. I was actually quite touched by that."

Ruby's hand rests on my arm. "You should be. The president's right, y'know? About all of it. You're a great man with a good heart and no issue doing terrible things to those who deserve it. The perfect combination."

She beams at me. I see love and pride in her eyes. I lean forward, and we kiss until my heartrate increases. When she moves away, her expression has changed. It's softened into sympathy and concern.

"Adrian, I have to say something. I want you to know this is one of those times when I'm not being an asshole to amuse myself, okay?"

I smile. "Okay."

She takes a deep breath. "What happened in Tokyo

was... tough. It was tough on everyone involved but especially on you. I love you. I respect you. There are times, even now, when I still actually fear you a little a bit. I'm in awe of who you are and what you're capable of."

I nod, trying not to go red. "But?"

"But... you're only human, and right now, you're recovering from something that has likely changed you forever. Physically and mentally. Are you sure you're up for this?"

I reach out and brush the hair from her face, tracing the back of my hand down her cheek.

"I'm tired and sore, but I'm fine. I'm still me. Miley broke me physically. Of course, she did. Christ, the whole world saw her do it. I'd be an idiot to try and deny that. But mentally?" I tap my left temple with my trigger finger. "I'm as strong as I ever was."

Ruby smiles patiently. "Newsflash, hot shot: you were never that strong mentally, and we both know it."

I glance away. "Yeah. Fair point."

"Let me ask you this. And again, I'm in full *not an asshole* mode here. How are you managing the pain we both know you're still in?"

I know what she's asking me and why. I developed a dependance on the painkillers I was initially given, quickly and completely. They needed to be that strong because I had been beaten to within an inch of my life. But they were addictive. I hit them hard to help me get through the violence I needed to commit. I can't believe how strong Ruby was to stand by me. I wasn't worried that they came close to destroying me. What hurt was how close they came to destroying *us*.

It's a genuine concern, and I'm grateful she asked.

"I'm managing it fine," I say. "Look."

I reach into my back pocket and pull out a thin cardboard box of drugstore painkillers.

"I take them only when I absolutely have to, and even then, I stick to the recommended dose. They're not super effective, but they take the edge off. I'm healing every day, and the stronger I get, the less I need them."

Ruby looks at the box, then back at me. I see her body tense, the way it does when you stop yourself from moving.

I hold the box out to her. "It's okay. Check them."

Reluctantly, she takes the box and looks inside. She sees the two foil sleeves of tablets. One is half-empty.

"I've had them a few days," I add. "See? Only when I have to."

She looks away as a tear escapes down her cheek. She tosses the box aside on the bed and looks at me.

"I'm sorry for asking," she says. "I'm sorry for doubting you. I just—"

I place my hand on the side of her face and use my thumb to softly wipe the tear away. "Hey, you don't have to apologize. I know why you're asking, and I appreciate it. I might make bad choices sometimes, but I learn from my mistakes. It's the only reason I'm still alive after two decades of doing this shit."

Ruby nods and places her hand on mine. She leans into my palm and closes her eyes as a warm smile spreads across her beautiful face. When she opens her eyes again, any sadness and doubt has gone.

"Okay," she says. "So, how does this all work? Where do we start?"

I lean back against the headboard, momentarily holding a hand to my ribs as I search for comfort.

"Well, I haven't said I'll do it yet. I have twenty-four hours to think about it."

"Oh, please. We both know you're going to do it."

"We do?"

She springs to her feet and stands before me, bouncing on the spot like a cheerleader about to start her routine.

"Of course, we do. You'll never turn down the opportunity to prove someone right when they tell you how good you are. Besides, I know better than anyone that when the shit's about to hit the fan, you'll always try to help."

I smile, feeling my cheeks flush a little. "That right?"

She jumps back on the bed, landing on her knees beside me, and rests her hands on my stomach. "Yup. Because despite the fact that you're one of the best assassins to ever live, you know, deep down, that you will always use your wonderfully violent talents to help people."

"I guess."

"I guess? Adrian, where are we right now?"

I look around the room and shrug. "In a hotel."

"Which city, dickhead?"

"Washington."

"Right. And what happened last time you were here?"

"I made the front page of every newspaper in the world before my death was faked by a clandestine organization of assassins who eventually tried to kill me."

Ruby laughs. "Exactly! There are few people who can do what you do. That's why Schultz asked you to do this. And that's why you're going to say yes. This isn't something you will ever allow yourself to walk away from."

I struggle to my feet and walk over to my coat. I take out the flash drive and stare at it.

"What's that?" asks Ruby.

I hold it up for her to see. "This contains ten personnel files. Ten candidates for the team. I need to pick three, then recruit them."

She reaches over the side of the bed and retrieves a laptop from a bag next to the bed. She opens it up in front of her and holds out her hand.

"So, what are you waiting for? There's work to be done, bitch."

We smile at each other.

God, she never ceases to amaze me.

People say there's someone for everyone. That one person you're destined to be with. I thought I had already loved and lost mine. When Janine was taken from me, I never wanted to find anyone else. I never believed I could. I was lucky to meet Tori. She personified everything about the new life I was trying to build. She loved me for who she thought I was, and it was amazing for a while. But it all went to shit when she found out who I really was, and she ended up a casualty of my old life, like so many others.

But then Ruby came along. It's like I made her in a machine. She's perfect for me in every way. That's when I realized the saying is wrong. There isn't just one person for you because people change. The man I was pre-Adrian Hell... there was one perfect woman for him. It was Janine. But she's gone, and so is the man I was back then. Same goes for Tori. She was perfect for the man I was trying to be when we met. But she's gone now too, and so is he.

There's one perfect woman for the man I am now, and I'm looking right at her.

"Well, hang on a sec," I say. "When we access this drive, we have twenty-four hours before it wipes itself. We can't start until we're one hundred percent on board."

Ruby shrugs. "And?"

"And... I haven't said I'll do it yet. This is a big deal. I'll only agree to it if you'll do it with me. Me and you, side by side."

She smiles. "I know. Do you think I would let you do something this important without me?"

I smile back. "Well, I thought that might be the case. But I wasn't about to speak for you or make any assumptions."

"I go where you go," she says. "Without you, life's too boring to waste my time on."

"Okay, then."

I take out my phone and make a call, placing it on speaker as it rings out.

Schultz answers. "Buchanan owes me fifty dollars."

I frown. "What do you mean, Mr. President?"

"He bet me fifty bucks you would call within three hours of the sales pitch. I said you'd call within two." He pauses. "Ninety-six minutes. He owes me fifty dollars."

"Glad I could help."

"So, what's it to be, son? Can I count on you?"

I let out a heavy breath and look at Ruby for confirmation. She nods.

"Yeah, I'm in," I say. "On one condition."

"Name it."

"Ruby's in with me. She and I are gonna run this thing."

"I recruited *you*, son. Not your girlfriend."

"She's every bit as capable as I am. She's also the only person in this world I trust completely. You think I'm working for you without someone to watch my back, you're insane. Sir."

Schultz sighs down the line, causing static through the speaker.

"Fine. But she's your responsibility."

"Suits me." I wink at her.

"Have you looked at the files yet?"

"We're about to."

"Okay. Pick your three and go get 'em. You have six days.

24

You have a direct line to me. I'll arrange whatever you need to get the job done. There's an address on that drive. An abandoned RAF base in London. That's where you'll get them to meet and where you'll train them."

"London?"

"The U.K. will know you're there, as a courtesy, but they won't know why. It has to stay that way."

"Okay. Six days?"

"November eleventh."

"I'll be in touch."

"Godspeed, son."

The line clicks dead.

I toss the flash drive to Ruby, who immediately slots it into the side of her laptop. I move over and sit beside her.

"Time to go to work, baby."

She smiles. "Yes, sir."

I recognize the mischievous glint in her eye as she opens the first folder. Images and documents flood across the screen.

Let's see who we're dealing with.

4

I'm sitting opposite Ruby, eating breakfast in the hotel's restaurant. I'm tired, but the coffee is flowing, so I'm sure I'll manage. It's busy but not crowded. Not exactly five-star, but I don't exactly care. They serve coffee and food, so I'm sold. I can see Ruby discreetly looking around at the décor. She has that *this isn't The Ritz Carlton, but it'll do* look on her face.

We stayed up late last night. Sadly, it wasn't for the usual reasons when I'm awake until the early hours with Ruby. We were engrossed in the personnel files of the potential recruits for Blackstar. With the limit on how long we could view the files, we worked into the night to narrow ten people down to three.

We did.

Now we just need to recruit them.

Ruby sips her coffee. "So, where do you want me?"

I raise an eyebrow as I finish chewing my toast. "Honey,

we're in a restaurant. They frown on that sort of thing here..."

She rolls her eyes and throws a packet of sugar at me.

I laugh.

"You know what I mean, asshole," she says, smiling.

"I do." I pour some more coffee. "The two in the States should be easy enough. We'll take one each."

"What about the third?"

"I'll get him."

"You sure? That's a long-ass flight."

"It is, but it'll be the trickiest one, and I don't want you in that situation."

I see her eyebrow flick up. I'm about to get the Ruby Special, I think.

"And why's that?" she asks. "Don't think I can handle it because I'm a woman? Think I need to be protected by the big, strong man? Don't think I—"

I hold my hand up. "Okay, knock it off, Beyonce."

Ruby sticks her tongue out playfully.

"We just need to play to our strengths here," I say. "You would be best served heading down to North Carolina, I think."

"Okay. That's the Marine Recon guy at Camp Lejeune, right?"

I nod. "Sergeant Lincoln March, yeah."

"What are we saying to these people?"

I shrug. "No more than we have to at this stage. Best thing to do would be to stroke their egos a little bit. Big them up, make them feel special for being chosen. I guess they are, to be fair."

"You think that will work?"

I shrug again. "That's how the CIA recruited me."

She tuts. "Imagine my surprise."

"Whatever. It's how I recruited you from that nuthouse a couple of years ago."

She glances away. "Whatever."

"Yeah, exactly!"

We share a laugh.

"So, that leaves you with the chick in Spokane?" she asks.

"Yeah. Makes sense. It's quicker to fly from there to the third guy than it is to fly from here. I don't want to be too close to the deadline."

"I guess we're lucky that two out of three are on base."

"I don't know if it's luck, really. The military just isn't as busy as it used to be. A lot of them are grounded for now."

"True. Not much action going on." Ruby pauses. "Not that it's a bad thing."

"Yeah, a lot of global issues are being handled by Globa-Tech. Well, by the U.N., but it's the same thing, for the most part."

"Why is that? Surely, GlobaTech would appreciate the help."

"I guess it's because involving your military in the affairs of another country can be viewed as political. That's a can of worms we've just about shut for the first time in fifty years. No one's in a rush to open it again. GlobaTech are neutral because the U.N. is neutral. There's no agenda or hidden motivations. They just want to help."

While 4/17 was tragic beyond measure, it's hard not to admit that, on some level, it did actually achieve what Cunningham wanted it to. I'm not saying there weren't better ways to go about it, but this is probably the closest we've come to world peace in our history.

But millions paid for it with their lives. That's not something we will ever recover from. Countless generations will always remember what happened that day. They will always remember the cost of the foundations upon which this new world is being built.

I just wish it could've been different. It *should've* been. I should've done more.

Blackstar can be my way of making up for it. That's how I justify this to myself. I might not have been able to prevent the disaster, but at least I can help clean up the shit that's emerged in its wake.

Those of us who are left to live in this new world deserve that.

"Do you think the military will ever get back to the way it was?" asks Ruby.

"I hope not. If it does, it'll be because the world needs it to. That would mean we've gone right back to where we were before all this, and the sacrifices we all made were for nothing. I hope every country learns from this."

"Same. Although, we both know, probably better than most, that evil will always exist."

I sigh. "That's why we're here—to make sure the people fighting it are still equipped to do the job."

Ruby sits back in her chair, nursing the mug of coffee in her hand. She stares blankly at the liquid as it swirls around in front of her.

"Crazy to think the concept of war can evolve," she says.

"It's unavoidable. When people change, so do their actions. For years, there has been conflict in the Middle East. We got involved with Iraq and Afghanistan. India and Pakistan were at each other's throats for years, as well as everyone else's. Russia and China always had some beef they involved people in. And for what? It always boiled down to money and religion."

Ruby laughs to herself. "Look at us, sitting here engaging

in the moral debates of history. We've probably killed more people between us than most serving soldiers ever will."

I smile at the irony. "Fair point. Although, we actively avoid trying to kill innocent people. And we certainly never hide behind bullshit reasons or agendas. I'm not saying it's completely different, but it's not the same. Say what you want about what we do, but at least it's honest."

"Yeah, you're right. Just makes you think, though. All this..." She gestures to our table, then to us. "The reasons might change, but the results will always be the same."

"It will. You're right. It's the nature of the beast. We're here to make sure the good guys can still hold their own in the fight. That's all. Probably the most noble thing I've done in a long time."

Ruby smiles softly and leans forward, placing her hand on mine. "Now we both know that's bullshit. I refer you again to the last time you were in this town. You knew what it would mean for you if you did what you did. But it needed to be done, and you did it anyway." She sits back again and finishes her coffee. "You ask me, the world would be a much better place with more men like you in it, Adrian."

My cheeks flush with color. Ruby and I aren't exactly a typical romantic couple, but every once in a while, she'll surprise me.

"Thank you."

She waves a dismissive hand. "Don't get me wrong. You're still not all that. You did just get your ass handed to you by a little girl, after all."

She smiles as I flip my middle finger at her.

"Actually, I think you'll find most of my aches and pains are a result of being blown up on a boat, not from the torture or the subsequent fight."

Ruby stands and pushes her chair underneath the table.

Then she moves to my side, leans over, and kisses my forehead. Staying close to me, she whispers, "By an itty... bitty... *girl.*"

Then she turns and leaves.

I watch her walk away, which is a sight to behold.

"I guess I'll grab the check, then?" I shout after her, prompting a few people sitting close by to glance over.

Ruby simply waves her hand without looking around, then disappears out of sight.

5

I step off the plane at Spokane International Airport and stand on the blacktop of the private runway. I look over at the main terminal as I stretch out the stiffness accumulated on the seven-hour flight.

I didn't fly commercial, but it's still uncomfortable spending so long on a small plane. At least I wasn't paying for it.

I check my watch.

These time zones are going to kick my ass when all this is over.

A rental car has been prearranged for me. I stroll over toward the main building and head inside. My business is beyond top secret right now, but there are still some official hoops I need to jump through. Our illustrious leader has given me a government ID to help the process along.

I flash it to the various security checkpoints scattered through the airport, and I'm ushered through without fuss, much to the chagrin of the hundreds of passengers forced to line up like normal.

I navigate the sea of travelers, avoiding larger groups where possible by dodging through the gaps in the crowd. I'm in the unfortunate position of still being recognized. It's hard to avoid when I made global news multiple times in just a couple of years. It's usually okay walking along the street, but whenever I'm in crowded areas—especially ones with large TVs showing world news channels twenty-four-seven—I sometimes get the odd side glance. Despite Ruby's argument to the contrary, I don't like the attention.

From stepping out of the plane to reaching the main entrance of the airport, it's taken me about fifteen minutes. I see the rental desk over to the right. There's a small line of people. I'm happy to wait. I could flash my badge and be a dick about it, but I have plenty of time, and I'd rather not cause a scene.

Five minutes later, I step up to the window. The woman sitting behind the glass gives me a warm smile. I keep the small talk to a minimum and hand her the details of my rental booking. Two minutes later, I'm outside with the keys, scanning the nearby lot for my sedan.

Having an inconspicuous car is great for wanting to blend in when you're on the road. It's not so great when you're trying to find it in a parking lot among fifty of its clones, all painted in variations of the same goddamn color. How the hell am I meant to—

Never mind. Found it.

It's a Lexus. Big and roomy. Dark gray. A hybrid too. Its battery is good for fifty miles or so. The gas tank kicks in when the battery's depleted, but it self-charges as you drive and reactivates when it's full. Efficient and environmentally friendly.

The technology behind the solar, self-charging roads I drove on in Dubai a couple of years ago hasn't quite made it this far west. It's a shame, but I'm guessing it's just a matter of time.

I don't drive much, and I've never really been into cars, but the smooth, near-silent purr of this Lexus as I fire it up gives me chills.

Now for the most important part...

I tune the radio to find a rock station. It takes me almost a minute to find a local station playing Whitesnake.

I smile to myself.

Perfect.

I grip the wheel and take a deep breath. This is it. As soon as I leave the lot, I'm on the clock. Serving Uncle Sam. Trying to recruit the military's best and brightest without telling them what I'm recruiting them for.

Much the way Julius Jones did with me, all those years ago.

Too many years.

I've come full circle, it would seem. I'm rejoining the big, scary war machine to go and find people to be the next me. The student becomes the teacher and all that.

I ease out of the lot and head along Flint Road, toward the highway.

In the immortal words of David Coverdale himself... here I go again.

13:23 PST

Fairchild Air Force Base is only fifteen minutes away from the airport, so the drive is painless enough. The base is commanded by an outspoken colonel, whom I'm hoping I don't have to make nice with. When I told Schultz who my picks were, he assured me that my visits with them would be authorized.

Well, for two of them, anyway.

I've been on military bases before, though not for a long time. They're like small, self-contained towns. They have residential areas, shops, restaurants, schools, and a post office. Up to a thousand people could be living full-time on the base, and Fairchild is no different.

The person I'm looking for is on active duty but is currently stationed on base, testing new UAVs. I'm assuming I need to head for the hangars.

I turn off the highway and head along South Rambo Road.

Ha! Rambo...

A half-mile later, I take a right and turn into the base. There's a checkpoint outside the Reserve Center. I present my credentials and am permitted entry without question. I see the hangars away to my left and follow the road toward them.

I pull over near some other vehicles and kill the engine. I take a moment to look around and get my bearings.

Okay. Showtime.

I get out of the car and stretch again, being careful not to overdo it and aggravate one of the many things still hurting. I had to dress for the occasion, so I'm wearing a tailored gray suit. No tie.

I hate this, but Ruby said she thought I looked hot, so I'm tolerating it.

I grab my overcoat from the back seat and shrug it on over my jacket. It's November, and I'm standing out in the open directly below Canada.

Let's just say I've been warmer.

There's an icy wind tearing around the base. My old man would've called it a lazy wind. It can't be bothered going around you, so it goes straight through you and chills you to the bone.

I walk toward the nearest hangar, positioned beside a runway. I approach three men in fatigues who are standing outside it. They look over as I reach them.

"I'm looking for Captain Vickers," I say. "Can one of you point me in the right direction?"

One of the men, who looks younger than he probably is, looks me up and down. "Can I help you?"

I look at him. I see the double wings, front and center. Airman. First class. Just doing his job.

"You can show me where Captain Vickers is."

"I'm sorry. And you are?"

I show him my new ID. "In a hurry."

He shrinks back a couple of steps and swallows hard.

I could get used to flashing this thing around. Saves me having to threaten people.

"Follow me, sir," says the airman.

He leads me along the side of the runway, toward the third hangar. He slows and points to an open door cut into the larger hangar doors, which stand defiantly closed.

"The captain's inside, sir."

"Thank you."

I head for the door without looking back. I'm greeted by a buzz of activity when I step inside. A metal walkway runs along the walls. Equipment stations are positioned in the middle on all three sides, looking down over the wide-open central area. The hangar is filled with airmen and technicians, all seemingly focused on the source of the deafening noise in here: a small drone buzzing around above.

I survey the large area, scanning the faces for the one I came to see.

On the far side, up on the walkway, I see a woman dressed in fatigues, standing behind a console. She appears to be the one controlling the drone.

Hello, Captain Vickers.

Keeping to the side, I make my way around and climb the steps. I stop a respectful distance away from her. Now that I'm closer, I can see her chestnut hair is neatly tied back. I see the laser focus in her eyes as she operates the drone. Her hands instinctively control the joysticks in front of her.

She has a strong, confident posture. Justifiably so. Her military record is incredible.

"Can I help you?" Vickers shouts.

The couple of technicians standing with her don't react. I guess she means me.

"I mean you, suit guy," she says, as if reading my mind.

I step to her side. "You look busy. I didn't want to distract you."

"I am and you're not. Are you here to see me?"

Her eyes never leave the drone.

"I am. Is there somewhere we can speak privately?"

"Not right now. Come back in a couple of hours."

I smile. "Yeah, that's not how this is going to work. Your colonel knows I'm here to talk to you. This is the highest priority, Captain. I'm gonna need you to put your toy down now. I'm kinda on the clock here."

Vickers glances sideways at me, frowning, but doesn't say anything.

It takes her a couple of minutes, but she carefully lands the drone in the center of the hangar. She nods to the technician beside her, then steps away from the console and looks back at me.

"Follow me."

She leads me down the steps and back across the hangar floor, toward an office in the corner. She steps inside and moves behind the desk, putting her back to the left wall. I close the door behind me and close the horizontal blinds hanging over the glass pane.

She gestures to the seat opposite her as she sits down. I remain standing.

"So, what can I do for you?" asks Vickers, clasping her hands together on the desk.

Let's see how good my sales pitch is, shall we?

"First of all, what I'm about to say doesn't leave this room. If word of this meeting finds its way out into the real world, I'll know it was you who leaked it. Then you'll be in more shit than you can comprehend."

She shrugs. "We're not here. Got it."

"Excellent. Now, do you know who I am?"

She shakes her head. "Should I?"

"I guess not. Did the colonel tell you to expect me?"

"He didn't. I've been locked away in here the last couple of days. What's this about?"

"I'm a... contractor, I guess, for the government. I'm here to recruit you."

She smiles politely. "The Air Force beat you to it. Sorry."

"It sure did," I reply, returning the gesture. "Jessica Vickers. Although, you prefer Jessie, right? Born March 7, 1988, in Goose Creek, South Carolina. Joined the United States Air Force in 2014. Just over a year later, you became the first woman to ever complete Combat Controller Training, making you both a trailblazer for women in the military everywhere and a member of one of the most elite units the

Air Force has. Your record is exemplary. Your piloting skills are unrivaled. You were understandably highlighted and fast-tracked by the brass, which is why you've reached the rank of Captain in a little over five years. Given there's little opportunity to see action nowadays, you've been assigned here to help develop and test new drone technology. Did I miss anything?"

Vickers is staring at me blankly.

I hope I remembered all that correctly. I memorized her file on the flight over here.

She recovers. "Yeah, that... that about sums me up. I'm sorry—who are you?"

"The name's Adrian. I've been tasked with putting together a team. Kind of a *best of the best* thing. I want you to be a part of it."

"I don't understand. I didn't apply for anything. Was I put forward in some way?"

"You were on a list of ten names compiled by leaders of every branch of the military at the request of the president. I was told I could pick three. I picked you."

Her eyes are still slightly wider than normal. Disbelief. Shock. Confusion.

"Why?" she asks.

I sigh. "Do I have to recite all that stuff about you again? Honestly, I've already forgotten half of it. You're good, Jessie. You're better than good. You're incredible. I want you on my team."

Vickers frowns. "And what's the purpose of this new team, exactly? What would I be doing?"

I try to hide a wince of dread. I hate the answer I need to give.

"I can't tell you," I say. "Not right now. Not until you're on board."

"Okay. Well, I appreciate you coming to see me and your theatrics of quoting my record to me."

"Theatrics? I thought that was pretty cool."

She rolls her eyes. "Oh, Jesus. Look, I'm happy where I am. Another twelve months, I could be looking at a promotion to Major. You don't impress me with a half-assed attempt at cloak-and-dagger bullshit that you're clearly not comfortable with in the first place."

I frown. "Half-assed? I worked on this."

"And you really need to stop repeating what I'm saying. It's annoying."

"Annoying?"

I smile. She doesn't reciprocate.

"Fine," I say with a sigh. "This isn't one of those things where you're the first choice, but there's plenty more where you came from if you say no. I'm also not here to blow smoke up your ass. You're it. The only choice. I don't need someone *like* you, Jessie. I need *you*. You and the other two names on my list. You're the only ones who are gonna make this work."

Vickers stands and moves around the desk. She stops in front of me and folds her arms across her chest.

"And what is *this*?" she asks.

"It's a chance to make a difference. To take the fight to the real bad guys and actually protect people."

"What bad guys? There aren't any wars to fight anymore. We just get paid to sit around and watch GlobaTech Industries stop anyone still trying to step out of line."

The disdain in her voice is hard to miss. I can imagine a lot of people in the military share her view.

"I do real work here," she continues. "The technology I'm helping develop and test has real-world applications. It can help get vital supplies to hard-to-reach areas without risking human life. It can replace technology and communications to the nations that were blown back to the Stone Age by 4/17. I'm a key part of that here, and I won't walk away from it."

I nod. "That's great. Honestly. You might not like it or agree with it, but GlobaTech has been doing that for two years, and they're better and faster at it than you. Your talents are wasted here. I'm giving you the chance to blaze some more trails and put your substantial set of skills to better use."

"Doing what?"

"I still can't tell you. But I will say this. You think there aren't more wars to fight? You're wrong. Not only are you wrong, but you're woefully ill-equipped to fight the wars that are coming. Like it or not, GlobaTech aren't. They're currently the only ones out there on the front lines, and they need help. The government asked me to train a team, so they're up to the task."

Vickers steps away, seemingly appeased and curious. She sits on the edge of the desk and looks at me.

"When you say the government is doing this..."

I smile. "I mean the president of the United States and a few others who are important enough to remain anonymous."

"Right. And you."

"And me."

"Seriously, who are you? Really? You're not a spook. You're not military."

"I'm..."

I pause, debating how much to say. I can't tell if this conversation is working or not. I absolutely can't mention anything about Project Blackstar yet. But I need to say something to get her to take this seriously.

Screw it.

"Let's just say I helped get President Schultz elected."

Vickers narrows her eyes. She stares at me, confused. Then her face relaxes. Her eyes widen. Her mouth hangs open.

"You're him," she exclaims. "You're *that* Adrian, aren't you?"

I nod solemnly. "I am."

"Holy shit."

"Jessie, the president and I have a history. As most people know, I've had a rough couple of weeks, but he called me and gave me the same hard sell I'm giving you. I know it's a lot to ask for you to have a little faith, but you have to trust me. This team... it's the real deal. As real as it gets."

She stands and paces away, walking a slow line back and forth beside the desk. I see her eyes dart back and forth at the floor in front of her—a sign of how hard the cogs inside her head are turning.

Eventually, Vickers stops and looks at me. "I can't just be reassigned. That's not how it works. First, I would need to speak to the colonel and—"

I hold up a hand. "Let me stop you right there. First, the colonel doesn't get a say in anything. This is so far above his pay grade, it's in orbit. Second, this isn't reassignment. If you agree to this, you would be leaving the Air Force. Officially, you would be granted an honorable discharge, for the purposes of keeping up appearances on your military record."

She frowns. "Then what?"

"Then you would disappear."

She doesn't say anything.

I smile. "How's that for cloak-and-dagger bullshit?"

"This is a lot to take in. I mean, I have to—"

"You don't have to do anything, Jessie. Why do you think you were on the shortlist in the first place? No immediate family beyond an elderly mother. No partner or spouse. No dependents. Few friends. You were picked for a reason."

"But I—"

I reach into my pocket and take out a card. I hand it to her.

"What's this?" she asks.

I nod to it. "That's the address of a decommissioned Air Force base in London. Be there at nine a.m. on the dot, five days from now."

"I haven't agreed to any of this yet. In fact, so far, I've said nothing but the exact opposite."

"I'm sure you'll change your mind when you've had some time to think about it. Your country needs you, Jessie. I've seen your record—and your psych profile if I'm being completely honest. There's a good fight to be fought. You don't strike me as the kind of person who walks away from that."

I head for the door.

"Hey, hang on," she calls after me. "You can't just leave."

I open the door and look back at her. "Five days, Captain. I'll see you there."

Then I leave.

I walk at pace across the hangar, toward the entrance. I've got another flight to catch in an hour, so I need to get moving.

I think back to how that meeting went and shake my head.

Your country needs you.

Jesus, Adrian.

If she doesn't show up, I can guarantee it's because I said that.

6

One of the benefits of having your own money—or, in this case, using someone else's—is that you can afford to circumnavigate logistical issues other people might face.

For example, I've been in the air about an hour. I left Spokane without issue. Whether it was a successful trip remains to be seen, but the job's done, and I'm onto the next one. But I'm flying a direct route to a place where there aren't any direct commercial routes. I can do that because I'm sitting inside a private jet that's been borrowed from the CIA.

Aside from a change of clothes, the only thing I have with me is a large briefcase. Its contents aren't exactly something I could stow in the overhead on a commercial flight, but I figured I'd rather have them and not need them than... well, you know the rest.

Another benefit of flying private and working for the government.

My next recruit is currently in Pakistan.

I say *currently* because he wasn't there yesterday and won't be there two days from now. I'm operating within a small window of opportunity. Thankfully, I have plenty of time to think about it. This flight is apparently going to take over seventeen hours and cross several time zones.

For all I know, I'm either going to land twelve hours before I took off or three days after.

Christ.

Before I get too deep into this flight and the file reading, I'll check in with Ruby.

I pick up the sat phone beside me and call her cell. She answers quickly.

"Hey," I say.

"Hey yourself," she replies.

I smile at the sound of her voice.

"How did it go in North Carolina?"

"Good. I think. I don't know. It turns out I'm not great at the cloak-and-dagger hard sell."

I laugh. "I know the feeling. I used the phrase *your country needs you* at one point."

"Okay, I wasn't *that* bad..."

"Gee, thanks. I reckon Vickers is on board, though."

"Same with Link."

"Link?"

"Yeah, Lincoln March. He said he prefers Link."

"Uh-huh. And was he flirting with you when he said it?"

"Possibly."

We share a laugh.

"Not getting jealous, are you?" Ruby asks playfully.

"Depends. Could I take him?"

She pauses. "I dunno... he was a big guy. *Lots* of muscles. Kinda cute too."

"Whatever."

She laughs. "Are you doing that face?"

"What face?"

"You know, the face you pull when you're super unimpressed and struggling to resist the urge to reach for your gun."

I glance out the window next to me, trying to see my reflection. I'm scowling a little, and my eyes are blank canvases of hatred and general displeasure.

Huh.

"Yeah, I'm doing the face."

Ruby laughs harder, causing some static on the line.

"I didn't even realize," I continue. "Do I always look like this when I'm not happy?"

"You do. It's cute."

"Okay, I might not have known I do it, but I doubt *that's* the reaction I'm going for."

"Oh, don't get me wrong. It's scary as Hell. Your death stare would make a grown man wet his pants. It just doesn't work on me. I react that way for different reasons."

I laugh to hide the fact my cheeks just flushed with color, despite the fact that there's no one here.

"Jesus! Still... nice save."

"Thanks! I gotta protect my man's fragile ego somehow."

"Yeah, given you take great pleasure in making it fragile to begin with."

"Why, whatever do you mean?"

We laugh again.

"I miss you."

"I miss you too. You all set for the final name on the list?"

I look at the folder on the seat opposite me. I had to print it out, so I could read it without carrying a laptop around with me.

"I will be by the time I land."

"When will that be?"

"Ah, I have no fucking idea. These time zones are weird."

Ruby sighs. "When did you leave Spokane?"

"I dunno. Just after three?"

There's a slight pause.

"Okay. You'll land a little after eight p.m. tomorrow night, local time."

I frown. "How the hell did you work that out?"

"There's an app on my phone."

"Really? They can do that?"

I can almost hear the eye roll.

"Christ, you're old."

"Hey, I'm not old. I'm traditional."

"No, Adrian. Thanksgiving is traditional. You're antiquated. Like the dinosaurs. Oh! Can I call you Tyr*adrian*saurus Rex?"

"No."

"What about *Hell*ociraptor?"

"I'm hanging up now."

"Killersaurus?"

"Bye, Ruby."

"Wait, I have more..."

I end the call and toss the phone onto the seat next me. I spend the next few minutes staring blankly out the window, watching the ocean of clouds below me float by.

I'm not old.

Am I?

??:??

.   .   .

I must've fallen asleep. I check the time, but it's unlikely to be accurate. I have no idea where I am, and I don't care enough to ask. Light's fading outside, so I've been out a while.

I stand to stretch my legs and back. I pace along the cabin, occasionally cracking my neck.

This is a nice plane. I've been in a few over the years. I don't typically do well in private jets. Having been hijacked in one and forced to jump out of the other as it exploded, my opinion of them is tainted. But this is nice. Thick carpet underfoot. Plenty of legroom. The leather on the seats is soft and doesn't squeak when I try to get comfortable. The pilot and copilot were friendly.

Could be a lot worse.

I sit back down and pick up the file. This last guy won't be easy to recruit.

I start reading his bio.

Lieutenant Adam Rayne. Born October 3, 1984, in Portland, Oregon. Joined the U.S. Navy in 2008 and spent five years working toward the rank of Lieutenant. He then applied for the SEALs and spent the next three years training. Passed with relative ease and was assigned to SEAL Team Three in March 2016. Been with them ever since. They operate in the Middle East, and while they've been quiet the last eighteen months or so, his team is currently deployed on a covert mission in Karachi. Details are sketchy, even with the level of access the president gave me. Given how badly Pakistan was affected by 4/17, my guess is that some of the old-school terror groups are vying to become lords of the rubble.

There are some things GlobaTech can't get involved in, apparently.

So, I have to infiltrate a SEAL team currently on a

mission and steal one of their best guys without anyone knowing.

Easy.

Rayne's record is outstanding. Seventeen confirmed kills, which by military—and legal—standards is good. Over thirty successful campaigns during his tenure with the SEALs. To be consistently that good at this level is impressive. Besides the Rainbow guys and Delta, the SEALs are top of the food chain. Definitely not guys I would choose to fuck with, even on my best day.

I say, on my way to fuck with them, with my best days waving in the rearview.

If I can get this guy on board, Blackstar will be a force of nature. Vickers comes from the most elite unit in the Air Force. Ruby's guy is a recon specialist for the Marines. Rayne is an active SEAL. I've been known to have my moments too.

Schultz will be getting his money's worth, for sure. Whatever he and Buchanan are worried about, if my team can't handle it, no one can.

7

Ruby was right. I landed in Karachi about three hours ago. Here, I'm on my own. Even in this delicately civilized new world, the U.S. isn't keen on sending operatives into countries in this neck of the woods. The Pakistani government knows the SEAL team is here. It doesn't know I am, and I aim to keep it that way. I might have more stroke than usual right now, but I'm not a diplomat.

The plane is being refueled and will be ready to go when I am. I have to make this quick. And subtle.

Ha! Best of luck, sunshine.

Nice to see my inner Josh is still cheering me on.

Rayne's SEAL team is currently holed up in an abandoned farmhouse twelve miles northwest of the city, close to the Hub River. Their mission is to gather evidence on the remains of a terror cell reportedly hiding out in the area. If they make a positive ID of their primary target, they have orders to take him out.

A battle left behind from a war that's long gone.

The political minefield is apparently too sensitive for GlobaTech and their peacekeeping parade. An old-school problem requires an old-school solution.

I'm parked a half-mile west, on a road that winds around the side of a low mountain range on the banks of the river. An unbarricaded ridge offers an elevated view of the area with little chance of being seen.

I have a battered and dusty Jeep, graciously loaned to me by the Jinnah International Airport's long-term parking lot.

Well... I say loaned. It's more borrowed.

Well... I say borrowed. It's more stolen.

I stole the Jeep.

I'll give it back. I just needed something inconspicuous, which rules out a rental firm at the airport. And I have no contacts here, so no favors to call in.

It'll be fine.

Rayne and his team chose the farmhouse to hunker down in because it has direct line of sight across the river, toward a run-down store just under a mile away. It sits alone on an intersection in the middle of nowhere, on the outskirts of a small town.

According to the intel I've been given, that store's back room is currently harboring a terrorist.

My guess: the team are going to sit tight until the early hours—probably three a.m. or thereabouts. Then they'll make their way toward the store on foot. They'll scan the area, likely with heat vision technology, confirm the target is on site, then take him out and retreat into the shadows until morning. Then they're on the first ride out of here.

It's a good plan. It makes perfect sense, and I'm sure the team has trained for it exceptionally well.

I almost feel bad that I'm about to ruin it.

I pull my coat tighter around me and hunch my shoulders. You think Pakistan, you think the Middle East. You think deserts and mountains. You think uncomfortable warmth. What people don't tell you is that, in November, it's just as fucking cold as everywhere else. I'm standing here in the middle of the night, in the mountains, in November. It's thirty degrees and it sucks.

My hands tremble against the low temperature as I hold my binoculars up to my eyes, looking at the farmhouse. I'm working on the educated assumption that the SEALs will want to rest before their mission. They will take it in turns to catch a couple of hours, with one or two of them acting as a sentry.

No sign of movement yet. I just need to be patient. Pick my spot. I'm about eight hundred yards away, so maybe ten minutes on foot at a steady pace. There's little cover, although I have the mountain path blocking me from line of sight for most of it.

There are seven members of the SEAL team. I need to incapacitate six of them, so I can talk in peace to the seventh. I'll need to start with the sentry when he walks the perimeter.

And there he is.

A man has appeared in the doorway, which faces south, away from the river and back toward Karachi. He walks away from me, out of sight around the far side of the single-story building. I wait until he reappears, completing his circuit.

It's just him. That means six are still inside.

Time to move.

I stride back to the Jeep and open the briefcase resting on the passenger seat. It's big and cumbersome to carry around but worth it. I ignore the sniper rifle and pick up a handgun designed to fire tranquilizer darts. I also pick up a grenade and a black cloth bag.

I lock the door and set off walking, pinning myself to the inside of the road that leads down the mountain trail and right past the farmhouse. I need to stay out of sight until the last moment. I'm dressed in black, and I'm definitely not expected, so I should be fine.

I slide the gun into the inside pocket of my overcoat. The grenade goes in my left outside pocket. The bag goes in the right pocket.

Let's see how good the current best of the best really is.

23:31 PKT

I'm crouching behind a large rock approximately thirty feet from the western wall of the farmhouse. The sentry is maybe ten seconds away from completing his circuit and walking into view.

I need to be quick. I need to shoot him with the dart and get to him before he drops, so as not to alert anyone inside.

The tranquilizer contains a cocktail of sodium thiopental and diazepam—anesthetic and sedative. These things are tricky. A regular dose will knock a grown man out cold for about an hour. Too high a dose, he might never wake up again. Combining low doses of multiple liquids results in double the effects with minimal risk. I might need to help the process along a little, but he should be out pretty quick, with no long-term side effects.

I take the gun out, check the payload, and wait.

I reckon six seconds until he rounds the corner.

Five.

Four.

Three.

Two.

Shit. He's early.

I pop up and fire, aiming for the thin strip of flesh visible beneath his gear, at the side of the neck.

He doesn't see me before the dart hits him. I'm within arm's length of him before what's happening registers on his face. I lunge toward him and clasp a hand over his mouth and nose. I step behind him, wrap my other arm around his neck, and apply just enough pressure to aid the tranquilizer and knock him out.

It takes maybe eleven seconds.

I lower him gently to the ground and check his pulse. He's breathing, slow and shallow. He's out and he'll be fine.

Step one, done.

Now for the fun part.

I lean against the wall and peer around the corner, looking at the sole entrance to the building. The bricks are weathered and crumbling. The mortar has cracked and fallen away in places, and the paint is peeling almost everywhere. It's a miracle the structure is still standing.

The door is only a couple of feet away. It's standing slightly ajar. No indication of movement inside. I reach into my pocket and pull out the grenade. This little trinket is one of the last things GlobaTech designed for the DoD before ending their contract. It's a combination of a flashbang and a gas grenade. The flash of light is still there to disorient, but instead of a loud bang, the explosion distributes a gas similar to the anesthetic used in dental surgeries. The effects confuse and sedate people caught in the blast, making them easier to overcome. There's none of the negative side effects of the old bang, which caused permanent hearing damage, and the gas isn't anywhere near toxic enough to affect long-term health.

Perfect for evening up the odds when the numbers aren't in my favor. Like now.

I pull the pin, keeping the lever depressed. I count to three, then step out. I whistle loudly as I toss the grenade through the open door, then hold it shut. I whistled to make sure everyone had their eyes open. After a momentary pause, the grenade goes off.

I wait thirty seconds, then slowly open the door and peer inside.

All six men are stumbling to the floor. Each has one hand clasped over his eyes as the other desperately searches for anything to hold onto. Their movements are already sluggish.

I step inside as quietly as I can. I might have a serious advantage, but I'm still in a room full of Navy SEALs. I need to play this smart.

I take a deep breath and quickly move around the room, checking their faces before delivering short, incapacitating blows to each of them. The third guy I come to is Adam Rayne. I hurriedly throw the bag over his head, then drag him along beside me as I clean up the rest of the room.

With all five men down, I haul Rayne outside. He drops to his knees but doesn't try to remove the bag. I take a moment to catch my breath. I hear him groaning with confusion beneath the bag.

"Take some deep breaths, son," I say. "You're outside now. You'll be fine. You're not in any danger. I'm not your enemy."

He coughs and mumbles but says nothing.

I'm breathing heavily, trying to slow my heart rate. I

hoist Rayne to his feet and place a hand on his shoulder, pushing him firmly ahead of me.

"Come on. We're going for a stroll."

We set off up the hillside, toward my Jeep. It takes a few minutes for him to find his words.

"Who are you?" he asks.

"I'll answer all your questions in due time, Adam," I reply. "I need you to listen to what I have to say first, then you can ask me whatever you want."

"My... my team. Are they—"

"They're fine. Just sleeping. They'll wake up in a few hours with a hangover from Hell, but they're otherwise unharmed."

"How did you—"

"All in good time, son. We're nearly there."

Truth is, talking and walking uphill in the cold isn't helping me get my breath back. I need a couple of minutes.

23:54 PKT

Rayne's leaning against the hood of the Jeep, hands clasped in front of him. I'm standing a few feet away, facing him.

I asked him nicely not to fight back or try to remove the bag. He's complied without argument, partly because he's thinking like a SEAL and playing it smart. Also, enough of the gas affected him that he isn't exactly firing on all cylinders right now. He doesn't know who I am or what's really happened, so starting a fight when he can't even see would be stupid.

I step toward him and pull the bag from his head. He recoils, squinting despite the lack of natural light. I watch him struggle to acclimatize. He's about my height. Similar build. There's a tattoo of an eagle on the side of his neck. He stares at me, frowning.

"What do you want?" Rayne asks.

"Do you know who I am?" I ask.

He shakes his head. "Should I?"

"I guess not."

"So, again, what do you want?"

I casually point a finger at him. "You."

"I don't understand. Where's my team?"

I gesture over my shoulder with my thumb. "Asleep in the farmhouse. Like I said, they'll be fine in a couple of hours."

"Do you know what you've done? Do you have any idea—"

"I've just single-handedly taken out an entire team of Navy SEALs without breaking a sweat, just to have a civilized conversation with you. Most people would be flattered."

His expression softens to one of disbelief. As it does, I notice his eyes change. Even in the faint moonlight, I can see how dark his eyes are. It's hard to tell where his iris stops and his pupil starts. When he first looked at me, his stare was as hypnotic as it was cold. But now, despite their natural darkness, his eyes seem to light up his face.

I think it was Shakespeare who said the eyes are the windows to the soul.

This guy's soul would be as interesting as mine.

Rayne sighs. "Seriously, man, who the fuck are you? How did you even know we were here?"

I pace toward the car and rest beside him on the hood.

"Honestly, I've come to realize that I'm not that great at the covert sales pitch, so I'm just going to level with you. I'll tell you what I can, but you need to understand that there are some things I can't tell you right now."

"Okay..."

"I'm with the U.S. government. I guess you could say I'm helping them on a consultancy basis. I've been asked to recruit people for an elite team that would answer directly —and only—to the president. I was given a list of ten names from all branches of the military. I had to narrow it down to three, then recruit them."

"And you want me?"

I nod. "You made the cut, yes."

"Mind if I ask why?"

"I've seen your record. It's exemplary. You're one of the finest men ever to make it to the SEALs. It was a no-brainer."

He shrugs. "Thanks, I guess. So, what's the team for?"

"That... I can't tell you. Not until you've signed up. Just know that you'll be on the front lines, doing more good than you've ever done before."

Rayne falls silent, staring blankly at the dusty road beneath his feet.

Finally, he says, "That's not a bad sales pitch."

I smile. "Thanks."

"You got many more of these to do?"

"You're the last one."

"The other two join up?"

I shrug. "I hope so. I'll find out in a couple of days."

"What do you mean?"

I reach into my pocket and pull out a card, which I hand to him.

"If you're in, be at that address, nine a.m. sharp, three days from now."

Rayne takes the card, then looks at me. "I can't just... up and leave. There's a protocol."

I shake my head. "Not for this. Not for me. The people at the top of the food chain who need to know about this already do. If you want in, you're in. Just pack your bag and hop on a plane. No questions asked."

"Ah, I dunno, man. I worked my whole life to become a SEAL. This is all I ever wanted. Plus, you haven't exactly given me much to go on here. You showed up in the middle of the night, in fucking *Pakistan*... you took out a squad of SEALs and offered me a job without telling me anything about what it entails. And what? You just expect me to go along with it?"

"I wouldn't say I expect you to, but it would make things a lot easier if you did."

He pushes himself away from the hood and paces away, idly kicking a couple of stones on the ground. When he turns back to look at me, his eyes have changed again. His expression is firmer.

"Sorry, whoever you are. That ain't me. I need to know I'm doing something for the right reasons. I made peace with the fact that I do bad things for a living long ago. But the end always justifies the means. That's how I sleep at night. How do I know this isn't some crazy CIA shit with an ulterior motive? Not like *that* hasn't happened before."

I smile. I like this guy. Kinda reminds me of me, only younger.

Huh. Maybe I shouldn't introduce him to Ruby...

"That's a valid concern," I say. "So, I'll throw you a little caveat. My name's Adrian Hell. I know a thing or two about underhanded government bullshit, and I'm giving you my word that's not what this is."

Rayne looks at me, eyes narrowed with uncertainty.

"Adrian Hell? Why does that name sound familiar?"

I take a deep breath. "You been on social media in the last few weeks?"

He shrugs. "Not really."

"Okay. How about the news a couple of years back, during the short-lived North Korean invasion and—"

He snaps his fingers and points at me. "No fucking way!"

I shrug humbly.

"You killed President Cunningham," he says.

"I did. In my defense, the piece of shit deserved it."

Rayne shrugs. "No arguments there."

I smile again. "So, are you in?"

"I dunno, man. Can I think about it?"

"Sure." I pause. "Well?"

He rolls his eyes. "Funny."

"Thanks. You've got three days." I point to the card in his hand. "If you're not at that address by then, forget we ever spoke. Forget all this. Word of it gets out, I can promise you we'll meet one more time, and that meeting will end differently."

He smirks. "That a threat?"

I nod. "It is. Orders from up high. This is beyond any definition of top secret you've ever heard of. From the president himself. Can't risk anyone finding out about it."

He relaxes a little. "Fair enough."

Silence falls. The piercing wind gently swirls around us. I shiver involuntarily.

Rayne suddenly looks toward the farmhouse, then back at me.

"Shit! What about my mission? My team? How the hell are we going to explain any of this?"

I stand. "Oh, yeah. Almost forgot."

I open the door and retrieve the briefcase. I lay it on the

hood and open it. Rayne moves beside me and stares at the content.

"Whoa..."

I smile. "Yeah. Ain't she something?"

I take out the parts of the sniper rifle and begin assembling it.

He reaches out tentatively, as if hesitant to touch it.

"It's one of three rifles collectively known as the Holy Trinity," I explain. "It was confiscated by GlobaTech a couple of years back. I know the guy in charge and asked for it back. He kindly obliged."

"I've never seen anything like it," he says. He points to an engraving on the stock. "What's that?"

It's a small emblem, etched into the frame with gold. Three bullets standing on end.

"That means this is number three in the Trinity."

"Where are the first two?"

I shrug. "No one knows. These things are the stuff of legend."

"Okay. Why do you have it here, then?"

With the rifle fully built, I move around the front of the Jeep and stand facing the river. I flick the legs of the stand down and rest the rifle on the hood.

"I'm doing you a favor. Let's call it a gesture of goodwill."

Rayne frowns. "Which would be... what, exactly?"

"I'm going to complete your mission for you, so your boys don't get in trouble."

He stares at me, stunned silent.

"Grab that spare scope from the briefcase." I position myself behind the rifle. "You can walk me through it."

With my legs spread shoulder-width apart and my back straight, I lean forward and line up my right eye behind the scope of the Trinity rifle. For a split-second, my mind is overrun with flashbacks of the last time I held this gun. The last time I looked through this scope.

It was two years ago, and I was staring at Josh.

I shake the images from my head.

I focus on the store at the intersection, a little under a mile west. Rayne moves beside me, holding the scope to his eye.

"You see it?" I ask him.

"Copy that," he says. "Point nine miles. The wind's coming in from the northeast. Five point three miles per hour."

He's getting the details from the HUD on the spotter's scope.

"Sounds about right," I say. I adjust the dial on my own scope to compensate.

We watch, frozen with purpose.

"There," he says after a couple of minutes. "The window on the south wall. Top right."

I nudge myself a millimeter to the right.

"I see it," I say. "Can you zoom in, get a positive ID?"

"On it."

I wait.

I have to say, I'm impressed with him. He's held his own so far. He's been patient. He's questioned me without being confrontational, despite me trying to goad a reaction out of him. He's shown me he's a man of principle, and the moment the gun came out, he was straight to business, no questions asked. Not only that, but he's given me an accurate read of a shot from a mile away while fighting the effects of a mild sedative.

I definitely made the right choice with this guy.

"Okay, I see him. That's a solid confirmation on the target. Got a good visual."

I pause. My finger's resting on the trigger.

"You sure? It's dark, and he's a mile away."

"That's affirmative. One hundred percent. The target is in the window. His back is to us."

"Okay..."

The shot is already lined up. Fifteen hundred meters isn't exactly straightforward, but his assessment of the shot was sound. Plus, I'm me.

I take one breath and squeeze the trigger gently. The shot rings out, echoing around the mountains like a shockwave.

One Mississippi. Two Mississippi.

I watch through my scope as the target's head disappears. I stand and begin disassembling the rifle without another thought. Rayne lowers his scope and looks at me.

"Holy shit. You made that look... effortless."

"What can I say? I'm good."

"I mean, I'm not bad with the long gun. But I know guys who are exceptional by SEAL standards, and they would struggle with that shot. You barely had time to line it up."

I take the scope from his hand and toss it in the briefcase, then close it.

"Yeah, well, that's the problem with people like you. You think too much. This gig is about instinct. You trust your gut. Always. You see a shot, you take it. You don't go through a forty-step checklist and file a report for every bullet that leaves your magazine. That's not how the world works. Not anymore."

I put the briefcase on the passenger seat, then walk around to the driver's door. I open it and look over the roof at Rayne. He's staring at me blankly.

"Three days," I say to him. "I hope you make the right

choice. You're too good to be wasting your time in the minor leagues."

I climb in and start the engine before he has the chance to reply. As I flick the headlights on, he steps back, out of the way. The glare of the lights cuts through the darkness like a laser beam. I look at Rayne through the passenger window. His dark eyes glisten with the spark of life.

I smile to myself as I drive away, leaving him in my rearview.

Yeah... I reckon he's in.

8

I've been asleep for almost two days. I'm still not entirely sure I know what time it is. I headed straight for the airport after talking with Rayne and left Karachi about one a.m. From there, I flew straight here, to London. I lost five hours in the process, which essentially means that I've just lived through two thirty-hour days.

I'm not sure my brain can process that, never mind my body.

The team is due to arrive tomorrow, so Ruby and I are taking some much needed down time and strolling around London. Not exactly the weather for it. I can't honestly remember the last time I was in the U.K., but I do remember it was cold and wet pretty much year-round.

We're walking along the banks of the River Thames. Across the water stand the Houses of Parliament. There are a lot of people around, all rushing with their heads down, focused on their destination.

Reminds me of New York. Perhaps just a little smaller.

Ruby's beside me, linking my arm with hers. She seems relaxed and content. Every now and then, she closes her eyes for a moment and lets the wind hit her face. She smiles as her hair dances around her.

"You okay?" I ask her.

She looks at me. "Uh-huh."

"You sure?"

"Of course. Why?"

"I dunno. You just seem..."

She laughs. "What?"

I shrug. "You seem at peace."

She holds my gaze, staring at me with those dazzling emerald eyes. Then she looks ahead, resting her head against my shoulder.

"I am. I'm happy to be with you. I'm happy to be here too. I've never been to London before."

"It's been a while for me too."

"Isn't this where Josh grew up?" Ruby asks. I hear hesitation in her voice.

I smile with bittersweet recollection. "Yeah. Not where we are, though. I think it was a place called Croydon."

"Did you ever come here with him?"

"Only once, back in the D.E.A.D. days."

"Never as Adrian Hell?"

I shake my head. "Never any cause to. Not a big market for assassins here. I think everyone's too polite."

She smiles. "Yeah, this place is like Canada, except they get the names of things wrong and serve food in newspapers."

I laugh. "Oh, if Josh were here now, he'd be all irate and British about such a sweeping generalization."

We share the moment of reprieve.

"It's a shame you never came back here with him, though," she says. "He must've missed his hometown."

I shrug. "I don't know. He was in the military his entire adult life. I don't think he was sentimental about where he was. He was all about the job."

"I guess."

We climb a flight of cracked, concrete steps beside a large fountain, which brings us out onto Westminster Bridge. We head left, crossing the water, heading toward Big Ben.

"Speaking of which," I say, "do you think we managed to get all three recruits?"

Ruby doesn't hesitate. "Damn right, we did. That's one hell of a team. No way they won't step up."

"I hope you're right."

"Do you not think so?"

"I don't know. Maybe. I'm pretty confident Rayne is in. From what you said the other day, March is likely on board too."

"You mean Link?"

I glance over to see her smiling mischievously.

I roll my eyes. "Whatever. It's Vickers I'm not sure of. She seemed the most skeptical. I just think I could've done a much better job of convincing her."

She squeezes my arm with hers, offering some friendly reassurance. "Quit doubting yourself. We both believe this Blackstar gig sells itself. And we believe in Schultz. That's why we're here. If the president can convince us, we can convince anyone."

I smile. "Yeah, I guess you're right."

"Bitch, I'm always right!"

I laugh. God, I love her.

"Come on," she says. "Let's enjoy the last day of peace. Buy a girl a drink already."

We reach Big Ben and stand for a moment, gazing up at the towering structure.

"That is a big fucking clock," I observe.

Ruby laughs. "You missed your calling as a tour guide, babe."

She steps away from me and begins gesturing with her arms in the middle of the sidewalk.

"If you look to your left, you will see a big fucking clock. And to your right, the statue of some old bastard in a hat."

I start laughing. People move around her, casting confused glances, to which Ruby's oblivious of.

I pull her toward me and kiss her, then take her hand and dash across the street between gaps in the traffic. We head along Parliament Street. A sign says Trafalgar Square is at the other end. There's bound to be a bar along here somewhere.

I look at her. "Did you just call me *babe* back there?"

Her eyes pop wide. She places a hand over her mouth. "Oh, shit. Did I?"

I grin. "You did."

"Oh my God, how embarrassing!"

I poke her arm playfully. "You love me."

"Shut your goddamn face right now, I swear to God."

I laugh. She joins in a moment later, unable to keep up the illusion of offense any longer.

We walk in a comfortable silence for a few minutes, casually navigating the busy sidewalks. We take in the vibe of a foreign city, forgetting the challenges that await us in the days and weeks ahead.

I see a building up ahead that makes me stop in my tracks.

Ruby looks at me and sees the surprised look on my face. "What's wrong? You okay?"

I nod toward the building. "The Red Lion. It's a bar."

"Great! We can get a drink."

I shake my head. "It's... I know that place. I forgot it was here, but..."

"What is it, Adrian?"

"Josh used to drink in there when he was a kid. The one time we came here, back in the day, he took us there."

"Are you sure? There must be hundreds of bars called that in this city."

I shake my head. "That's the one. It was near Trafalgar Square. I didn't think about it until I saw it."

"You wanna go inside?"

"I... I don't know."

I had told her about using the Trinity rifle in Pakistan. About what it meant to me. About the memories it brought back. She pointed out that I lost someone I cared about, and it's not difficult to see something that reminds me of him in my everyday life. She said it's just evidence of how important Josh was to me. How big a part of my life he was.

She's right. It's not something I should be afraid of or run away from. But it's still hard. A casual reference or a silly joke that triggers a memory of him is fine. But when it's something significant... I struggle to suppress the guilt.

"Come on," Ruby says, pulling me gently toward the bar. "Let's walk where he walked. Drink where he drank. It'll be nice."

She smiles to offer comfort. I smile back to hide my pain.

When I hesitate, she pulls me again.

"What better way to honor his memory than by bringing it back home for him?" she says.

Damn, she's good.

Finally, I nod. "Yeah, okay. Let's go."

"Good. Besides, do you really think he would condone you delaying me getting a drink?"

I chuckle. "Probably not."

We head inside and walk over to the bar. It's not over-crowded, but it's busy enough that there are no visible empty seats.

The interior looks a hundred years old. Dirty white walls with black paneling. Thick, wooden beams in the ceiling. The bar looks brand-new, though. It has a clean and polished mahogany surface, with brass fittings. The wall behind it is stocked with liquor.

I signal to the man behind the bar for two beers. He nods. A few moments later, he places two large glasses down in front of us.

"What the hell is that?" asks Ruby, studying the glass.

"It's a pint," I explain. "And I believe you're drinking something called Dizzy Blonde."

She glares at me. "The fuck did you just call me?"

I roll my eyes and point to the pump on the bar. "It's the name of the beer."

Her expression softens.

"Oh." She takes a sip. "Why is it room temperature?"

I take a gulp myself. Not bad.

"No idea," I say. "But these people eat from newspapers and drive on the wrong side of the road, so it's probably best not to question their traditions."

We move to the end of the bar and stand, taking a moment to glance around. My gaze settles on a table in the corner, by a window overlooking the street. There are four chairs positioned around it, all currently occupied.

Ruby sees me staring. "What is it?"

I nod toward the table. "When Josh and I came in here... that's where we sat. Feels like yesterday."

Ruby smiles and raises her glass. "To Josh. I can't believe he drank this shit."

I smile and raise mine, clinking it against hers. "To Josh."

She takes a sip, shuddering slightly as she swallows.

"What do you think he would make of Blackstar?" she asks.

I think for a moment. "I think he would've gotten behind it. Even if he were still at GlobaTech. *The more, the merrier*, he would say." I pause, smiling fondly. "Did I ever tell you about the bar fight he and I got into in Chicago?"

She shakes her head. "I don't think so."

"It was a few years ago now. We stopped off on our way to Pittsburgh."

"Trent?"

I nod. "Yeah. It had been a long day on the road, so we stayed overnight in Chicago. Went into this bar. Dark, dirty, rock music playing—that kinda place."

"So, your favorite type of bar, then?"

"Exactly. We were sitting near the pool table. There was a group of kids there, being all loud and obnoxious and carefree."

She smiles. "Those bastards..."

"Then a song came on, and Josh just... he went off into his own little world. Picked up his air guitar, and suddenly, he was performing to a sell-out crowd. He never gave a shit what anyone thought of him. And not in the way that people say when they secretly do care. I mean genuinely. Not one shit. This was when he still dressed like an extra from *Point Break* too."

She laughs along, enjoying the story.

"So, I was distracted about going after Trent, understandably. But I saw some of the girls were checking him out. They probably liked the fact that he didn't care. Anyway, one of their boyfriends clearly noticed too. Didn't take too kindly to it. Not that Josh was actively doing anything, but you know how kids can be."

Ruby closes her eyes, laughing. "Oh, no..."

"I let him know that he might have some shit heading his way. He asked me not to shoot anyone, which was a fair request. But I just sat back and watched. Told him he needed the practice after hiding behind a desk for so long, booking my plane tickets."

"I bet he loved that!"

I wave it away. "Ah... I just said it to fire him up. Couldn't have him being gun shy."

"So, what happened?"

"The guy stepped up to Josh and started mouthing off. He had no idea! Josh didn't even lift a finger. He just belittled and embarrassed him so completely by being sarcastic, the guy just shrank away with his tail between his legs."

She laughs. "Sounds like Josh."

"Yeah. Problem was, the guy tried to save face by getting physical with his girlfriend, who had been smiling at Josh."

"Sonofabitch..."

"I obviously wasn't going to let that slide, so I stepped between them. Pushed the girl behind me and explained in no uncertain terms to the guy that he was risking his long-term health. As I walked away, the dumb prick swung a pool cue at the back of my head. I spun around and caught it in my hand. Poor kid nearly shit his pants. Ended up having to put him down. We left shortly afterward to avoid any more drama."

"My hero," Ruby says with a warm smile.

I shrug it away. "Wrong is wrong. I don't care who you

are. Josh spent the next morning telling me how scary I can be. The rest of that trip, you already know."

"I do." She takes another sip of her pint. "You two made one hell of a team. Best in the business for a long time."

"Yeah, we did. That was more his doing than mine, but still... it worked." I pause to take a gulp of my own drink. "And now I have you."

"Damn right, you do."

"You're not as good at being my secretary, but you're undoubtedly deadlier and better-looking. A fair trade-off, I'd say."

We laugh together.

Ruby gestures to her drink. "This stuff's growing on me."

"It's not bad, is it?"

"Let's enjoy ourselves today, Adrian. Take our time. Relax. Drink. Tomorrow will be here soon enough."

I hold my glass up again for another toast, which she reciprocates.

"Sounds like a plan."

After all, I have plenty more stories about Josh I can tell her.

I hear his voice in my head.

Hey. You're not going to tell her about that waitress in Madrid, are you?

I smile to myself. "Did I ever tell you about the time Josh and I went to Spain?"

Asshole.

9

The old RAF base is on the outskirts of a town called Enfield, bordered by Epping Forest. It has a wide perimeter fence. Long-empty guard towers stand on either side of a rolling gate topped with barbed wire. There's a lot of flat, open space—once a small network of roads to navigate between runways and hangars.

One building stands alone in the middle, low and decaying. A large hangar stands at each end of the compound, like towering bookends, leaving lots of open space in between.

Inside, some of the walls are crumbling. I think it was previously used for SAS training, which is why there are bullet holes everywhere. But the place is still intact and operational.

Most of the rooms inside stand empty and in darkness. The doors are either closed or missing. But one room is

74

alive. The fluorescent lights buzz overhead. The door is open and inviting. Three chairs are behind three small desks, facing a larger desk that overlooks the classroom with a whiteboard behind it.

Pretty obvious where the team should go.

The only other room showing signs of life is the one I'm currently standing in with Ruby. It's the operations room, used to monitor the whole base via security feeds from the cameras scattered around the place. Thankfully, they all still work.

"You ready?" asks Ruby.

"I am," I reply confidently.

"It's just... you've never taught or trained anyone before."

"True."

"And you're not exactly the most patient person..."

I smile. "Also true."

"And that room is about to fill up with an awful lot of ego."

"Yet none will be as big as mine."

She slaps my arm. "That's my point, asshole."

I smile again. "Ruby, relax. Honestly, this is the easy part. Getting them here was the challenge."

"Yeah, well, they're not here yet."

I check my watch. "There's still time. Patience, my young Padawan."

She sighs. "Jesus Christ, I'm dating a twelve-year-old."

I glance at her. "That's frowned upon in most cultures, y'know?"

"Adrian, I swear to God, I will shoot you right now."

I start to laugh, but I see something in her eyes. She's only semi-serious about shooting me, yet she seems... anxious.

"Are you okay?" I ask.

Ruby shrugs and avoids eye contact. "Of course, I am. Why wouldn't I be?"

"I dunno. You tell me. But you're clearly not."

She goes to speak but hesitates, which isn't like her. I wait to let her find the right words. She struggles with opening up about as much as I do.

She paces away and rests against the edge of a desk against the opposite wall.

"I just think... I don't know. Did we think this through properly?"

I frown. "How do you mean?"

"I mean this... me and you... getting involved in Blackstar. Everything we've done, everything we've worked for... was it all for nothing if we just wind up working for a boss and a paycheck like regular people? We're not regular people, Adrian. We don't have regular lives. Why are we really doing this? Why are *you* doing this? Honestly."

I think for a moment.

"I won't bullshit you and say there isn't any selfish motivation behind it. You know me too well. But first and foremost, I believe this is the right thing to do. I know Schultz, and I know GlobaTech. They wouldn't be spooked without good reason. Whatever they're worried about is bad enough that they would ask *me* to help. You said it yourself... I can't say no to that. And neither can you."

She smiles briefly. "The difference between us, Adrian, is that you can't say no to what's right... whereas I can't say no to *you*."

I look at the floor, willing the color to stay out of my cheeks.

"I don't know what to say to that. Thank you."

"You don't have to thank me, Adrian. I love you and

respect you, and I'd follow you into Hell if you asked me to. I only ask because—I can't believe I'm about to say this—my spider sense is tingling."

I suppress my half-entertained and half-proud grin. She's being serious, and this isn't the time for me to be an asshole about it.

"Honestly? Mine too. I don't doubt the motives of Schultz or GlobaTech, but I don't think anyone involved is as prepared for what's coming as they think they are. I've made a career out of being around when the shit hits the fan. There's something in the air. Has been for a couple of years. When the storm finally hits, I'd rather be where I am now than sitting at home, resisting the urge to kill some two-bit drug dealer for pocket change because I'm bored of my fourth attempt at retirement."

Ruby smiles. "Is that the selfish motivation?"

I nod. "It is."

She walks over to me and kisses my cheek. She takes my hand in hers and looks me in the eye. "Despite everything we've done, I'm still a comfort zone kinda girl. That's all."

"Ain't nothing comfortable about the zones we live in."

She laughs. "You're not wrong. But it's still safe because it's what I know. What I'm good at. All this..."

She trails off.

"What is it, Ruby?"

She sighs. "All this is exactly what you and Josh would get involved in. I'm not him, Adrian. I can't do what he did. I'm just worried I won't be any use. That I won't live up to—"

I lean forward and kiss her, cutting her off mid-sentence. I place a hand on the side of her face and hold her against me. When we part, her eyes are sparkling and alive.

I smile, trying to offer comfort and reassurance.

"Ruby, if the only thing you do is help keep me in check

and keep my head in the game, you're already ten times more valuable than anyone else could ever be. Including Josh. He spent years keeping my Inner Satan on a leash and giving it some slack when the situation called for it. If he ever broke free, Josh helped rein him in again. But you... you don't care about the demon. You care about the man. You keep *me* strong, so I can control my own Satan, and that's something Josh could never do. So, quit comparing yourself to him, okay?"

She blushes and nods but says nothing.

"But you're also one of the most capable and, frankly, violent human beings I've ever had the pleasure of knowing."

She bursts out laughing and gently punches my shoulder.

I shrug. "What? You are. And I can't think of anyone I'd rather have beside me running this thing. All the reasons Schultz wanted me for this are the same reasons I want you."

Ruby kisses me again. "Thank you. That helped more than you know." She glances at one of the monitors beside us. "Now it looks like we have work to do."

I look over and see three figures walking through the main gates, between the guard towers. They appear to be talking to each other and looking around, as if questioning if they're in the right place.

I smile. "Sonofabitch. We got all three."

"Yeah, we did." Ruby holds out a fist for me to bump, which I do. "Is everything ready?"

"It is. Time to go to work."

09:03 GMT

. . .

I waited until they all found the classroom and took their seats before heading over to meet them.

I linger in the doorway long enough for them to all notice me, then step inside. They're all wearing civilian clothes, which can't help but show off their impressive physiques.

I nod a courteous greeting to Vickers and Rayne in turn, then approach March. His caramel skin shines under the bright lights. I extend a hand, which he takes.

"You must be Sergeant March," I say.

"Yes, sir," he replies. His voice is deep and booming.

"But you prefer Link, right?"

He smiles. "Yes, sir."

"My colleague has told me a lot about you, Link. Glad you decided to come on board." I move over to my desk and perch on the edge, folding my arms across my chest. "Now that we're all here, I can perhaps fill in some of the blanks I had to leave. Firstly... Captain Vickers, Sergeant March, Lieutenant Rayne. While your ranks are impressive and well-earned, they're no longer needed. From now on, I'll address you as Jessie, Link, and Rayne. If that's a problem for you... tough."

Jessie shifts in her seat. "With all due respect, I don't care what you call me. I just wanna know why I'm here. We all do."

I nod. "Fair enough. This is Project Blackstar. It's a covert unit put together at the request of President Schultz. It consists of the absolute best that the U.S. Armed Forces have to offer. We have an Air Force combat controller, a Marine sniper, and a Navy SEAL. This isn't a competition. I'm not here to blow smoke up your ass. If you weren't good, you wouldn't be here. But you are, so check your ego at the door and get over yourselves. This will be unlike anything you've done before. All the training you've had... it'll only get you so far. I'm here to take you further."

Link clears his throat. "Maybe I missed something, but... who are you?"

I smile. "I'm Adrian Hell."

His eyes grow wide. "The assassin?"

"That's me."

He shakes his head with disbelief. "This is fucked up."

"Well, you're not wrong, Link. Now I'm gonna be honest with you. This project doesn't operate on a need-to-know basis. I won't hide things from you. You answer to me because that's the way the president wants it, and I'm ultimately responsible for what this team does. But you will always know what I know, and as far as I'm concerned, you're all equal partners in this."

Rayne slowly puts his hand up.

I look over at him. "You don't need to do that. We're not five."

He lowers it again.

"What's Project Blackstar for?" he asks. "There must be two dozen black ops outfits across the military and the CIA, not to mention Delta and the Rainbows. What's so different about us?"

"Good question. Here's the inside scoop, Buttercup: GlobaTech Industries is the leading military force on this planet. Like it or not, their private security force is easily inside the top fifteen biggest armies in the world. Especially after 4/17. Also, like it or not, one of their guys is typically worth three of anyone else's. One of the perks of near-unlimited funding. The U.N. hired them for a reason. The world is changing. The art of warfare is changing with it.

GlobaTech are leaders of this new world because they're the ones shaping it."

Jessie scoffs. "Sounds like someone has a real hard-on for the *mighty* GlobaTech. Why not just go and work for them?"

I move over to her desk and stand in front of her, my hands in my pockets. "Because they can't afford me. Also, because they didn't ask. The president did."

I idle back over to the desk and rest against it once more. "What many people don't know about GlobaTech is that they have an elite unit that answers only to the director. These guys are as good as it gets, and they deal with all the dirty things that governments won't touch. They do it quietly and they do it well. They don't have the limitations you people do."

Link frowns. "Such as?"

"Such as red tape. Such as politics. Such as agendas. You three might represent the top one percent who have a little more leeway than the rest, but you still have limits and restraints. You have rules of engagement and treaties and laws. Hell, you can't even blow your nose without written permission from a three-star general, let alone kill anyone. You can't always do what needs to be done because you have to be seen to be nice and fair when you're doing it."

Jessie shrugs. "That's the world we live in. That's society. That's the rule of law. This isn't the Wild West."

I nod. "Except it's not. Not anymore. That isn't the world we live in now. GlobaTech are a victim of their own success in a lot of ways. They've left every major world military behind. Their men are better equipped and better trained. Their tech is groundbreaking and, for the most part, unrivaled. No country can compete with them. That's why they're out there fighting the good fight for the U.N., and you guys are stuck on base, testing drones and training cadets."

"I wasn't," says Rayne. "I was out in the field."

I look at him. "Yeah, you were. Fixing a problem left over from the pre-4/17 world, surrounded by so many political landmines, no one in their right minds would touch it."

"Except the SEALs."

"Exactly. Except you. My point is, you guys don't know the fight what's out there anymore. The enemies are getting better. Smarter. They're attacking in ways you don't understand. GlobaTech do, and President Schultz is done allowing the United States to be left behind. He wants our country to be prepared for the battles ahead. That's why he's asked me to recruit and train a team that will serve as his personal answer to GlobaTech's elite unit. That is Project Blackstar."

"Okay, hold up," says Link. "You just got through telling us we're the best of the best, right? No offense, but what are you going to teach us? I know who you are. I imagine most of the world does. You were on the internet less than three weeks ago being tortured by a fucking teenager. What are you gonna do? Show us how to get our ass kicked?"

Jessie and Rayne don't say anything, but they look at me expectantly.

The guy has a point. Thankfully, I anticipated this kind of reaction. It's understandable. I've been where they are. I know how their minds work.

I nod slowly. "You're absolutely right, Link. What do I know? I was beaten and tortured within an inch of my life in front of a global audience. What a lot of people don't know is that she was the daughter of an assassin and had trained with the Yakuza. One on one, she would give any one of you a run for your money. She fought without restraint. She fought for vengeance, not justice. She was violent beyond modern comprehension. She personified everything about the bad guys in our new world. She wasn't motivated by religion or greed. She wanted to burn it all down just to see one man suffer.

"But I still beat her. I *survived*. Because I'm just like her. I always have been. I've been that way for twenty years—long before it became fashionable. I'm the only person qualified to train you because I've been at the top of the food chain in both worlds since you three were in high school."

They exchange glances, unsure of how to respond.

"So, what exactly are you going to train us to do?" asks Rayne.

I pace in front of them. "Everyone has a bad day at the office sometimes. But I'm standing here with you, and that bitch was blown up on a boat. See, it doesn't matter how you play the game... so long as you win."

I move to the door and lean against the frame, staring back at them. They're all sitting casually in their seats. They all look like they accept what I said because they don't believe it's real. Like they're humoring me.

That's about to change.

"The world we live in now is different. The way you have all been trained is outdated. You are among the elite in your specific branches of the military, which means you likely have fewer limits than most. You're trained to think outside the box. That's great. But you still fundamentally operate within the boundaries of the world you know. Limits are limits, regardless of how many there are. It's my job to remove them completely."

Jessie frowns. "So, what? We're going to be allowed to break the law?"

I shrug. "We're going to be allowed to ignore it if we have

83

to. That's a responsibility few people wouldn't abuse. You're all here because I trust you with that responsibility. And so does the president."

"This is insane," she mutters.

I ignore her. "The new world... the aftermath of 4/17... it's a battlefield you've never fought on before. It's not about bombs and bullets anymore. It's about money and influence. The theater of war has been privatized. Governments are becoming redundant. They can be toppled overnight by a fucking social media post. You need to stop thinking within the confines of the world you grew up in because that world is gone. You need to start thinking in ways that would have never occurred to you three months ago."

"Like what?" asks Link.

"I need to know you can improvise. Deal with new problems in new ways. Beat the enemy at their own game. Your training began the moment you sat down. See, underneath each of your seats is a bomb, connected to a pressure trigger that activated the moment your ass touched the chair. You stand up, you die."

"Are you serious?" exclaims Rayne.

I smile. "Deadly."

Jessie narrows her eyes. "Bullshit."

"Take a look," I say, shrugging.

I can see none of them believe me, yet no one's standing up in protest. Doubt is a powerful tool. Link shuffles to his left, closer to Rayne, so he can see underneath Jessie's chair.

His eyes bulge. "Holy shit!"

She looks over at me. "Are you fucking kidding me?"

"You're insane!" yells Rayne.

"Quite possibly. And no, Jessie, I'm not joking. Welcome to your first lesson, kids. You have ten minutes to leave this room. If it takes you one second longer, I'll assume I made a mistake, and you'll be sent back to your old units—whether you're alive or not." I make a show of checking my watch. "I'll be outside. *Tick-tock*."

I smile and walk out of the room, leaving the deafening silence behind me.

10

I'm standing out in the open, facing the entrance to the building. All three of them have just walked outside, aiming handguns at me. They likely found the guns in one of the other rooms.

I check my watch.

Eight minutes. Not bad.

They stop a few feet in front of me. They all look pretty pissed.

Link steps forward and places the barrel of his gun to my forehead. I smile at him, which only angers him further.

"You're fucking insane!" he yells. "You could've killed us!"

I shrug. "But I didn't. I had faith that all three of you would find a way out of there, and you did. Just goes to show I was right to choose you for the team."

He forces the barrel against my head. The rim indents

my skin. "I should drop you where you stand and walk away. Pretend this whole thing never happened."

I raise my eyebrows. "Feel free."

Behind him, Jessie and Rayne exchange a concerned glance. Their own weapons waver in their grip. But Link stands firm. He appears more pissed than the others.

Interesting to see how the natural dynamic between the three of them has taken shape. He's clearly assumed leadership, despite Jessie holding the highest rank outside of this. They must have discussed how they were going to handle this once they escaped. I wonder if threatening to shoot me was unanimous.

I watch Link's finger slip in and out of the trigger guard. He's hesitant. Unsure of himself because of how confident I am.

"What are you waiting for?" I ask. "You're right. I'm clearly insane. Years of being the best killer who ever lived has taken its toll on my state of mind. I could've killed you all back there. You should leave me rotting with a hole in my head. Forget you ever saw me. Go back to your unfulfilling lives, killing nothing but time for no reason whatsoever."

He grits his teeth. "I'll do it, I swear to God."

"I know. You're one of the best marksmen ever to gain acceptance into the Marines. You could put a bullet between my eyes with that thing from the other side of this base. I just tried to kill you. What are you going to do about it?"

His eyes narrow. The barrel of his gun lowers slightly.

Jessie steps forward, to his side. "Come on, Link. This doesn't solve anything. Let's just go."

"Yeah, man," adds Rayne. "We're fine. No harm, no foul. Leave this nutjob to his presidential crusade."

I smile and look him straight in the eye. "What's it gonna be, Link? Can you just let this go?"

He holds my gaze for a few moments, then grits his teeth and reaffirms his aim.

"Fuck you," he says.

Then he pulls the trigger.

...

...

...

He frowns when nothing happens.

I screw my face up. "Aww. A little performance anxiety there, big guy?"

He lets out a guttural scream and drops the gun, then throws a right hook.

I expected he would. I could argue he deserves at least one free shot. But he isn't getting it.

I take a step back and deflect the blow, then step forward again, sliding my front leg between his legs. I hook my foot around the back of his ankle and give him a firm nudge with my shoulder. He stumbles back, falling heavily to the ground.

The scene freezes. Jessie and Rayne lower their weapons, looking down at Link. I take a couple of steps back and wait. Eventually, once the embarrassment has come and gone, he gets to his feet and dusts himself down. The three of them stand there, staring at me.

He's even more pissed now. He takes one step forward but stops when I point to his chest, grinning. A red dot just appeared on it. The others stare. Their expressions change from anger to resignation when multiple red dots begin appearing on all of their bodies.

All weapons are dropped. All hands are raised.

"Goddammit," mutters Jessie.

I let the moment sink in. They all look defeated. I'd feel bad for them if this weren't so funny.

"You're all amateurs," I say finally.

"Hey, screw you, man," says Rayne. "We—"

"You didn't check the chairs in the classroom when you first got here. You found the weapons but didn't question why there would even be weapons on a disused Air Force base. I'm sure you checked the mags to see if they were loaded, but you didn't check to see if the firing pins had been filed down. Then you rushed out here, pissed off and not thinking clearly. You were desperate to get revenge and didn't stop once to consider the possibility that I might not be alone. And now look at you. Standing there like idiots in the firing line of fifteen laser sights."

None of them speak. Jessie lowers her gaze, likely annoyed at herself. Rayne glances away, probably thinking the same. Link stares at me, still trying to be angry but knowing I make a good point.

I sigh. "You three are meant to be the best and the brightest the U.S. military has to offer, and you just got beaten—badly—by an unarmed, aging hitman. Was I wrong? Do you not deserve to be here?"

No answer.

"Let me tell you how I beat you," I say. "It was purely psychological. It wasn't about bullets. I knew every move you were going to make before you made it. Each one of you is an open book. Remind me to play you all at poker for money when we're done here... Jesus Christ. You trusted your environment. Your entire thought process happened within the confines of the world you were trained to exist in. *That's* what I'm going to train out of you."

"This is crazy," says Rayne. "There are certain things that are fundamentally accepted in life. I mean, who walks into a room and immediately thinks to check for a bomb under their seat?"

I raise my hand and shrug. "I do. Thinking like that is the only reason I'm still alive. Remember, it's not paranoia if the bastards are really after you. I'm going to train those fundamentals out of you. Get you all thinking the way I do. That's how you survive against the new threats in this world. That's how you're going to beat them."

Jessie clears her throat. "Okay. Point made. Now could you... y'know... call off your snipers? These dots are making me uncomfortable."

"Oh, yeah—sorry." I look over my shoulder. "Ruby! You can wrap it up now."

A moment later, the dots disappear. Everyone lowers their hands and stares behind me in disbelief. I glance back to see Ruby walking toward us. She was hidden behind one of the concrete pillars holding up the guard tower to the left of the main gate. She's strutting confidently and smiling. As she stops beside me, the team notices she's also holding a laser pen.

"You're shitting me," says Link.

Ruby shakes her head. "Nope. That was me."

"But... how?"

She takes out her cell phone and waves it at them. "Remote control. There are a dozen of these pens attached to tripods all along the perimeter back there. Pretty easy to control them. It's a simple app."

All three of them look at me, their mouths collectively hanging open.

I grin. "I told you earlier. The fights we're about to face are psychological. The enemies use their minds, not their guns. Technology and social media are more dangerous than they've ever been. The old way of fighting just doesn't cut it anymore."

Rayne starts laughing. "Damn. You're good, man. I'll give you that."

I shrug. "Thanks. Now, any questions?"

No one speaks. Link still looks a little sore, but he's visibly calmed down a lot since I put him on his ass.

"No? Excellent. Be back here tomorrow. Eight a.m."

I turn and start walking away. Ruby follows me. I don't look back to see what the team's doing. I think today's lesson hit home.

Ruby's grinning broadly.

"What are you so happy about?" I ask.

She leans in a little. "All that back there... how you handled them... that was hot."

I roll my eyes and laugh. "Thanks."

"Being a teacher suits you. Maybe when we get back to the hotel, you can give me detention... keep me behind after class?"

We look at each other. Her eyes are sparkling and alive.

I smile. "Yes, ma'am."

FIVE MONTHS LATER

11

I bought a penthouse apartment a few days after training began. I quickly realized that London was a good place to lay down some roots for the team. I'm not exactly shy of a dollar or two, so I told Schultz I would foot the bill for the location, so long as he could square things with the U.K. government about us being here.

It's overlooking the River Thames, in a district of London called Chelsea. It's one of the more upmarket areas, which kept Ruby happy. She and I live here. The rest of the team were given budgets by Uncle Sam to find their own accommodation. I told them I don't want to know where they're staying. I don't have anything to do with their private lives. The only condition was that they chose somewhere low-key and stayed invisible.

The penthouse has become the unofficial headquarters and meeting place for Blackstar. We found the old RAF base was too far away from the city to be practical. Here, we're close to the airport, should we need to travel, and it's a nice enough area that privacy is the default setting for any residents.

I walk across the street, enjoying the cool breeze and the early sun, and head inside. I take the four flights of stairs two at a time and head inside the apartment. Everyone looks around when I enter. It's a large, open space, separated into distinct areas. Windows run almost floor to ceiling on the left, offering a nice view of the river. There's a huge circular sofa in the middle of the room—sunken into the floor, with two steps in the middle—facing the wall nearest the door and the TV mounted on it. Beyond that is a kitchen, with a wide center island that forms a horseshoe path around the counters and appliances. Ruby's over there, drinking coffee. Jessie, Link, and Rayne are spread across the sofa, watching TV.

"Hey, Boss," says Rayne. "You seen the news?"

I shake my head. "Not yet. Let me guess... another C-list celebrity has updated their pronouns."

"If only. No, there was a siege yesterday at some office building in New York. A company called Tristar Security. Apparently, one guy stormed the place and took out a bunch of their security personnel."

I glance at the news report on the screen as I walk over to the kitchen.

"Don't look at me. I was here."

"They're saying he worked for GlobaTech."

I stop and look around. "Really?"

"So they say."

"Well, I would bet money on that not being the case, but it's not our concern. Until somebody tells us to get involved with Tristar or a rogue GlobaTech operative, we need to stay focused on the matter at hand."

Jessie gets to her feet. "Which is?"

I move around the kitchen island and pat Ruby lightly on the ass to move her to the side. She rolls her eyes and smiles.

"I'm glad you asked, Miss Vickers," I say. "Everyone gather 'round. I got us a gig."

They stride across the apartment. They're all dressed casually. All appear alert and motivated. There's a bounce in their step and a focus in their eyes that I can't help feeling proud to see.

It's been a good five months. Smooth, for the most part. Link has been the most difficult to win over. I don't know if he's still sore about what happened on the first day, but the first few weeks, he was clearly reluctant to listen. My patience wore thin pretty quick. It was Ruby who reined me in, reminding me why we chose the guy in the first place. It wasn't for his sparkling personality. It was only after the first couple of assignments that he warmed to the idea of answering to me. I honestly wouldn't say I was friends with anyone on the team, but there's a level of respect and courtesy that makes it easy to do the job.

They're a great team.

They each stand in front of me, leaning on the counter expectantly.

I open the file in my hand and spread the contents across the surface.

"We have a new mission," I begin. "I had a call with the president earlier today."

"Earlier?" asks Link. "It's not even nine-thirty. What time did you get up?"

I smile. "Too goddamn early. But for stuff like this, I need to be in a secure location, which means I'm up with the sun."

"Where did you go?" asks Jessie.

"A conference room in the headquarters of MI5. Courtesy of the British government. I have a secure line to the White House whenever I need it and a secure server there to receive and print information like this."

She nods. "Nice."

"What can I say? They're a friendly bunch over here. Anyway, these are satellite surveillance images taken by the CIA of Pancevo."

"Never heard of it," says Rayne.

"Me neither, until about an hour ago. It's a small, rural town north of Belgrade."

"Serbia?" says Link. "That place ain't ever gonna be a vacation spot."

I smile. "Probably not. They're images of a suspected arms deal that took place inside the last thirty-six hours. It's an abandoned warehouse in the back-end of nowhere."

The images are high-quality black-and-whites that show four men standing beside a stack of large crates. One crate is open, but the angle doesn't show what's inside.

Opposite them are two more men. One is significantly larger than the other.

I point to the smaller of the two. "This guy's our target. Not much is known about him. He goes by the name Holt, and he's currently high up on several watchlists around the world as a key figure in the black-market arms trade."

"This doesn't sound out of the ordinary," observes Link. "Why has this been given to us, instead of being handled through normal channels?"

"And who's that big bastard with him?" asks Rayne.

"The big bastard is why we've been given this mission," I say. "I don't know his name, but I know he's an assassin. A highly sought-after one with a good reputation. It was assumed I would know where to find him."

Ruby leans in next to me and studies the image. "Yeah, he does look familiar. Don't know his name, though."

"So, do you?" asks Jessie.

"Maybe, yeah. The target is Holt, but his bodyguard might be the best way of finding him."

"What makes this Holt guy so special?" asks Link.

"He's one of a few people who have stood out in the post-4/17 world," I explain. "A constant presence in the growing community of assholes looking to profit from the misfortune of others. As you all know, the landscape has changed. All the wars you three were trained to fight have gone, leaving a gap in the market, which people like Holt are trying to fill."

"Is this not a GlobaTech thing?" asks Rayne.

I shake my head. "They have their hands full. For now, this is being treated as an isolated issue. However, Holt is a big fish. The concern is that whatever he's selling could be linked to whatever GlobaTech and the president are worried about."

"Which we haven't been given any information on..." quips Link, not hiding the frustration in his voice.

"I don't know what to tell you," I say. "When I know, you'll know. For now, they're keeping their cards close to their chests. I suspect that's because they either don't have the evidence to support their theories, don't know who to trust, or both. I'm not the biggest fan of our illustrious leader, but I trust him to do the right thing. That's why I signed up for this, and that's why I recruited you all. I also trust GlobaTech. If they're worried about something, there's good reason. Until that's deemed our problem, we go where we're told."

Link rolls his eyes but concedes with a nod.

"Okay. This is the plan. I want you three to head to Serbia. Find out everything you can about what Holt is selling and whom he's selling it to. Ruby and I are going to Paris to track down Holt's bodyguard."

Ruby smiles. "Yay, Paris!"

Jessie sighs. "We definitely got the wrong end of *that* deal..."

I smile. "We work to our strengths. It's your own fault for being so good."

She shakes her head and smiles. "Whatever."

"So, why Paris?" asks Rayne. "Is there a secret club for assassins there or something?"

He smirks. The others laugh with him.

I shrug. "Pretty much, yeah."

He frowns. "Wait. Seriously?"

I nod. "There's an underground community of assassins and fixers that operates around the globe. Some places are more high-profile than others. There's a guy in Paris who runs a casino. He might be able to help. So, that's our first stop."

"Thought you were retired?" says Jessie. "Doesn't your membership expire or something?"

I smile. "It's not an *actual* club. I was the top of the food chain in that world for a long time. I have plenty of favors to call in. Like I said, we're playing to our strengths."

Link stands straight and picks up the photo of Holt and his bodyguard. "When do we leave?"

I shrug. "How soon can you get to Heathrow airport?"

He smiles. "That's my kind of answer."

I gather the contents of the folder together and hand it to Jessie. "Good luck, folks."

There's a murmur of thanks from the group as they hustle across the apartment and out the door.

Ruby's standing beside me, quietly sipping her coffee. She's wearing a large hoodie and leggings and looks incredible.

"You okay?" I ask her.

"Mm-hmm." She nods. "I'm gonna go pack for Paris. I assume we're leaving as soon as possible?"

"That's the plan."

She brushes her hand over my arm and back as she walks away, toward the bedroom.

She didn't say much during the briefing, and she's surprisingly subdued, considering I just told her she's going on an all-expenses-paid trip to Paris. Something's definitely bothering her.

I'm sure she'll tell me when she's ready.

12

Paris is beautiful at night. Lights line the streets, reflecting off the water of the Seine. The Eiffel Tower stands like a beacon, watching over the city. The traffic is busy without being intrusive. The people move at an easy pace along the sidewalks, content in their own world.

If I were here for any other reason, I'd be in awe.

Ruby and I are walking hand in hand along the banks of the river. I'm wearing a tailored black suit, which she complimented more than once before leaving the hotel. She's wearing a blood-red evening gown. It clings to all the right places, and she looks incredible. It's elegant and classy, yet she somehow still manages to wear it on the right side of slutty, which is her safe space when it comes to formal fashion.

The cool breeze is more refreshing than brisk. We walk with purpose but with no great hurry. I can see our destination on the other side of the river. There's a bridge up ahead that will lead us there.

While the silence between us is comfortable, it isn't natural. Taking Ruby to Paris and telling her to dress formally is like taking a kid to Disneyland. She would be excited beyond words. Yet she's remained uncharacteristically subdued since we left London yesterday. We know each other well enough to know when to give each other space, but even I can tell there's something bothering her.

"You okay?" I ask her.

She smiles almost reluctantly. "Sure. Paris is lovely."

"It is. I know we're here on business, but I figured you'd be a little more... I dunno... happy. This is your kinda town."

"I am. It's great. Just focused on the job. That's all."

Now I know something's wrong.

I stop and pull her to the side, turning her to face me. Then I lean against the waist-high wall that overlooks the Seine.

"Contrary to popular belief, Ruby, I'm not an idiot." I smile to try and keep the mood light. "Something's been bothering you since the briefing yesterday, and it's been too long for you to not say anything. What's going on?"

Ruby's eyes search mine. I see the internal debate behind those hypnotic emeralds. She bites her lip, then exhales heavily.

"Fine." She pauses. "Are you sure you're ready for this?"

I frown. "For what?"

She gestures around her. "This. Paris. The mission. Where we're going."

I shrug. "Why wouldn't I be?"

"Because..." She sighs. "Can I be honest?"

I smile. "Are you ever not?"

"I think you're underestimating the situation. I think us

being involved in Blackstar, with Schultz, has given you tunnel vision. You're being sloppy, and you're better than that."

"What do you mean?"

"You came here as if it's just another day at the office. Adrian, you walked away from this world two years ago. Low-level contracts in Tokyo notwithstanding, you're retired. You know how our world works. Someone steps away, and someone else steps up. I'm worried your reputation isn't what it used to be."

I sigh. "I don't give a damn about my reputation. I never have. I don't need anyone to tell me how good I am at this."

"I know you don't. But if you think a reputation isn't currency in this game, you're a bigger idiot than I thought."

"I know it is. I like to think I've done enough over the years to—"

"You walked away, Adrian. You weren't killed, which is the single biggest reason for retirement for people like us. You walked away. *I* know why. *You* know why. But everybody else? They will see it as you quitting and admitting you can't do this anymore. Most of the great and impressive things you've done lately were done behind closed doors. The only thing anyone in our world knows for sure about you now is that you got beaten to within an inch of your life by a little girl."

I roll my eyes and go to speak, but she points a finger at me before I can say anything.

"And before you start, I'm not making fun of you or belittling Miley's skills. She was about as deadly an adversary as you've seen in a long time. She was well trained and shockingly violent. But she was young and motivated. That's what people saw. They saw the next generation almost killing the previous one." She points across the river, toward the building we're heading for. "Everyone in there knows who you are. Of course, they do. But they also know there's little evidence anymore to suggest you're anything like the Adrian Hell you used to be. I know you are, but perception is everything. When we walk in there, I'm telling you right now, it will be like a shiver of sharks smelling blood in the water. You need to stop being so... *you* about this."

I don't say anything, letting her words sink in. She's clearly been holding that speech inside a lot longer than the last twenty-four hours. Her breathing is heavy. Her eyes are locked on mine.

"A group of sharks is a shiver?" I say eventually.

Ruby rolls her eyes. "It was on an Attenborough thing the other week."

"Look, I appreciate your concern, but you're worrying about nothing. Of course, I know the value of a good reputation. Josh taught me that. It's how I became the man I am. Living long enough to voluntarily walk away from this life is proof enough that I'm still me. Look at Ichiro. He was the same."

She shakes her head. "No, he wasn't. He was respected for walking away because of what he had done, not because of who he was. He didn't build his legacy on the back of good marketing. You did, and it worked brilliantly. But they're two different things."

I take a small step back from her. "What are you saying? That I'm a fraud?"

She screws her face up. "What? No! Jesus, Adrian, have you not been listening? I'm not denying who you are. I'm trying to tell you that after two years, nobody cares anymore. Your reputation allowed you to secure a lot of high-paying work. Work that no one else had the chance to get. You also made a lot of enemies who tried to hire these people to kill you. That was a big payday a lot of good assassins had to turn down because we don't hunt our own. But I'm worried you're going to walk in there as if it's the good ol' days, expecting to be welcomed back with open arms and treated like the king you used to be. Adrian, you're so driven by the purpose Blackstar has given you, I think you're blind to the fact that the only value your reputation is good for here is as a notch on someone's ammo belt."

I shake my head. "Feel better getting that all out?"

She stares at me blankly. "What?"

"I love you, Ruby, but this overbearing mother routine you sometimes do is tiresome. You're worrying about nothing."

She chuckles humorlessly. "Oh, fuck you, Adrian. Fuck you! Don't you *dare* dismiss me. Is this how you were with Josh when he tried to help? Hmm? Was he too afraid to be honest with you because of how you'd react? Because I can stay silent, Adrian. I can keep my peace if you want. If that would make life easier for you. If you want to walk around in your own self-importance. If that's what you want, fine." She pauses. "No wonder he walked away from you."

Her last words hang in the air. Her visible anger doesn't mask the immediate regret.

She sighs. "I'm... I'm sorry. I didn't mean that. I just—"

I hold my hands up. "No, please—say what you really think, Ruby. Don't sugarcoat it on my account."

"You know I would never—"

"No, you're right. He did leave me. He did walk away. Because I told him to!"

I raise my voice, and it takes her by surprise. Her eyes widen slightly. Her expression softens.

"He spent well over a decade keeping a gun out of my mouth," I continue. "He made me who I was, and I owed it to him to live that life. I didn't just walk away for me, Ruby. I walked away for *him*. He deserved better than being my full-time carer. He was my brother, and I loved him. But I knew I was a burden to him. He should've been so much more, so much sooner. But he wasn't—because of *me*. He died because, even after I stepped back so that he could have his own life, he got dragged down into my shit, and that's on me. I live with that every fucking day, so don't you tell me I'm being sloppy or naïve or careless!"

Ruby says nothing. Her eyes glisten as tears form in them. Her hand absently moves to cover her mouth. A couple of people glance out the corner of their eye as they walk past, not daring to get involved in a domestic on the street.

I look momentarily to the sky, then stare back into Ruby's eyes. "Do you honestly think I still believe I'm the same man I was ten years ago? Twenty years ago? The mind and the spirit are still strong, but I know my body's betraying me. However, I'm still as deadly as I ever was. I *walk around in my own self-importance* because that's who Adrian Hell is. That's how he became the man he did. How he earned the reputation he has. The reputation *I* have. Being that way is all I know anymore. *You dance with the one who brung ya*, Ruby. Josh helped make me this way because he knew it was the only way I'd survive. I do this to honor him. Maybe I'm too good at playing the role because you clearly think I'm a fucking idiot." I point across the river. "You think I don't know *exactly* what's waiting for me inside there?"

She shakes her head. A single tear escapes down her cheek.

"You want a peek behind the curtain, Ruby? You want to really know what goes on inside here?" I tap my temple with my finger. "What happened with Miley five months ago scared the shit out of me. She made it look easy. Yeah, I still beat her, but doing so nearly killed me faster than she almost did. I hate the idea of not being able to do this anymore. The only thing I can do to compensate for that is play on my reputation. There's an old saying: you either walk like you're the king, or you walk like you don't give a fuck who the king is. There will be a thousand bullseyes on my back the second I walk through those doors. Of course, there will. But you know what? Every single killer in there will take one look at me and know that trying to get that notch on their ammo belt still isn't worth it. Because I'm still me, and that ain't gonna change until someone puts a bullet in my head."

I pace away. My breathing is fast and shallow.

Maybe I was keeping something inside that I needed to get out too.

I stop and turn around to look at Ruby. Her arms are folded across her chest. Her eyes are wide and sparkling with tears. She's shaking a little. Possibly because of the temperature. Possibly not.

I feel bad for snapping like that. But I won't apologize for it. It needed to be said, as much for my benefit as hers. She has doubts, and I understand that, but I need her to see I'm still the man I always have been. I need her to believe in me.

If I lose her, I lose everything.

I step toward her, and she moves to meet me. She reaches out and places a trembling hand on my arm.

"You should have said something sooner," she says softly. "If I'd known, I—"

I smile. "I think we both should've spoken up sooner. Things might have been said in a healthier way if we hadn't bottled it up and waited to erupt."

We embrace beneath the pale moonlight. The gentle rush of the river beside us is the only sound in the world. We hold each other for what feels like an eternity.

When we part, she looks up at me and smiles. "I'm sorry for doubting you."

I shrug. "I'm sorry for giving you reason to."

We kiss, then she holds my hand. We set off walking again, heading for the bridge ahead.

"So, you're ready for this, then?" Ruby asks.

I nudge her playfully with my arm. "Always."

13

It took a few minutes for us to compose ourselves and for Ruby to fix her makeup. We spent another minute or two double-checking we were both okay. We're good now.

Hand in hand, we head inside the *Palais de Platine*—the Platinum Palace. It's the fanciest casino in Paris and caters to the most pretentious assholes that high society has to offer. It's also a safe space for assassins to hang out and find work. It's managed by a slimy, yet respectably effective controller called Remy Fortin. He coordinates the handlers who arrange work for people like me. Occasionally, contractors will work direct, but we usually try to stay away from the business side and stick to what we know.

There are numerous establishments like this around the world. Each one is overseen by someone like Fortin. A lot of assassins have their regular haunts. It's how they network. Personally, I always tried to avoid places like this. Not really my scene.

Ruby and I walk in through the large revolving doors. The glass is as clear as crystal and held in place by thin, golden frames. We stand just inside the entrance, taking the place in. There's a loud, civilized rumble of chatter and activity in the air. Background music is barely audible. Sounds classical, like something you would hear in an elevator.

Everyone is dressed in tuxedos and gowns. It's hard to tell the upper-class pricks from the trained killers. At first glance, nobody pays us any attention. We're simply two more well-dressed people in a casino. Nothing to see here.

"How do you want to play this?" asks Ruby as she looks around at the opulence with awe.

I smile to myself. It's good to have her back.

"We should try to blend in, lie low," I reply. "Fortin might not even be here. No sense in drawing unnecessary attention to ourselves."

She looks at me, smiling. "Since when are you subtle?"

I grin back. "Well, I didn't learn it from you."

"Asshole."

We laugh together and make our way further inside, climbing the few marble steps that lead to the main floor of the casino. It's not quite Vegas, but I can taste the wealth in the air. Tables and slot machine are all occupied by people who seemingly enjoy handing over their money.

To each their own, I guess.

Ruby gestures toward a Blackjack table to our left. "You wanted to blend in..."

"Yeah, I guess we'll have to play something while we're here," I say, rolling my eyes. "Come on."

As we head over to the semicircular table, I notice the first couple of reactions from some of the guests. Nothing much. Just the occasional sideways glance, followed by a hushed conversation.

I guess word will soon travel. Probably the right move to bide our time. Let the attention come to us.

I sit in an empty chair to the right of the dealer. He's a short man, probably in his late twenties, with a thin mustache. It's either a fashion choice, or he's simply too young to grow a real one. I can't tell.

He acknowledges my arrival with a courteous nod. I place a hundred-Euro bill on the table, which he quickly exchanges for chips—two fifties. The other players pay me no heed.

I shuffle for comfort in my seat, fidgeting against the tie I had to wear. Ruby stands behind me, resting a hand casually on my shoulder. Ever the glamorous companion.

I bet fifty and am swiftly dealt two cards. I'm familiar with the game. I'm not exactly *Rain Man*, but I know enough to play it properly. I have to beat the dealer's hand to win.

I have a two and a queen.

The dealer works his way around the table, dealing cards on request and collecting his winnings as he goes. He reaches me. I tap my finger twice on the table, signaling for another card.

A nine.

"*Vingt et un*," he announces. He adds another fifty chip to mine and pushes them both toward me.

"Did you win?" asks Ruby.

I shrug. "It would appear so."

"Damn. Why have we never done this before? Ooo, you should bet a *thousand* next time!"

I glance back at her. "*That's* why."

"Oh, whatever," she huffs, crossing her arms. "You're boring."

"I'm also rich, and I intend to stay that way by not gambling all my money on a game of cards."

I stack my three chips together, then toss one back into the mix for the next hand.

The dealer waits for all bets to finish, then deals the cards.

I get a four and an eight.

I wait my turn, then tap the table for a card.

He deals me another four, giving me sixteen in total. There's a good chance the dealer will beat such a low hand if I stick, but there's a high risk of going over twenty-one if I take a fourth card.

Screw it.

I tap the table again.

A seven.

Damn it.

"Did you lose?" asks Ruby.

"I did," I reply, sighing. "Thankfully, I still have the same amount I arrived with, so I haven't lost anything, really. Let's hope I don't have to play this for long. We know how my luck tends to run."

She absently runs her fingers through the back of my hair. "Play a couple more hands, then we'll go get a drink at the bar."

"Yeah, okay."

Just then, a waitress appears at our side, expertly holding a silver tray in one hand, carrying two cocktails. Both Ruby and I turn to look at her. She's wearing a short black dress and high heels, with white shirt cuffs on her wrists, like bracelets. She looks like a Playboy bunny without the ears.

She smiles at us both. "Sir, madam... compliments of the house."

She hands each of us a drink in turn. Her English is good, despite the heavy French accent.

"Our host has requested that you join him in his private booth," she continues. "If it is convenient now, would you care to follow me?"

Ruby and I look at each other and shrug.

I get to my feet and nod to the waitress. "Sure. Lead the way."

She turns and walks off, still balancing the tray in her hand, despite no longer carrying drinks.

Ruby leans in and whispers, "That didn't take long."

"No, it didn't," I reply. "Not sure if that's a good sign."

"Guess we're about to find out."

We follow the waitress across the main floor of the casino, attracting more and more looks from the patrons. A mix of curiosity and disdain. Judging by how many people have stared, I'm starting to think there aren't many here who didn't earn their fortunes by murdering people.

At the far end of the room are three steps, leading up to a raised area covered by frosted glass. A velvet rope barricades the way. The waitress unhooks it and gestures us both through. The steps are central and lead to a narrow walkway formed by the two areas shielded by the glass. To the left is empty. To the right is a man wearing a white suit with a black shirt and no tie. He's sitting in the middle of the booth, behind the table, with two women on either side of him. Each one is wearing a short dress and heels and appears to have applied her makeup with a shovel.

The man looks up at us and grins. His teeth are so white, they glow in the dim lighting.

Remy Fortin.

"Welcome, *Monsieur* Adrian," he says, then turns his

attention to Ruby. "And *Mademoiselle Rubis*... the jewel of Paris, no?"

He laughs at his own remark, looking at his harem for support. They all giggle on cue.

His skin is flawless, hiding his advancing years. His hair is dyed jet-black and smoothed back against his head like an oil slick. He wears the permanent expression of a man who thinks he knows something other people don't, and his smile is, in my opinion, more like the creepy sneer of a child molester.

I don't like Remy Fortin.

Neither of us respond. I smile politely.

He continues. "When my little birdies told me Adrian Hell, the man, the... *légende* had walked into my establishment, I admit I was surprised. I heard you had left us mortals behind."

I nod. "Something like that, yeah. I'm happily retired."

Fortin gestures to the casino. "And yet..."

"Just a bit of personal business. I need a favor. Some information. Figured you were the best person to ask."

He laughs. "Oh, Adrian. Flattery will only get you places when you look like these ladies. You want to talk business. Let's talk." He offers me a space in the booth with a wave of his hand. "Please."

I step forward and place my drink on the table but remain standing.

"Thank you, but I won't take up too much of your time. I'm just looking for someone." I take a folded printout of the photo of Holt's bodyguard from my pocket and hand it to him. "The big guy at the back is one of us. I want to talk to him."

Fortin studies the photo. His face gives nothing away.

After a moment, he tosses it onto the table and shrugs. "I

do not help my clientele hunt one of our own. You, of all people, should know this, Adrian."

"That's comforting to know. But I'm not working a contract. Like I said, this is personal. I just want to have a conversation with him. Do you know where I can find him?"

Fortin shakes his head. "Even if I did, I would not share these details with you. We maintain discretion at all times here, as we do in all of our establishments across the world. Again, you know this, Adrian. Surely, you cannot expect me to pass such information on?"

I sigh and glance at Ruby. She rolls her eyes and gives me an almost imperceptible shake of her head, confirming my fear that this is a waste of time.

I look back at Fortin. "I understand. Thank you for your time and hospitality. Ruby and I will leave you to it."

Fortin leans forward, bringing his arms around from behind the ladies next to him and resting his hands on the table. "You wish to leave so soon? The night is still young! Sit. Drink. We can reminisce about your tales of legend, hmm?"

I smile as a courtesy. "As appealing as that sounds, we have places to be. It was good seeing you, Remy. Look after yourself."

He sits back and grins, flashing his teeth. "I always do, Adrian. I always do."

I step back and allow Ruby to walk away first. I quickly follow without looking back. As we head back across the casino floor, I notice that the looks we're getting have grown less subtle and less confused. I'm suddenly aware of how we're surrounded by people who are obviously not happy to see us.

Ruby had a point.

"One last drink?" she asks as we pass the bar.

I shake my head. "Ah, I think we should probably leave."

She glances around and sees the staring.

"Hmm, good point. This seems to have gotten real awkward, real quick."

"Certainly feels that way. Come on."

We walk outside, relishing the late spring breeze. The streets are busy with nightlife. The traffic is mostly taxis.

We set off walking west, toward Place de la Concorde. I can see the obelisk stretching up into the dark sky up ahead.

"Now what?" asks Ruby as she links my arm. "I can't say I'm surprised we got nowhere with that sleazeball, but hitting a dead end already is a real blow."

I smile. "We're not done yet. Remy Fortin might be the top of the food chain in Paris, but he's not the only game in town."

14

We grabbed the first taxi we saw and headed northeast, putting the Seine behind us. We cut through the ninth *arrondissement* of Paris and approached the eighteenth. It was a short drive—no more than fifteen minutes. We got out a little before our destination, close to the Sacré-Cœur Basilica. The streets are quieter here. Little traffic and few people. At times, the only sound is the clacking of Ruby's heels on the ground.

Some of the buildings around us are nothing short of an architectural masterclass. The gothic designs are lit from below to give them an eerie majesty in the dark of night.

Since leaving Fortin's casino, my spider sense has been in overdrive. I got a really bad vibe as we were leaving that place. Too many people were looking at us like sharks at feeding time. Not that we can't handle ourselves. Individually, we're both extremely capable. Together, with our backs to the wall... we're unstoppable.

That said, it's a hassle we don't need. Especially when we're trying to keep a low profile overseas.

"Where are we going again?" asks Ruby.

"There's a class system in our world," I explain. "Same as any other area of society. Fortin is the upper class. But Josh always insisted on keeping good relations with everyone. People like me and you wouldn't necessarily look for contracts from the working-class equivalent, but these guys have their ears to the ground at all times. They see the truth of the world. I think Fortin can sometimes be out of touch with that."

"Right. And you think these people will help us?"

I shrug. "If we ask nicely, why not?"

We walk on, ever aware of every dark corner, every out-of-place noise, every minute change in the wind. Paranoia saves lives.

"Have you thought about what happens next?" Ruby asks after a few minutes.

"What do you mean?"

"I mean the endgame... the point to all this. We've had a strong start, and you've done a great job bringing this team together. Seriously."

I shrug. "They didn't need much work, really."

"Maybe not, but they weren't a cohesive unit. The day we met them, Link tried to shoot you in the face."

I laugh. "I do make a unique first impression."

She rolls her eyes. "My point is, we're on a roll here, which is great... but what's the point? Nothing we're doing is really that far beyond the capabilities of anyone currently on the government's payroll. We're meant to be Schultz's answer to Buchanan's team at GlobaTech, right? So, when are we going to be given something to do that justifies the time and money spent on us so far?"

"That's a good question. Honestly, I don't know. I think the missions we're being given now have been sitting on someone's desk in their *not worth the trouble* pile. I think Schultz and Buchanan believe there's something coming, which they're trying to preemptively prepare for. I also think they're operating on limited intel and gut feelings. We'll know more when we need to, I guess."

"And until then? We carry on collecting our government salary like good little employees?"

I shrug. "It's not a bad salary."

Ruby sighs. "Yeah, it's a good salary. I just never pictured us working for someone else."

"Honestly, me neither. But I'm too old to play the game anymore, and we've both earned our retirement. This keeps us busy and has the added bonus of being the right thing to do. That's how I justify it to myself."

"Yeah, you're right. I guess I just never pictured us as the good guys, either."

I smile. "Our world is too gray for the simple concept of good and bad. I never considered myself a bad guy, even after twenty years in the business. I just did bad things for what I believed was a good reason."

"More justification?" she says with a grin.

"I gotta sleep at night somehow, right?" I point to a narrow side street up ahead. "This is it."

We turn onto the street, which is little more than an alley. It's barely wide enough for a car to drive down. The buildings on either side are mostly run-down. Some of the doors lead to the rear entrances of stores on the main street, but a lot of them are barricaded shut; the buildings are long abandoned.

Trash bags line the left sidewalk. Discarded needles and

beer cans spill out of holes in the bottom, likely caused by rats scavenging for food.

Ruby doesn't even try to hide the disgust on her face. "Where the hell are we? And what the *fuck* is that smell?"

I glance around and notice multiple puddles near the walls of the buildings.

"My guess would be piss," I say casually.

She grimaces. "Christ. This contact better be worth it."

I point to a man squatting low on his haunches, leaning against the wall beside a rotting wooden door. He's completely covered by the long, loose coat he's wearing. It's dark and stained. Only a hand pokes out of the end of a sleeve. His fingers toy with a small animal that's sitting next to him.

"We're about to find out," I say.

"Please don't tell me that's your contact."

"Probably not. But this is definitely the right place."

We approach the man, keeping a little distance between us. Mostly because of the smell.

I study the hunched figure for a moment. A sliver of jawline is visible beneath the hood.

"I'm looking for Corbeau," I say.

The man looks up, revealing his face. He grins, flashing the four remaining teeth still clinging to the inside of his mouth. His eyes glisten with madness.

"*Êtes-vous perdu, mon ami?*" he asks.

I glance at Ruby, who looks as bewildered as I do.

I shake my head. I picked a bad night to leave my Pilot and Ili behind.

"Sorry, I don't speak *coward*," I reply. "I'm here to see Corbeau. I know this is where he lives."

The man tilts his head from side to side, examining each

of us in turn. His grin fades. Next to him, the ragged creature he's fussing over hisses.

"My cat... he does not like you," he says. His English is broken. His accent is thick.

Ruby takes a step back.

"*That* is not a cat. What *is* that, seriously?" She looks at me. "Adrian, what is that thing?"

It's a cat... or, at least, a close approximation of one. There's no fur, and scabs cover its thin, fleshy body. Its ears are pointed, although half of one is missing. Its claws are long, and its legs are frail. I can see its ribcage through its skin.

"I'm not here to impress something that looks like the stomach of another animal," I say. "I'm also not here for any theatrics and gimmicks. I'm here to see Corbeau, and I won't be asking again."

The cat hisses again and curls up behind the man, sheltered by his coattails. His grin returns, more from curiosity than laughter.

"It is not polite to speak of my friend in this way," he says, stumbling on some of the words. "This cat belongs here. The two of you do not."

"Hey," says Ruby. "Go tell your boss that Adrian Hell and Ruby DeSouza are here to see him. See if *he* thinks we don't belong here."

The man sighs and glances back at the cat. "My little friend, he... came to me when his owner died. He, too, was a friend of mine. Stabby Joe, we called him."

Ruby's eyes go wide. She shakes her head with disbelief. "Fucking... *who*?"

The man looks at me. "Surely, you will have heard the name Joe Valane?"

I shrug. "Can't say I have."

"Oh, *monsieur*, Joe Valane... he was the master of the—" He raises his hand and slashes the air with an imaginary blade. "Moved like the night itself. You never heard him until his steel... it was pressing the flesh, you know. Hence the name... Stabby."

His accent prolonged the word. *Stah-beee*. Jesus.

"How did he die?" asks Ruby.

The man shrugs and screws his face up. "Meh, somebody, they... shoot him while he eat."

"Well, that's what you get for bringing a knife to a gunfight," I say. "Sorry about your friend, and sorry about insulting that... thing back there. But we're in kind of a hurry, and patience isn't really my thing, so if you could go get Corbeau, we can leave you to be homeless in peace."

Before he gets the chance to say anything, the door next to him opens from the inside.

I glance over at Ruby. "Looks like someone's inviting us in."

"Great," she mutters. "I'm *so* glad I wore heels."

We head inside, not bothering to look back. We enter a small, narrow vestibule, with stairs descending in front of us. The walls are damp and cracked. The air tastes stale.

I go first, walking down the metal staircase. I try to ignore the straining of the bolts beneath our combined weight. It's longer than it looks, and it seems to take an age to reach the bottom.

When we do, we step off into a large, underground warehouse. The roof is high, with a row of small windows just below it, maybe thirty feet above us, that look out at the street.

As Ruby moves next to me, I hear her gasp at the sight before us.

"Oh my God..." she whispers.

"Yeah," I say. "This is something else."

Sprawling out before us is a bustling shanty town—the slums of Paris, tucked away beneath the streets, hidden from the judgmental eyes of the public who would rather live in blissful ignorance.

Makeshift wooden stands are scattered about like a market, forming a natural pathway through. We set off along it, glancing without slowing at the stalls we pass. Food, clothing, weapons—this place has everything.

There are so many people here. I imagine a lot of them are simply homeless, as opposed to professional assassins either lying low or operating at the bottom of the food chain, looking to move up.

I had heard about this place, but I've never been here until now.

Ruby is attracting a lot of attention. The men stare for obvious reasons. The women seem fascinated by her clothes. I glance at her. She looks uncomfortable. On edge. I can't tell if she's getting ready to run or getting ready to fight.

Three men approach us, emerging from the crowds and forming a line to block our path. We stop in front of them. I wait for someone to say something. Whoever talks first is usually in charge.

The man in the middle looks us both up and down, then smiles.

"*Monsieur, mademoiselle*, welcome," he says. "Allow me to show the way, eh?"

He gestures for us to follow him. There isn't really an alternative option.

The men lead us through the small town and into an area covered by plastic sheets hanging from above. In here are several large units formed by wooden frames, which appear to serve as places to sleep. There are lots of stained mattresses and tents. Some are occupied; some are not.

We finally stop in front of a unit much larger than the others. Inside is a tattered sofa, with a man standing on either side, discreetly holding silenced SMGs. Sitting on it is a third man, who's wearing a long, stained overcoat similar to the man we saw outside. He's overweight without being obese. His gray hair stands out against his dark, mottled skin. He's looking at us, grinning with yellowed teeth.

"My, my," he says, his voice booming in the underground acoustics. "This is truly an honor. Do you know who we have here, boys? We are in the presence of greatness, I swear on my soul."

I hold his gaze, saying nothing. Beside me, I feel Ruby's body tense. I suspect her patience is wearing thin, and she's one of the few people I know whose tolerance for games is as limited as mine.

"I heard you were in my city," he continues.

"Word travels fast," I say casually.

"It does for me. Tell me, how is Remy?"

I shrug. "He's a slimy, selfish piece of shit with ideas above his station."

A moment of tense silence falls on us all. Behind me, the three men who brought us here shuffle on the spot. On either side of the sofa, grips are tightened on weapons. The man on the sofa stands, showing his full height and width. He walks up to me, holding my gaze. Then another smile spreads across his face. I reciprocate.

"Adrian, it is good to finally see you, no?" He extends his hand, which I shake. "Tell me, how is our mutual friend doing?"

"He's doing great, last I heard."

Ruby looks at me. "You two know each other?"

I nod. "Ruby, this is Corbeau, king of the Paris underworld."

He offers a courteous bow. "My lady, it is a pleasure."

Her eyes narrow. "Mm-hmm, I'm sure it is. And your mutual friend is…"

"Ichiro," I say.

She raises her brow. "No shit!"

"Yeah, these two go way back. Ichi happened to mention him to me in conversation once. When the name sounded familiar, we connected the dots. It's a small world." I look at Corbeau. "You've got a hell of a community here. I'm impressed."

He shrugs humbly. "It isn't much, but it is home to so many souls."

"Contractors?"

"Some. Mostly, to those forgotten by the world above. I provide them sanctuary and protection. They provide me with eyes and ears around the city. Nobody sees a homeless person sitting in a doorway. But the homeless person sees everything."

"Does that include your man outside?"

Corbeau laughs. "He is our security. Our doorman."

I raise an eyebrow. "He looks like Gollum with a crack-pipe. You should upgrade."

"He is… unique, for sure. But he is effective. He would not be out there if that were not the case."

"I thought he was just there to feed Stabby Joe's cat," says Ruby, perhaps a little too offhandedly.

Corbeau throws her a glance but ignores the quip.

"I assume this is not a social visit, *Monsieur* Adrian?" he asks me.

"It isn't."

I reach inside my jacket and take out the photo of Holt. I hand it to him, and he studies it carefully.

"I do not recognize this man," he says. "Should I?"

"That guy's name is Holt. I have a personal matter to discuss with him, but locating him is proving difficult. I'm here looking for the guy standing behind him. He's in the business. One of us. I was hoping you might know where I could find him."

"I see," he says, not taking his eyes off the picture. "And you think this man will lead you to Holt?"

"That's the idea."

"And what did our friend *Monsieur* Fortin say?"

I shrug. "That he didn't know and wouldn't tell me even if he did."

Corbeau hands the picture back to me. "I am afraid I must say the same. You know how our world works, *monsieur*. We do not work against our own."

"This isn't a contract. Like I said, it's a personal matter between myself and Holt. I just want to ask this guy if he knows where I can find him. No harm in that."

He paces away and takes a seat once more in the middle of the battered sofa. "Still, this is... how you say... a gray area for me. I keep people safe. I am trusted and respected because I guarantee secrecy."

"I know, but—"

"However, we are old friends, are we not? We discuss life and work, and should we happen to gossip a little... there is no harm in passing on a rumor, no?"

I smile. "I don't think so."

"Then it is settled. The three of us, we shall have a conversation as friends do. And I will tell you, my friends, of this rumor I heard of a man like the one in your picture. There is talk that he moved out of the independent scene after his last job. So good was his work, the client hired him exclusively. I hear the money was too good to ignore."

"Sounds like a good deal," I say. "You heard where this guy is? I would love to ask him about his career change."

"Sadly, there is no more rumor, *monsieur*—only information. That cannot be given for free."

"And what's the cost?" asks Ruby.

Corbeau seems to think for a moment. "Information can be given in exchange for work. One contract, and I tell you all I know with no harm to my reputation."

"No way." She looks at me. "Adrian, we're not here for this. If he isn't going to tell us, we should go. We'll find this guy another way. The team might be having better luck in Serbia."

She's right. Of course, she's right. We can't get involved in this kind of work. Not now. Holt's the priority. Besides, given our current status, going back to basics would likely be frowned upon.

However...

"Thing is, Ruby, no one's going to tell us shit for free. If at all. The team might have some luck tracking down the buyers, sure, but that's unlikely to lead us straight to Holt. This is the best chance we have of finding him quickly. We don't know what kind of time frame we're working with here. Best to assume it's a short one."

She sighs and goes to speak but stops herself. She purses her lips and looks away; the internal deliberation is evident on her face.

Eventually, she rolls her eyes. "Fine."

I turn to Corbeau. "What's the gig?"

He smiles at me. "The target is an aristocrat. A wannabe playboy whose trust fund lifestyle has seen him accrue large debts with some disreputable people."

I frown. "Okay. That sounds straightforward. Why hasn't this contract been done already? Why give it to us?"

"The target is Jean-Paul Reginald."

Ruby and I exchange a glance and shrug.

"Is that name meant to mean something to me?" I ask.

"The Reginald family is the last dynasty in France with links to the disbanded monarchy." He smiles again, but this time, it's laced with regret. "Nobody will take this job because Jean-Paul is too high-profile. He is a national celebrity. No payout is worth the risk of exposure."

"People are smart," observes Ruby.

"Indeed, *mademoiselle*. However, it is no secret that Adrian Hell does not want for money. And I suspect in these circumstances, information holds more value to you, no? Value enough to accept the risk no one else will."

Damn it. I should've anticipated this. We've walked right into the middle of a no-win situation and admitted that we have no choice to the person holding all the cards.

Amateur mistake, Adrian.

"Say we do the contract... what do we get?" I ask. "How can I be sure your information's worth it?"

Corbeau stands and places a hand on his chest. "I give you my word and swear on my friendship with Ichiro. You get this job done, I will give you the details of the last job the man you seek carried out."

Well, that isn't nothing.

I look at Ruby. "What do you think?"

"I think this whole thing fucking sucks," she says. "But... I have to admit, finding out exactly what Holt hired this guy for is the best lead I think we're going to get, and it could lead us to Holt himself."

"I agree. Finding out who he wanted dead could be crucial. So?"

"What?"

"I'm not doing this unless you're with me."

She holds my gaze. The smallest smile creeps onto her lips. She says nothing. She just nods.

I look at Corbeau. "Okay, you have a deal. Where can I find this Jean-Paul guy?"

His laugh booms around us. "Excellent! There is a charity gala tomorrow evening at the Musée Rodin. The crème of high society will be there, including *Monsieur* Reginald. He travels with security at all times, so this event will be your best chance."

"Consider it done."

"Do you need weapons? We have some quality stock here."

I smile. "I saw on the way in. But we're good, thanks. I never travel without some stock of my own."

"Then it is agreed. We shall meet again when you are finished."

Ruby and I take turns shaking his hand. Then we're led out by the three-man welcoming committee, back through the shanty town, to the metal staircase leading up to the street.

"This better be worth it," Ruby says as we climb the steps.

I let her go first, so I could enjoy the view. I'm not sorry.

"This part certainly was," I reply, smiling.

She glances back, sees me staring at her ass, and rolls her eyes. "Subtle."

"Not even a little bit. But this will be fine. Nothing we can't handle between us."

We open the door and step outside.

Oh.

Corbeau's security guard is lying on his side, with blood

pooling around his head. Beside him, the cat has been almost split in half by a bullet to its body. In front of us, in a large semicircle, I count fifteen men and women, all armed. They're facing the door, probably waiting for us. I recognize one of the women from Fortin's casino.

We freeze, standing shoulder to shoulder, looking out at the squad of assassins clearly here to kill us.

I look at Ruby. "Now *this* we might struggle with."

15

Neither of us take our eyes off the mob of killers covering the street. The way we came is blocked. We could head left, but I'm not sure how far we would get if we made a run for it.

"You carrying?" asks Ruby quietly.

"No," I reply, barely moving my lips. "You know the rules about the casino. No weapons inside."

"Shit."

"Yeah."

Come on, Adrian... *think*. What are the options?

There's no point running back inside. The door barely exists as it is. No way it would stop a hail of gunfire. We would be dead before we reached the stairs. I'm also not sure there's another way out once we're down there. Besides, I don't know if the assassins in there are any friendlier toward us than the ones out here. No guarantee we would be any safer inside, even with Corbeau's endorsement.

I'm not armed. I'm definitely not fast enough to outrun bullets.

Let her off the leash.

My Inner Satan speaks from the dark recesses of my mind. That part of my psyche doesn't say much these days. It's my Inner Josh that tends to get me through most things. But when the beast inside speaks, I always listen.

You might not have a gun, but you're far from unarmed.

That's a good point.

I glance at Ruby. "Hey, I haven't seen your Wild Child in a long time. She still in there?"

She turns her head slowly. As her gaze rests on mine, I can see all traces of humanity have gone from her face. The spark of her emerald eyes has gone. The dead orbs I'm looking into may as well be black. Her expression is deadpan.

Then she smiles.

Christ! I forgot how good she is. Forgot how similar to me she is. That crazy of hers... it's been almost four years since I've seen it. Not since I busted her out of the nuthouse to help me kill the president. But it must always be there inside of her, just below the surface. Waiting. And she just flipped it on like a switch.

Damn.

If she can get close to any of these assholes, it will stop them trying to shoot her for fear of hitting each other. Then she can really do some damage. It might even buy me a little time too. I flick my gaze beyond her, to the dead body lying next to the door.

I wonder if Stabby Joe's old friend was as good a security guard as Corbeau thought?

I wink at her. "You ready, sweetheart?"

Her maniacal grin widens, reaching her eyes without affecting them. "Baby's hungry. Baby needs to feed."

I smile as she slowly turns her attention to the group blocking our path. She locks onto one of the men standing directly in front of us. I see the fear and concern spread across his face.

"Go get 'em," I whisper.

Ruby sets off running, aiming for her chosen victim. She's in the middle of the narrow road before anyone reacts. She cartwheels into a back flip, kicking her heels off as she brings her legs up and over. She lands facing the guy, just over an arm's length away. I see her glance up at her shoes, currently flying through the air. She catches one and slams it into the side of the guy's head. I watch the long, thin heel disappear inside the guy's ear.

Fuck, that's grim. Still... it's effective, which is what counts now.

With the rest of them momentarily distracted, I dive to my right, rolling into a crouch beside the dead body. I quickly rummage inside the long coat, which is now even more stained thanks to the blood. My hand feels the comfort of steel in the pocket.

Bingo.

I don't even bother to check it. I pull it free, take aim, and start firing. Two men drop straight away. I clip a third, but he dives for cover behind a large dumpster.

I look for Ruby, who is lost in a huddle of deadly humanity. There's a group of five clumped together. I assume she's in the middle somewhere.

I resume firing and take out a couple more before the rest of them catch up and begin turning their attention to me. I start running left, past the entrance to Corbeau's underworld and along the narrow street toward freedom.

"Ruby!" I yell without looking around.

A few moments later, she's alongside me, sprinting bare-foot. The sound of automatic gunfire fills the air as we head left, around the corner at the end. The stuttering roar of bullets cracks and splinters the brick millimeters from my body before we disappear from the assassins' line of sight.

We don't slow down. Ahead of us is an intersection. The traffic is light at this time of night, but the roads are far from empty.

"Straight over," I manage, fighting for breath.

With a cursory glance in both directions, we run across, weaving through the gaps between the cars and ignoring the occasional blare of a horn.

There are more people on the sidewalks here. There seems to be a few restaurants around, which might explain it. I hope to God what's left of that hit squad doesn't start—

More gunfire from behind us, accompanied this time by a collective wail of screams from the people around us.

Never mind.

"How many... did you... get?" asks Ruby between deep breaths.

I wince, sucking in a deep breath through gritted teeth. I'm trying to ignore the stabbing pain in my chest it brought with it.

"I killed four... injured one," I reply. "You?"

"Took out two... disabled another."

Ahead, the road doglegs to the right, toward another intersection. This one only goes left and right. I point to a walkway directly in front of us across the street, between two blocks of stores.

"There. Come on."

We dodge more traffic at full speed. As we reach the opposite sidewalk, I risk a glance over my shoulder.

I see three—no, four guys following us, making no effort to hide their guns.

We head through the gap in the buildings, narrowly avoiding an assortment of tables and chairs that must belong to one of the restaurants here. It leads us to another street, but there's no road access from behind us.

"I counted fifteen... originally," I say to Ruby. "Six down, plus... two injured... leaves seven. There are... four... behind us."

She lets out a guttural growl of effort, digging deep for the energy to keep running.

"Let's hope... the other three... decided we weren't... worth it," she says.

Bullets pepper the ground at our feet. I look back again. The four in pursuit are gaining on us. Sadly, I'm not surprised. I can barely move as it is, and Ruby's feet must be shredded.

I twist my body as much as I can and fire the remaining bullets at them. I don't hit anyone, but it gives them something to think about. They hang back momentarily and split into pairs, each taking a side of the street, seeking shelter.

The hammer thumbs down on an empty chamber. I toss the gun aside. It's no use to me now. In front of us is a dead end. Nothing but a building with no entrance. The only way forward is to the right.

It leads us nowhere.

We're faced with the backs of apartment buildings. Three of them surround a large patch of communal grass, with a large tree in its center.

Instinctively, we both slow down.

"Now what?" asks Ruby.

"I'm thinking," I say, fighting for breath.

I look around. The buildings are too high to scale, which

is just as well. My days of *Spiderman*ing my way out of trouble are long gone. There's no path between the buildings to the streets beyond, either.

I don't need to look around to see where our pursuers are. I hear them turning the corner; their collective footsteps echo in the still night air.

Wait. What's that?

The building ahead. There's a light.

Is that a door?

No time to be wrong.

"Follow me," I say to Ruby.

Bullets punch into the thick bark of the tree, inches from my head and shoulder, as we run past it. There's a wooden fence in front of me, maybe five feet high. I'm in no condition to climb it, and it's too dark to search for the gate.

Screw it.

I drop my right shoulder, grit my teeth, and find an extra bit of speed. I feel my legs shaking with each step, but if I slow down now, I'll start thinking about how stupid an idea this is, and that won't get us anywhere except dead.

I shout out as I collide with the fence, hoping it's not secretly a wall.

It's not.

I crash through it, over-balancing and stumbling forward to the ground. Ruby vaults over me and continues running toward the light, which is indeed shining through an open door. I scramble to my feet, scooping up a piece of wood as I do. It might come in handy.

I'm in a large backyard, which I'm guessing is shared by the residents of the building I'm about to trespass in. It's too dark to make anything out, apart from the one guy standing outside, having a smoke. His confused expression is illuminated by the end of the cigarette. Given the lack of reaction, I have to wonder what exactly he's smoking.

I follow Ruby inside, hoping no one decides to start firing again. There are innocent people around now. I hate the idea of putting civilians in danger, but this is the only way to put some distance between us and the remaining assassins.

I see Ruby a few paces ahead of me. We're in a long, dimly lit corridor, which I'm hoping leads to the front entrance of the building. There's a maintenance room on the left. An open door leads to a laundry room on the right. Thankfully, there's no sign of anyone besides *Cheech* back there.

There's a stairwell on the right. Two elevators just past it. Then the entrance.

These guys are right behind me. I just heard a single gunshot.

Damn it.

So long, *Cheech*.

They're not going to stop. Neither I nor Ruby can keep this pace up for much longer. Then what? We've just led them back out onto the streets, where there's more innocent people just waiting to be caught in the crossfire.

This needs to end.

Ruby throws open the main doors and bolts right, along the street. I'm a few steps behind her, but I'm done running. I exit the building and turn left. I slam on the brakes, jarring my already burning thighs, and pin myself to the wall just beside the door.

Three.

Two.

I grip the plank of wood like a baseball bat.

One.

The first assassin in line behind me appears, slowing as he prepares to turn. I throw my hips around, then my shoulders, swinging like I'm in the World Series. The piece of fencing smashes into his face. He doesn't expect it. He doesn't have time to protect himself. His head lurches back, sending his legs flying forward and him crashing to the ground. I glance down and see the mess I've made of his face. Swollen and bleeding and broken. He isn't getting back up.

The second guy emerges, and I swing for him too. He manages to avoid the brunt of the impact. The wood connects with his shoulder, spinning him away to my left. He's disoriented but unlikely to be out for the count.

The final two men are in the doorway now, and they're ready for me. I grab the first one by his throat and drag him toward me. He's smaller than me and much skinnier, so he's easy to move. I spin him around and duck slightly, using him as a human shield in case anyone decides to start shooting.

With his back now to me, I hold him in place by his throat. I reach around and grab the hand holding the SMG. I clamp my hand over his and make a fist, forcing him to do the same. In doing so, he depresses the trigger. I step back, whipping his arm up as I do. A stream of gunfire spurts forth, shredding the last man in the doorway. The close-range assault tears him apart, and he drops lifelessly back inside the building almost instantly.

I step to my right, turning my shield to my left in the process. Keeping a grip on him, I do the same, riddling the still-stunned second guy with more bullets until the magazine is empty. He flails backward, crashes into the wall, then slides down to the sidewalk, leaving a thick trail of blood behind him.

Finally, I push my hostage away from me, creating some distance and allowing me to compose myself, ready for a one-on-one fistfight. I'm exhausted and sore and would give anything to go to bed right now, but I'm still going to kill this bastard with my bare hands.

He glares at me, snarling through yellowed teeth. In one swift motion, his hand disappears behind him and reappears a moment later holding a switchblade.

I let out a heavy sigh. I feel my shoulders slump forward slightly, a gesture of both fatigue and resignation.

Well, that's just cheating.

He cuts the air in front of him, trying to appear threatening. He'll be able to see how tired I am. He's unlikely to be fazed by his cohorts' deaths. The squadron of killers may have appeared together, but I suspect it was every man for himself in terms of taking me out. Any glory earned from mounting my head on the wall would be an individual prize, not a team effort.

A few seconds pass. Then I relax and breathe a small sigh of relief as I realize something he hasn't.

He wasn't alone, but now he is.

Whereas I *was* alone... and now I'm not.

Ruby sprints toward him from behind. She lets out a primal roar as she jumps, lifting both legs and driving both knees into the middle of his back. She then grabs his chin from behind and pulls his head toward her. As gravity does its work, they land heavily. Her knees are pushed deep into his spine; his head is pulled back farther than it's designed to be pulled. The snap of his neck is sickeningly audible.

She stands slowly, taking breaths deep enough for her shoulders to move. We look at each other, enjoying the moment of reprieve.

"You good?" she asks.

"Better than that guy," I say, nodding to the man lying dead at her feet.

"Any more of them? May as well deal with them while we're here, right?"

I shrug. "Don't know where the other three went. I'm in no rush to find out, either."

She nods. "Agreed. No sirens yet. We should get off the streets."

"We'll walk for five minutes in a random direction, then hail a cab to our hotel. Regroup there. Your feet okay?"

She glances down at them and shrugs. "I'll tell you when the adrenaline wears off."

We stick to the old rule—*when in doubt, go left*—and put the carnage behind us.

23:48 CEST

Ruby's taking a shower. We got back to the hotel about ten minutes ago. We weren't followed. There was no sign of the remaining three contractors.

I'm lying on the bed, staring at the ceiling, willing the last of the spots floating in front of my eyes to fuck off.

I'm not sure whether Fortin was behind the attack. My gut says he wasn't, although Ruby disagrees. Despite how much of an asshole he is, I don't think he was playing us when we met. He was right about reputation. He was also right about us not taking contracts out on each other. It's an honor thing. So, I don't believe he sent all those people after us. I think all those people saw us in the casino and, as Ruby feared, jumped at the chance to collect a couple of valuable scalps.

But the debate over Fortin's involvement is irrelevant. Our days in Paris are numbered. We need to get whatever information we can about Holt's bodyguard and get out of here before this turns into something my new diplomatic *get out of jail free* card doesn't work on.

I ease myself upright and reach for my phone, which is resting on the table just in front of me.

"Who are you calling?"

I hear Ruby's voice as I dial a number. I look around to see her padding across the room, wearing nothing but a towel. Her hair's still wet. She's trying to mask the winces of pain with each step.

"Just checking in with the team," I reply. "You okay?"

She nods. "I'll be fine, so long as I don't have to walk anywhere for a couple of weeks."

I smile regrettably. "If only."

The phone starts ringing. It's answered after a couple of rings.

"Yeah?"

I recognize Rayne's voice.

"Adam, it's Adrian. How's it going over there?"

He sighs down the line, blowing distortion through the speaker. "Slow but steady. We've done some digging, asked around, kicked in the doors of a few local pieces of shit... the usual."

I nod. "And?"

"And we have the location of the buyers. We're scoping the place out right now. Jessie's using one of her surveillance drones, so we can maintain a safe distance."

"Good work. Anything you're concerned about?"

"Not yet. We're just trying to determine how many people they have and get a feel for their routines. No sign of the goods Holt is selling to them, so we're thinking there might be a final meet, hopefully inside the next thirty-six hours. We have eyes on them."

"Keep me posted, would you?"

"Sure thing. How's it going in Paris?"

I shrug. "Not as great as we would've liked. Our being here seems to have triggered the local contractor presence. Already had a large hit squad chase us down tonight."

"Jesus! You both okay?"

"Yeah, we're fine. Not keen for another round, though. We might have a lead, but the information comes at a price."

"Which is?"

"Doing a job the rest of you don't need the details of."

There's a moment's silence. "Fair enough. It's your show, Boss. You need any back-up?"

"No, you three stay there. You're onto something, so let it play out. See where the pieces fall. Watch your backs out there, okay?"

"Always."

"Good man. See you in a couple of days."

I hang up and toss the phone onto the bed behind me. I lean forward, resting my elbows on my knees and my head in my hands. Ruby sits down beside me, links my arm, and rests her head on my shoulder.

"Everything okay?" she asks.

"Yeah, the team are on top of things over there. They have a line on Holt's buyers."

"I didn't mean with them, dumbass."

I smile. "Yeah. I'm fine. I'm just—"

"Too old for this shit," she says with me.

We laugh. She gets to her feet and stands in front of me, resting on the edge of the hotel room's desk.

"Seriously, Adrian, that's becoming a recurring theme nowadays. You're not too old for this mentally." She taps her temples with a finger. "Up here, you're more capable and deadly than you've ever been."

"But physically, I'm screwed, right?"

She shakes her head. "You're not screwed. You're not as young as you used to be, sure, but who is? You just need time to heal. You just tore up Paris and killed a dozen assassins at maybe forty percent. And that's being generous."

"What other choice do I have? We have to find Holt. That's the mission. We have to be ready for whatever Schultz and Buchanan are worried about."

Ruby crouches in front of me and rests her arms on my knees. I can feel the dampness of her skin through the material of my pants. She looks up at me and smiles. I can see the light returning to her eyes with each second that passes, slowly locking the monster behind them back in its cage.

"We will be. You have a team now, Adrian. Use them."

"I am..."

"You're not. You're doing half the work yourself because you're a control freak who could win a gold medal in being restless. You could've easily sent Jessie and Link to Serbia, sent Adam and me here, then took a few days to continue healing, knowing everything was in hand."

I go to speak, but the words don't come. I suspect Josh or Satan caught them before they could escape, and with good reason. That's the second really good point Ruby's made since we got here. I should probably start listening to her.

I just nod and slowly lie back on the bed. A moment later, she's lying beside me, an arm across my chest, her legs over mine.

And then... peace.

16

Say what you want about the French, but they know how to make a good cup of coffee.

After everything that went down last night, Ruby and I slept like the dead. Unfortunately, the rest didn't last that long. We were awake with the sun and out of the hotel within fifteen minutes. Staying in one place for too long isn't an option anymore, so we'll need to plan the next stage on the move.

We're sitting at a small table outside a café. The Eiffel Tower is behind us, partially blocked by the nearby buildings. It's bright without being warm. The wind betrays the season, so sitting here requires my jacket as well as a sweater. Ruby is dressed in a far more practical outfit than she was last night—tight jeans tucked into knee-high boots with a low, wide heel. Her over-sized hoodie doubles as a short dress. I know she's also wearing three pairs of socks to cushion the impact on her injured soles.

All of our belongings are gathered into two bags, currently resting on the back seat of our rented convertible, which is parked in front of us. Clothing is in one. Weapons are in the other. I feel the comforting weight of a Raptor behind me—one of the custom weapons Josh had made for me. I'm not spending another second in this city unarmed.

I watch Ruby opposite me, absently sipping her fruit-and-nut-flavored latte. I don't know how she can drink that shit. It's coffee, not a goddamn dessert. I take a sip of my own. It's normal, black... with two extra shots of espresso in it that really hit the spot.

"We need to think about the hit Corbeau gave us," I say after a few moments of comfortable silence.

"We do," Ruby replies, nodding. "This Jean-Paul asshole is a prominent figure. A French socialite who travels with security at all times. That's what Corbeau told us, right? If he's at this charity gala, it will attract a lot of other people of similar social standing. That means all eyes will be on the event."

"That's what I figured, yeah."

"Well, you're pretty recognizable too, for a number of reasons—especially after last night. I think that rules out gatecrashing it. We need to think of another way to get inside."

I smile. "It rules it out for *me*."

She frowns. "What do you mean?"

"You're right. Too many people will either be looking for me or will recognize me at something so public. But no one will be looking for you. You rock up wearing a dress like last night, you'll walk right in through the front door like you belong there."

"Just like that?"

I shrug. "Just like that. I'm sure you won't find it difficult to get close to him. I noticed we have some UV aerosol in the kit Schultz arranged for us. You casually spray him with that, as if you're accidentally catching him with your perfume or something. That paints him for me."

"And you'll be... where?"

"Outside. On a rooftop maybe half a mile away, kneeling behind a sniper rifle. I'm not sure exactly where yet. We can scope that out once we're done here. But I'll switch to a UV lens, so I can see the spray on him. I'll line up my shot, give you the all-clear to get out, then pull the trigger. Job done. Easy."

She rolls her eyes at me and smiles, somewhat sympathetically, as if pitying me for being mindlessly optimistic. "Adrian, is it *ever* that easy?"

"No reason why it can't be."

"Then why hasn't Corbeau found someone else to do this job? Why offer it to us as payment for something important?"

"Ruby, people didn't avoid this job because it was difficult to carry out. They avoided it because the risk of exposure is too great. But I'm not exactly a stranger to that anymore, so I don't care. Besides, you can blend into those situations better than anyone. This is going to be the most straightforward thing we do here."

She falls silent, staring blankly ahead as she sips more of her coffee.

"I guess you're right," she says finally. "Maybe I'm overthinking it."

I shake my head. "No, you're approaching it with a healthy and justified amount of skepticism. As am I, believe it or not. I'm just looking at the big picture. We do this, Corbeau gives us the information we need to track down Holt's bodyguard. He should then lead us to the man himself, and we can finish our mission. Out of all that... with all the variables... a standard hit on a French aristocrat with bad debt and delusions of grandeur is definitely the easy part."

Ruby smiles. "Well, when you put it like that..."

"Exactly."

My phone starts ringing. I shuffle to retrieve it from my pocket, look at the number on the screen, then answer it.

"Adam, what's the latest?" I ask.

"We've tracked the buyers to an abandoned factory on the outskirts of Belgrade. This place could be the headquarters for 1960s communism. It's in the middle of nowhere. All gray and ominous. We have eyes on a total of six targets. We think this might be the final meet we were hoping for."

"That's good work. What's your plan?"

"We're going to sit tight and see if anyone else arrives. We have to assume they're here to meet someone. If we get lucky, we get Holt. If no one else shows, or if we think our window is about to close, we'll move in and capture whoever's there. Worst case, we just get the buyers, which isn't nothing."

"I completely agree. How do you intend to make the approach?"

"Link and I will be on the ground. I'll move in close to secure. He'll cover me from mid-distance. Jessie will hang back, giving us remote air support via her toys. It puts a pretty wide perimeter around the place, so they won't be getting far. As a back-up, Link will use your old trick of remotely controlled laser pointers, in case these assholes are feeling brave with the six-on-three odds."

I smile. "Nice."

"We'll subdue five of them and question the sixth. Depending on what we get out of them, we'll either finish them all there and leave them to rot or dump them all at the side of the road on our way out of town. That will be your call when the time comes."

I think for a moment. "I wouldn't approach this any differently. You have the green light, Adam. Watch your six. Good luck."

"Copy that."

He ends the call. I pocket my phone, then drain what's left of my coffee.

"How is the team doing?" asks Ruby. "That call sounded encouraging."

"It was. They've tracked down Holt's buyers. They're about to move in and see what they can get out of them."

"That's great. The three of them work well together."

I nod. "They do. I haven't once doubted the choices we made."

"That was Adam that called you again, right?"

"Yeah."

"Seems they've assigned themselves a leader in the field."

"He's the best candidate for it. Link's effective, but he's like using a sledgehammer to remove drywall. Not as much finesse or patience as the others, but he gets the job done no matter what. Same with Jessie. The shit she can do with those drones... she's an incredible asset. But her approach is a little stiff. She's too logical. She isn't capable of being spontaneous or thinking on her feet without questioning any decision five times. But if you tell her which direction to aim in, she'll deliver for you every time."

Ruby nods. "I agree. Rayne seems more comfortable with just doing things. He doesn't waste any time. He acts or reacts the second he has a clear objective." She pauses, then smiles at me. "He also seems to be the most comfortable with bending the rules."

I raise an eyebrow. "What's that look for?"

"He's basically a younger you."

She's probably right. I thought the same thing in Karachi when I recruited him. However, I feign offense anyway.

"Looking to trade me in for a younger model, are you?" I ask.

She laughs. "Please. Like I would ever find anyone else who would put up with my bullshit the way you do?"

I grin. "Well, you're not wrong there!"

She immediately screws her face up and throws a packet of sugar at me. "Hey! You're not meant to agree with me, asshole."

"Sorry. I was just putting up with your bullshit, like you—"

My words trail off. My gaze is drawn to the group of people walking along the sidewalk, heading toward us from our right. They're still a few hundred yards away. There's a real mixture in the large huddle—young, old, couples, kids, students... all shuffling together, focused on their own little worlds. Some are chattering into a cell phone. Others are listening to music. Some are talking to each other.

But three people in the group are doing none of those things. They're walking with hardly any additional body movement. They're not talking. They're not listening to music. They're not with anyone. But they do all have one thing in common.

They're all looking at me.

"What is it?" Ruby asks, sitting forward slightly in her chair.

"I think we might have some company," I reply.

She follows my gaze and sees what I see. She looks back

at me for a moment, then her gaze flicks to something over my shoulder. Something behind me. Her expressions changes to mirror mine.

"I think you might be right," she mutters.

I glance behind me and see three more people standing out from the crowd. This time, however, there's a big enough gap in the sea of pedestrians for me to make out the gun one of them is holding low, discreetly pressed against their body.

There are too many people around. I can't risk this devolving into what it did last night. But we're pinned in now. Flanked from both sides. Handling three killers each isn't ideal, but we could if we had to. That's not the problem. The problem is doing it without anyone around us getting caught in the crossfire.

"Shit, Adrian, what do we do?" asks Ruby.

I casually take the car key out of my jacket pocket and show it to her. "I drive. You shoot. Let's go. Now."

17

Ruby moves first. She vaults over the door and shuffles into the passenger seat. She's already reaching back into the weapons bag as I land in the driver's seat and start the engine. The three assassins in front of us stop, immediately making them stand out even more in the sea of people still going about their day, blissfully unaware of how bad shit's about to get.

Behind me, I hear people start screaming. I hear the commotion of a crowd, scared and confused, running in any direction they can.

"Go!" yells Ruby.

Smoke billows behind me as tires screech, partially masking us from the group back there. I slam my foot to the floor and speed away from the café. The street is narrow, but thankfully, the traffic is light. Almost immediately, I'm forced to swerve into the opposite lane to navigate around a vehicle driving too slowly. I glance at the group that were in front of us as I drive past, making eye contact with each one for a fleeting second. Two men and a woman. The expressions on their faces are hard as stone and twice as cold. I see one of the guys talking into a cell phone.

That's probably not a good sign.

I move back out to the right lane and speed up again. I'm approaching an intersection and a red light. A couple of vehicles are stopped there, which may cause a problem.

I grip the wheel and shuffle in my seat, trying to get comfortable. I think this car's an MX-5. I don't know—Ruby picked it. Whatever it is, it's not built for someone my size. I'm just glad there's no roof, so I can sit straight.

Ruby's sitting half-turned in the seat, facing me. She's holding one of my Raptors on her lap, looking behind us.

"Do you know where you're going?" she asks.

I shake my head. "Not a clue. Right now, I'm settling for anywhere those bastards aren't."

We pass a side street on my left. Out of the corner of my eye, I see a large black vehicle come speeding out of it. It slides loudly across the road, narrowly missing the back end of my car.

I glance in my rear view. It's a 44. Mercedes. I see a driver and a passenger glaring out at me.

"Ruby, is that—"

Automatic gunfire fills the air. More shouting and screaming from bystanders is carried past us on the wind as the needle tips fifty.

"Never mind."

Ruby balls up on the seat beside me, getting as much cover as she can behind it. I sink down into mine as much as the legroom allows.

This is the problem with a convertible: there's little to no protection from bullets. They should warn you of that when you rent them.

"You gonna fire back at any point?" I shout over.

I feel her glare at me. "I'll fire at *something* in a minute! I'm trying not to get my head blown off."

"Fine. Just try to—" The dull, stuttering *thunk!* of bullets punching through the body of the car distracts me. I look in the rearview again. "Hey! This is a rental, fuckface!"

Ruby pops up in her seat and fires off a few rounds as I reach the red light. It isn't going to change in time. There's a line of cars heading toward us from across the intersection. Some are heading right past us. Others are turning left, moving across us. I need to get around the stationary cars in my lane before the oncoming traffic reaches us. Then I need to get across the intersection without being T-boned by cars turning.

Easy.

Adrian, you're not exactly known for being the best driver. Are you sure about this?

Josh, now isn't the time for the glass to be half-empty. Be positive or be quiet.

Fine. I'm positive this is a stupid idea.

I sigh. I hate myself sometimes.

"Hang on..." I say, gripping the wheel tight enough to lose color in my knuckles.

I accelerate, moving into the left lane and around the cars in front of me. Horns blare as I'm now faced with another car speeding toward me. I yank the wheel right, zipping back onto my side. The car shoots past me, missing me by inches.

Ahead, I see another car turning left, about to cut across me. I step on the gas, accelerating way beyond the speed limit in an attempt to get past where that car's about to be.

...

...

...

I clear it. I must've been a couple of inches away from getting clipped. The car coming from my left slams its brakes on. Again, horns sound out, but I ignore them. I imagine the driver would prefer to be alive and pissed off, as opposed to the alternative.

I need to get on a freeway—get some room to move where there's unlikely to be many people.

Next to me, Ruby pops up on one knee and starts firing, resting on the back of the seat for balance. In the mirror, I see the Mercedes take the same path I just did, cutting it even closer to stay in pursuit. A few rounds find their mark but do little to deter them.

She sits back down to reload.

"We really need to get out of Paris," she says, breathing heavy with adrenaline.

I nod, staying focused on the road. "I know. After tonight, hopefully, we can."

"If we make it to tonight..."

"We will. We just need to—"

Up ahead, I see another vehicle speed out of a side street. It fishtails across the road before settling directly in front of us. Another black car. This one's a BMW. A man leans out of each rear passenger window and takes aim with an assault rifle.

I slam the brakes on. "Oh, fuck! Hold on!"

The car lurches forward, throwing Ruby against the dash. She grunts from the impact and bounces back against her seat. I yank the wheel left, sliding sideways and lining the car up with the next left turn along. Then I hit the gas again, taking us off the main road.

The street is narrow, more like an alley. A thin strip of sidewalk, littered with trash, runs along either side of a single lane.

"You okay?" I ask.

Ruby's just composing herself in her seat. "Yeah, just—watch out!"

Shit! There's a car heading straight for me!

I brake and swerve, mounting the curb on my right and scraping Ruby's door against the wall of a building. Thankfully, the oncoming vehicle did the same. We just about squeeze past each other, but we both lose our driver's side mirrors in the process.

I grimace. "Ah, fuck. There goes the deposit."

"Well, at least it doesn't matter as much about the mirror I just lost over here," says Ruby. "Have you taken us the wrong way down a one-way street?"

I quickly look around, but there are no signs. "It would appear so."

"Nice going..."

"I'm sorry. I could've always stayed sandwiched between the two cars full of assassins shooting at us, if you'd have preferred?"

Gunfire interrupts us. We both duck instinctively.

"The Mercedes followed us," says Ruby. "And they're gaining."

I let out a grunt of frustration. "I see them."

Up ahead, this side street leads out onto another main road. Cars are moving quickly in both directions. No way I'm getting out of this intact.

"Seatbelt."

"What?"

I speed up, reaching back to put mine on. "I said, *seatbelt*. Now."

Ruby looks ahead and sees the stream of traffic we're heading for.

"Oh, shit." She fumbles for her belt. "Adrian, tell me you know what you're doing."

"Okay. I know what I'm doing."

She places her hands on the dash, bracing herself. "Are you lying?"

"Yes."

"What!"

"You told me what to say. You didn't say it had to be the truth."

She pushes back against her seat as we approach the end. "I swear to Christ, if we die here, I'm gonna kill you."

We burst out into the street. I brake hard and steer left, moving across both lanes of traffic. The first lane, the vehicles are moving left to right. By some miracle, I find a gap and slide through it.

Tires screech. Horns blare. People nearby scream.

Uh!

My body jolts. I hear the sound of metal buckling behind me.

Ruby grunts as she's thrown sideways into me.

Shit.

Not so lucky with the other lane. A car moving right to left just clipped the front of our car at speed, sending us spinning. I wrestle with the wheel, turning into the spin to try and even it out.

I grit my teeth, snarling through the effort. "Fuck, fuck, fuck! Hold on!"

We complete a full rotation and half of another, then rock to an abrupt stop facing the opposite way I had intended. I immediately look down the side street we just came from. The Mercedes wasn't as fortunate. They must've gotten T-boned from the left, as they're now stationary a little way past the side street, facing away from us. A significant dent has appeared in the passenger side.

No time to waste.

"Ruby, get ready."

I start the engine again and set off in the direction we're facing. Ruby doesn't need to be prompted. We both live on the same wavelength, and she knows exactly what to do.

I slow as we draw level with the Mercedes. She turns in her seat, extending her arm and taking aim with my Raptor. She fires multiple rounds through the window. Both the passenger and the driver flail in the seats as they're peppered with bullets.

I speed away. Ruby sits back in her seat, reloading the weapon.

"Now can we get out of here?" she asks.

I nod. "That's the plan. I'll head for the freeway, which will take us out of the city. We'll lie low until tonight, then head back in quietly, ready for the hit."

She sighs. "This better be worth it."

"No reason to think Corbeau won't deliver. Ichiro chooses his friends carefully. I trust his judgment."

We fall silent as I navigate a few back streets, eager to put some distance between us and the chaos behind us. It will undoubtedly have attracted the attention of the police, so we need to be far away and driving like everyone else, so as not to stand out.

Ruby reaches behind me and draws the second Raptor from my back. She holds them both low and smiles.

I glance at her. "What?"

She looks at me. "These weapons are incredible. They have no right to be as lightweight as they are, given the power they pack. Their accuracy is off the charts. I don't know how Josh made these."

I smile. "GlobaTech have some talented R&D guys."

"No denying that. But these things... they're better than any other handgun out there. By a long way."

"You say that like it's a bad thing."

She shakes her head. "It's definitely not a bad thing. I just... I don't know. Think about it. Josh made these handguns for you, with instructions to deliver them to you should he die. They're literally the best handguns in existence. On a different level to anything else."

"Right..."

"And now here we are, working for the president, running a team whose sole purpose is to be better than anything the military has because we need to be ready to fight a war that no one else is even close to being prepared for. Am I the only one here who sees the comparisons?"

I focus on the road ahead in silence for a moment, thinking.

Finally, I say, "You think Josh anticipated whatever Schultz and Buchanan are worried about, figured I would be involved at some point, and made these so that I was equipped for the new fight and ready for it before anyone else?"

Ruby raises her eyebrows and shrugs. "I think Josh was smarter than you or I could ever hope to be. I think he read the game better than most. And I think he knew you better than anyone." She waves the two guns at me. "In a lot of ways, these things represent everything Schultz asked of you."

"And you don't think it's just a coincidence?"

She shakes her head. "I don't think the universe is lazy enough to allow coincidences. Adrian, I've just used one of these things, and doing so made me feel... invincible. Like I had an unfair advantage over everyone else. I don't know how else to describe it."

I laugh. "Welcome to my world. Why do you think I'm so confident all the time?"

"Because you're an asshole." She sticks her tongue out playfully. "I'm just saying, I think when we finally get out of this crazy town, it's something we should explore. See if these weapons are Josh's way of trying to tell you something."

If it were anyone else, I would dismiss the whole idea as clutching at straws. But I trust Ruby's instincts, and I know she wouldn't say anything if she didn't believe there was something to it.

I also know Josh better than anybody ever did, as he did with me. Ruby was right—he saw the world in a way few others ever could. He definitely understood *our* world better than anyone. He was always really good at chess. I never played him. Never had the patience. But his ability to see how things would play out was extraordinary. Easily the only reason I'm still alive. If anyone could've seen the way things would play out post-4/17, it was him. Maybe working with him is exactly why Schultz and Buchanan are on edge. Maybe he saw the ripples, and now they're preparing to ride the waves.

Of course, they were going to come to me.

I follow a sign that says the *autoroute* is two kilometers away. Pretty sure it's French for the freeway. It leads me onto a wider and busier road. There are four lanes—two running in each direction. I see a walkway up ahead, bridging over the road—likely an alternative for people to get across, given there's no sidewalk or lights here. On the left is a long line of trees, separating this road from the city streets. On the other side is a steady stream of low commercial and industrial buildings. I think the river is behind them.

I see the tip of the Eiffel Tower in my rearview, shadowed against the cloudless blue sky. Beside me, Ruby rests her head back and closes her eyes. Her hair waves in the wind as it blows against us.

"Do you think Fortin really was behind all these contractors coming after us?" she asks, raising her voice a little to be heard over the noise of the wind.

I think for a moment. "I still think it's unlikely. Although, I promise you, if I find out he was, I'll be heading back to that casino to do more than just play Blackjack."

She says something I can't make out. I lean over a little.

"What's that?"

"Bridge," she says.

"I don't think Bridge is a game you play in casinos. And I didn't mean I'd spend more money there. I meant—"

"Bridge."

"Huh?" I glance across and see her staring ahead, her eyes fixed and unblinking. "What's wrong, Ruby?"

She points through the windshield. "Bridge. Bridge. Bridge!"

I frown and follow her gaze. We're approaching the walkway that stretches over the four lanes. I can make out the people standing on it. Six, to be exact. All are looking down over the railing at the road. At this speed, we're maybe five seconds away from being directly beneath them. From here, I can clearly see one of the people is holding something up, resting it on their shoulder.

Oh, shit.

Six people on the bridge. Six assassins last seen by the café. Coincidence? Unlikely.

No such thing, according to Ruby.

I squint against the sun. "Are they holding—"

"A rocket launcher?" Ruby nods. "Yes. Yes, they are. Can we think about moving now, please?"

If they fire at us, they'll either hit us—which would suck for us—or miss us, which would likely suck for everyone else. I can't let that happen.

I check the mirror and weave through the traffic, away from the bridge.

"You are shitting me..."

Ruby looks at me. "What?"

"The BMW is back and right behind us."

"Fuck! We're pinned in. Adrian, we have to—"

"I'm thinking! Gimme a second."

I barely have a second. Three at most.

I need to avoid the onslaught from the bridge. I need to lose the car behind us.

I could always... no. That's silly.

I have to... damn it, I can't. Not without crashing.

What if I... no. Wait, can I? I mean, I could. Would it work? It might.

Running out of time. Come on, Adrian.

Do it.

Really?

Yes, it'll be fine.

Satan, you have a really poor track record of being right about this kind of thing.

Trust me. Josh agrees.

Does he?

Excuse me! He absolutely doesn't! But to be fair, you have no other choice, brother.

Fuck it.

The lane ahead is clear. This will almost certainly—possibly—work.

"Ruby, place both Raptors on my lap, then grab the wheel."

"What? Why?"

"Just do it."

She does.

"Good. Now hold on tight, and whatever you do, keep the wheel straight. You ready?"

"No!"

"Perfect!"

I grab both guns and stand, putting a foot on my seat and pushing so that I'm wedged against the rim of the windshield. Then I stamp on the brakes. I raise both arms and lean against the windshield for balance. I twist my torso, so one gun is aimed at the bridge ahead of us and the other at the BMW behind.

I have to get this right. The shots have to be on target. Luckily, these are really good guns.

I fire three rounds out of each Raptor. With my left, I aim to the right side of the guy holding the rocket launcher. With my right, I aim for the driver's side mirror of the BMW.

The guy on the bridge instinctively jerks to his left. The driver of the BMW instinctively swerves to his right.

The rocket launcher fires.

I toss the guns into Ruby's lap and drop back into my seat, then take the wheel and hit the gas. A couple of meters behind our car, on the right side, the trajectory of the rocket and the path of the BMW meet.

The explosion is deafening. The heat from the blast immediately stifles the air around us, sucking the oxygen away. The sound of metal buckling and creaking is audible over the roaring flames.

Ruby screams.

"Christ!" I yell.

I try to steer away from the blast, but I'm not quick enough. The shockwave lifts the rear end of our car clear off the ground, spinning us away from the flames. Cars skid to a frantic stop all around us. One collides with the near side of ours, shunting us back toward the burning wreckage.

We rock to a standstill in the epicenter of the carnage. Around us, the radius of panic and chaos visibly expands. People flee from vehicles on both sides of the road.

"Ruby, you good?"

I look across. She's sitting upright in her seat, eyes wide and vacant. No blood anywhere I can see. Possibly some mild shock, which is understandable. She doesn't answer.

I place a hand on her arm. "Ruby, we need to move."

She jolts back into the moment and stares at me. "What? What happened?"

"Pass me a gun and grab a bag. We need to go. Come on."

She doesn't reply. She just nods. I take one of the Raptors from her, then reach back and grab one of the bags. She gets a hold of the other, and we climb out of the car, quickly navigating the sea of abandoned vehicles.

We approach the steps of the bridge from the left, putting them at our two o'clock. I can see all six assassins racing to cut us off, moving in a line, down toward the road.

Running at speed while carrying a bag is awkward and ungraceful. It also makes shooting while running that much harder. But sometimes, the only way to survive is to do unto others *before* they do unto you.

I don't hesitate.

I take aim and start firing. The first couple of rounds ping loudly off the metal railings of the steps. The next couple find their mark. I see two of the group drop away out of sight.

There's more gunfire at my side. I glance over to see Ruby following my lead. She takes out another one.

The remaining three return fire, forcing Ruby and I to separate. We dive away from each other to find cover. I roll behind a recently abandoned car. The engine's still running. I peek over the hood and see Ruby crouched behind the open door of another car.

We catch each other's eye and exchange a silent nod of understanding. I glance past her, back toward our rental and the burning BMW just beyond it. I think it's safe to say whoever was chasing us won't be doing so again.

The assassins ahead of us step onto the road and immediately fan out, forming a thin line across the outside lane. They have their weapons raised. They won't care about any collateral damage here. They just want us dead.

I can see some people still inside their vehicles. I see the fear on their faces. The tears in their eyes. Families huddled together. People talking into cell phones. I can't let anything happen to these people because of me. Too much damage has already been caused.

Ruby pops up out of cover, standing with her gun raised. "Hey, assholes!"

I watch in horror for a fleeting moment as all three snap their aim toward her in unison. Then I realize what she's doing.

I quickly stand, take aim, and fire three rounds.

BANG!

BANG!

I pause for a split-second to adjust.

BANG!

Three shots in quick succession. Three bodies drop to the ground.

I grab the bag at my feet and move around, keeping my

gun trained on the assassins, just in case. There's no need, though. I didn't miss. It's just habit.

Ruby does the same and meets me halfway, close to the foot of the bridge steps.

"You okay?" I ask.

She nods. "Yeah. You?"

"Yeah."

"Nice shooting."

"Thanks. Nice distracting."

"Thanks."

"Wanna get out of here?"

"I think we probably should."

"Me too."

She quickly shoves her Raptor in the weapons bag. I tuck mine away behind me, then we set off running, anywhere that's far away from here.

18

It's quite peaceful up here. Admittedly, given the last forty-eight hours, I could probably stand in the middle of the Rio Carnival and find it relaxing. But still, there's something calming about being alone on a rooftop, overlooking Paris beneath the burnt orange sky of dusk.

He says, looking through the scope of his rifle.

Shut it, Josh. I didn't judge you on how you relaxed.

Hey, what did I do that was so weird?

You sat there designing computer viruses and playing with spreadsheets, you fucking nerd.

That was useful!

I'm not saying it wasn't. I'm saying it wasn't your coolest moment there, sweetheart.

Truth be told, I miss his spreadsheets. He used to tell me all about whatever he was doing, knowing I wouldn't understand a word of it. But seeing him all excited about what he was working on always made me smile, so I happily let him talk at me when he needed to. It was probably the closest thing to meditating I've ever done.

I look over my scope, staring down at the activity below me. Guests have been arriving for the last half-hour. Ruby should be here soon.

There are only slivers of daylight left, but I still have good visibility of the Rodin Museum. It's lit up like a Christmas tree for tonight's event.

I'm kneeling behind a low chimney stack on the roof of a four-story apartment building south of the museum. I can easily see over the wall of the southern entrance, into the courtyard, and through the many large windows of the museum itself, which is around two hundred and twenty-five feet away. Maybe two-thirty. Assuming the guests will congregate on the upper floor, I'm looking down a twenty-degree angle. The air is mild and still, so no wind factor to account for. My rifle is effective up to around fifteen hundred meters... so, almost five thousand feet.

This shot is so simple, I don't even need to factor in gravity's effect on the bullet.

I'm using a Remington. The XM2010. I've used it a few times before, so I know how effective it is. Schultz arranged for our supplies, which might explain why we weren't supplied with GlobaTech weaponry. I guess he has to show he's supporting his own side in some way.

It's bolt action, and I have a .300 Winchester round chambered. I don't need more than that. At this distance, a fifty-cal' round would put a hole the size of a soccer ball in the north wall. I need to kill the target, not evaporate him.

Below, I see a white limo turn into the courtyard. It circles around and stops by the main entrance, facing east. A concierge opens the door. A moment later, Ruby appears. I can only see her torso over the roof of the limo, but as she ascends the steps and heads inside the museum, I can see the full, gold evening gown.

Damn.

It's split to the thigh on one side. Her hair is styled and flowing freely down to her shoulders. A small handbag on a thin strap hangs from her right shoulder. Her heels are precariously high, but that makes the level of grace she walks with even more impressive—especially given how sore her feet still are.

Pretty sure she's putting an extra shake in her hips because she knows I'm watching.

I smile. "And I thought I was the killer here. Holy shit."

The earpiece I have in crackles.

"You should be focusing on something other than my ass," says Ruby in a low voice.

"I can do both."

"Uh-huh. Just make sure you don't fire at the wrong target."

"Wouldn't be the first time."

She pauses at the stop of the stairs, in the threshold of the doorway, and glances over her shoulder, straight up at me. She won't be able to see me at this time of night, from that distance, but she knows I'm here. I look at her through the scope and see the stone-cold glare of disapproval on her face.

I smile again. "Love you too."

She disappears inside.

We spent most of the day holed up in a dirty, fifty-dollars-a-night hotel room above a vape shop. We needed somewhere no one would think to look for us. After two run-ins with squads of opportunistic assassins, we knew there would be more looking for us. The entrance to the room was around the back, in a cobbled alley too narrow for a vehicle to fit down. It was awful, but it was perfect.

We each took a long shower, changed into fresh clothing, then spent the day sleeping and planning tonight's hit. We built on the initial plan we formed when we got the job —Ruby would attend the charity gala as a guest, work the room until she found our target, then use a special spray to mark him for me. It looks like a normal perfume, but it sprays particles that will only show up under a UV light. She will get close to him and pretend to spray herself but actually paint him. I can then activate the UV filter on my scope and easily identify Mr. Reginald in the crowd. Given his social standing, he will no doubt be working the crowd too. I just need to wait for a clear shot. Shouldn't be too difficult, given how many large windows there are.

The only real obstacle was getting an invite to the gala in the first place. A quick call to Washington sorted that. Schultz immediately reached out to the French ambassador. Within five minutes, we had our ticket.

Of course, Ruby wanted to fully embrace her role in all this. She made a discreet call to a high-end boutique in Paris for the gown. I was tasked with organizing the limo on short notice—which wasn't easy or cheap.

Finally, in an effort to limit my exposure before going outside was absolutely necessary, I spent twenty minutes online, finding the perfect place to take the shot.

And here I am.

I glance right, past the cathedral, and look at the Eiffel Tower, lit up in the distance like a beacon. This city really is something. Maybe when all this is over, I should bring Ruby back here and actually enjoy the scenery and the culture. I think she would like that.

I turn my attention back to the museum, staring intently through the scope. I always keep both eyes open when using a long gun like this. It allows me to comfortably see my target while also being aware of my immediate surroundings.

I glimpse Ruby walking past one of the windows on the first floor, away to the right. She's holding a champagne flute and smiling. An elderly couple is saying something to her.

In my periphery, I see a fleet of vehicles pull up outside. I adjust my aim to focus on the entourage. There's a stretched black limo in the middle, with a sports car in front and two black SUVs behind it. The museum staff outside who are welcoming guests immediately begin to fluster, as if the arrival has knocked them off their game. The man who opened the door for Ruby begins pointing, directing other staff to the vehicles.

This must be the man of the hour.

A moment later, I see him. Jean-Paul Reginald emerges from the limo as if he owns the museum and everyone in it. From what Corbeau said about him, he might. He's flanked by two women who look like models. If I were a betting man, I would say they were probably hired for the evening. They have big smiles on their faces and seem to be relishing the fuss being made over them. But no self-respecting woman would look that happy around a douche-canoe like him.

His security detail then exit the other vehicles. There are ten in total—four from each of the SUVs and two from the sports car. All are suited and booted. All are wearing earpieces. That's some heavy-duty protection. Who does this guy think he is?

"Head's up. Pelvis has entered the building."

I hear Ruby choke on a mouthful of champagne.

"Thanks for that, asshole."

I chuckle. "Sorry."

"I think the name you're looking for is *Elvis*."

"Nah. This guy looks too much like a dick."

"Jesus. Where is he?"

"Just heading inside now. He's flanked by two whores and ten bodyguards. Be careful trying to get near him. Those guys aren't messing around."

"It's fine. Corbeau said this guy was related to French royalty, right?"

"Something like that, yeah."

"So, he was obviously going to have protection. Chances are, he has an ego as well."

"He does look like he thinks he's president of the entire world, to be fair."

"Exactly. Men with an ego are easy to charm. Trust me, I've been doing it for years."

"Hey! I'm holding a gun, y'know."

Ruby ignores me. I see her walk back across to the left. I adjust my scope to look ahead. There's a staircase leading to the second floor, which is visible in the central window. Reginald and his band of merry men are heading upstairs. I see Ruby linger casually at the bottom for a moment before following them.

"Watch yourself," I whisper.

Ruby sighs. "*You* watch me. I have a job to do."

She waits for a small group of guests to head up the stairs, then follows them, mingling with them for additional cover.

I hear her make passing conversation with one of the women near her.

She's a natural.

I shift my scope up, scanning the second floor. It looks like a wide-open floor up there. I see a bar at one end. The counter is white and looks illuminated from beneath. The wall behind it is neon blue, lined with glass shelves filled with spirits. There is some artwork and a few statues opposite, near the far-left wall. I'm guessing the museum has moved a lot of its collections to make room for tonight's guests.

Some of Reginald's security has lingered near the stairs. I see him beside the bar, although he's partially obscured by the wall. I can make out two guards, hovering behind him at a respectable distance, and one of the women, still hanging off his arm and laughing.

Back at the stairs, I see Ruby appearing.

"He's over by the bar," I say to her. "I don't have eyes on all his security. There are four next to the stairs. I see two with him. There might be more."

She doesn't immediately respond. I watch as she saunters past the security guards stationed at the top of the stairs. They all have their hands clasped professionally in front of them. I have to assume they're packing. I see one of them check out Ruby's ass as she struts past him. For a single second, I rest the crosshairs on the center of his forehead.

"Eyes front, asshole."

I see Ruby glance behind her and smile. "Now, now. Jealousy doesn't suit you."

"No, but shooting people does."

I follow her through the scope and see her approach the bar. She signals to the bartender.

"Pornstar Martini," I hear her say. "Extra lime, with a white wine sidecar."

I frown. "What the hell did you just order?"

"A girly drink. You wouldn't like it." She glances toward the window. "Okay. I see him. There are two guards and another whore on his left. You won't be able to see them."

"Okay. Wait until he's on the move to mark him. Then get the hell out of there. I'll do the rest. I'll wait until he's surrounded. The shot will cause more chaos that way, making it easier for you to slip away."

"That could take all night. We're already too exposed." Ruby pauses. "Okay, I have an idea."

I go to say something in protest, but I stop myself when I see her already on the move. It's too late now, and I don't want to distract her.

The barman places her drinks in front of her. She slams back whatever was in the shot glass, then picks up the cocktail glass and idles to the end of the bar, close to where Reginald is standing. She places her drink down and turns around at the corner, putting her back to him. The guards are to her side. I can't see clearly, but she must be directly behind him.

Ruby reaches inside her bag and takes out a small mirror. She begins putting some lipstick on. After a moment, she takes out some perfume and sprays.

I see Reginald's expression wrinkle. He turns around. He must've said something to her because a second later, she turns around to face him. She looks innocent and flustered.

"Oh my God, I'm so sorry!" she says.

I flick the UV filter on through my scope. I see the glowing purple patch on the back of his head.

I smile. She's good.

"I didn't realize," Ruby continues. "Don't worry. It's not a strong fragrance, I promise."

I see him gesturing with his hand as he's talking to her, but I can't hear what he's saying.

"Oh my God, wait... are you Jean-Paul Reginald?"

He shrugs.

"Oh, wow. I heard you might be here tonight. It's so great to meet you."

He shakes her hand, then brings it up to his face and kisses the back of it.

"I'm Ruby."

The woman on his arm turns away to face the window. She doesn't look happy.

"I'm in fashion. I flew in from Milan last night to be here."

Ruby shakes her head, smiling politely.

"You're too kind, Jean-Paul. But I'm here with my designer, Christian."

She reaches back to grab her drink and takes a sip.

"You have a private room here? Really? And what goes on in the private room?"

She takes another sip, then shakes her head.

"No, I've never played Baccarat. I'm not one for gambling. I don't really understand it. The only thing I really understand is fashion." She places a hand on his arm. "That is a *killer* suit, by the way! Saville Row?"

He shrugs.

She nods. "Armani, of course. You should meet my designer. He would love to work with you. Let me go find him."

He grabs her arm.

"Oh, no, I couldn't. I have to—"

He gestures past them, as if telling her which way to go. The guards I can see move. Their body language tenses.

I hear Ruby laugh nervously. "Well, if you insist on me joining you in your private room, how can I refuse?"

She's then led away, out of my line of sight. The other guards and woman walk into view, then back out of it.

The target, four guards, two escorts, and Ruby just walked toward the north side of the building, beyond the bar, out of my line of sight.

Shit.

"Ruby, what's happening?" I whisper.

No response.

I hear the faintest sound of a door slamming.

"Wow, this is nice," Ruby says. "Love the décor. So, how did you manage to secure a private room in the northeast corner all for yourself?"

Silence.

"Hey, what are you... get your hands off me, mother—"

I straighten and rest the rifle down at my feet, then press a finger to my ear. "Ruby? Are you okay? What's happening?"

I'm getting nothing but silence.

I have a bad feeling about this.

I listen intently for any sign of—

"Ah! Fuck!"

I yank the earpiece out as a high-pitched whine sounds on it, momentarily making my ears ring.

That happens when one end of the comms channel is destroyed. That means they found her earpiece.

Fuck.

I need to get inside. The problem is, that's going to make me extremely visible. That may bring with it a new set of problems, given there are now a bunch of reporters in the courtyard outside the museum, presumably covering the gala.

But I don't have a choice.

I lay the rifle down flat. It's hidden behind the chimney.

I'll come back for it later. Then I draw the Raptor from my back, check the magazine, and attach the silencer. I move low and fast toward the fire escape I climbed to get up here earlier.

Ruby's in trouble, which means everyone in that room is about ten minutes away from being very fucking dead.

19

Moving as fast as I can without drawing attention to myself, I walk into the courtyard I was looking down on a minute ago. There are a few cars still trickling in with guests, but it's quieter out here now than it was at the beginning.

Except for the gaggle of reporters hovering by the entrance. They must be holding out for a chance to scoop a big celebrity.

Well, I'm not doing interviews right now.

Thankfully, they're grouped together on the left of the steps leading inside. To the right, moving along the side of the museum, I see catering and waiting staff busying themselves.

That's where I need to be.

I take a wide path counterclockwise, circling along the right edge of the courtyard. I pass the gift shop and use the cover of the tall hedge to move unseen. I reach the end of it and pause, peeking around toward the entrance. There's maybe twenty feet between where I am and where I want to be. I have to be quick.

I appreciate the chances of a French reporter recognizing me is slim. That said, not long ago, I was incredibly visible to the world. I still have some of the war wounds to prove it. Those reporters over there... pacing idly around, chatting to each other, playing with their cell phones... they're bored. There's nothing worse than a bored journalist. They will try to make anything seem like a big deal just to have something to write about.

Seeing me here will be a big deal—especially when a bunch of people, including a prominent socialite, are found murdered. Won't take a rocket scientist to put two and two together.

I look away and walk quickly across the gap, heading down the side of the building, where catering vans are parked in a line. I glance back to see if anyone was paying attention.

Doesn't appear so.

I turn back around and walk straight into a waiter. We bump shoulders and both stumble away to the side.

I hold up a hand. "Excuse me."

The waiter looks at me blankly and says nothing. He probably didn't understand me. I start to walk away but stop myself after just one step. I look back at the waiter. He's wearing black pants and a white shirt, with a black waistcoat and red tie. He's about my height. About my build. There's an ID badge clipped to his waistcoat with no photo.

Hmm.

I look ahead to the entrance, which presumably leads into the kitchen. There's a security guard standing there.

Hmm.

I look back at the waiter and smile to myself. "*Bonjour*, opportunity."

I walk toward him as he approaches the open side door of one of the catering vans. I look around. No one is nearby and paying attention.

Perfect.

As the waiter leans inside the van, I take out my gun and slam the butt into the back of his head. He falls forward, instantly unconscious. I jump in beside him, drag him fully inside, then slam the door closed.

...

...

...

Three minutes later, I slide the door open and step out dressed as a waiter. My gun is tucked in the front of my waistband, and I'm using an apron I found in there to help hide it.

I quickly look around for something to carry, so I look busy. Inside the van is a small box containing slices of lemon.

That'll do.

I pick it up and walk briskly toward the side entrance. It's all about confidence now. Look like I belong here, and people will assume I do. I breeze past the security guard without making eye contact, twisting my body to avoid another waiter walking the opposite way.

And just like that, I'm inside.

Now to find Ruby.

The kitchen is bustling. A sea of chefs and waiters dash around in all directions. I see a tray of canapes resting on a counter near the swing doors that lead out onto the first floor. I scoop it up as I walk past and push my way through the doors using a shoulder.

Out here, guests are mingling, talking and laughing together, dressed like they could buy everything I own ten times over. It's not too busy here. The real party must be upstairs.

I thread my way through the people and head for the staircase. A short man with gray hair and a tuxedo steps out in front of me. Smirking, he reaches for a snack from the tray I'm holding. I don't say anything. I take one myself and hand him the tray. He grabs a hold of it, looking bewildered. I shrug as I shove the canape into my mouth and take the stairs two at a time.

Mmm. That was really nice. Pineapple and... something.

I step out onto the second floor and look around. The room is much larger than it looked through my scope. I see the bar where Ruby was standing maybe ten minutes ago. No sign of any of Reginald's security guards.

The back wall has two archways, one at either end, leading into another area of the upper floor. I couldn't see them from my vantage point. I know Ruby was led away from the bar...

I walk across the room and head through the right-hand arch. I follow the walkway as it narrows and winds to the left. The carpet here is blood-red. The walls are decorated with mahogany panels, with artwork hanging on them. There are a few people loitering and chatting. The corridor splits in the middle. I assume carrying on will lead me back around to the other archway, into the main room I just left. But I head right, toward another room at the front of the museum.

I emerge into a large open space, not quite as big as the one behind me. There's another bar directly ahead. Again, it's not quite as big. While the other one looks like a permanent fixture, this looks temporary, like it's only here for the evening. Long, red velvet curtains hang open at the tall windows that offer a view of the main courtyard below.

I look around. To my right is the door leading into the room there. It's standing open. I can see a handful of people inside, congregating around a display case in the middle. Possibly something to do with the charity gala.

I look left. The door to the separate room over there is closed. It's also guarded by two of Reginald's entourage.

Bingo.

A fellow waiter wanders by, holding a tray full of drinks. I gently tap his arm and smile.

"Hey, buddy, what's in that room back there?"

I gesture to it with a flick of my head. His brow furrows as he stares at me.

Right. French. Damn it.

I hold up a finger, signaling for him to wait a moment. I rummage in the pocket of my pants and take out the Pilot and Ili—necessities when traveling. I clip them into place in my ear and on my lapel, respectively.

"Okay." I try again. "What's in that room back there?"

The waiter glances over my shoulder and shrugs. *"I think it's a private room. Heard someone say there's an invite-only card game going on. I guess it's a bit of fun for the rich charity patrons."*

I nod as the translation comes through. "Right. Have they placed any orders that need to be delivered in there? Drinks?"

He shakes his head. *"We're not allowed inside. All staff were told that at the beginning of the evening. They have their own bar in there."*

Shit.

"Thanks, man."

I walk away, pocketing my devices once more. I need to get inside there, ideally without causing a scene out here. I need everyone here calm, so it's easier to leave once I have Ruby.

I head toward the room, then turn left along the corridor, back toward the main area. The two guards pay me no heed. I got a good look at them on the way past. They definitely have weapons inside their jackets. The bulge of the holster is noticeable.

I pause as soon as I'm out of sight and rest against the wall.

Come on, think. How can I get in there discreetly?

I stare blankly ahead until my vision blurs, lost in thought.

Maybe causing chaos out here is the way inside.

Huh?

Focus, dipshit.

The satanic part of my twisted subconscious isn't known for its tact.

However, as my vision clears and my mind stops wandering, I see that I might've been onto something.

Directly in front of me, mounted on the wall just below eye level, is a fire alarm.

I smile. I'm a genius.

I move to it and pull the lever, which immediately results in a loud and persistent wailing. The high-pitched, rapid beeping of the fire alarm sounds out. I walk back into the large room. People are exchanging confused looks, but no one's moving.

Typical. I should've set fire to the curtains.

Finally, a member of staff appears and begins ushering people out. As the crowd starts heading for the corridors, I approach the two guards.

"Hey, fellas, you gotta go," I shout. "Kitchen fire." I point to the door behind them. "I'll go tell everyone in—"

The one to my left moves forward and places a hand flat against my chest. He says something I don't understand. Judging by the way he's looking at me, I suspect it wasn't friendly.

Well, this makes things easier.

I grab his hand and wrist, then twist it counterclockwise. He's forced to move with his arm to relieve the instant pressure. As he doubles over, I lash out with my front foot, stamping down on the side of his leg. He drops to one knee, grimacing in pain. I quickly draw my gun and aim it at the other guard, who is just starting to react. I shoot twice.

Chest. Head.

The muted hisses of gunfire are lost beneath the ongoing alarm.

I place the barrel to the side of the first guy's head, which is roughly level with my stomach. I fire once.

Two down in no time. That leaves six, plus the target.

I yank the apron from around my waist and discard it. I'm holding my gun now, so wearing it just looks ridiculous. I twist the brass handle and throw the door open, then step inside, gun raised, ready to fire.

Oh.

Well.

Never mind.

I lower my gun and glance around the room. There's a circular card table in the middle, with three people sitting around it—two men and a woman. Guests for the evening, I assume. They're dressed formally and look terrified.

Over near the far wall, four of Reginald's security guards are slumped over one another in a large pool of blood. Next to me on the right, two more are sitting in leather armchairs, blood still trickling from fresh holes in their foreheads.

In front of me, Reginald himself is kneeling with his hands clasped behind his head. Up close, he looks greasy. Ignoring the fear currently dominating his wide, watering eyes, his expression is one of natural arrogance. Even now, there's a smirk etched on his face that makes me want to punch him. I get the impression that he looks down on everyone he meets.

Standing next to him is Ruby, who's holding a gun to his head. Her hair's a little more disheveled than it was when she first arrived, but other than that, she looks as stunning as ever.

All eyes in the room are fixed on me.

I wave my hand. "Hi."

Ruby glares at me. "What the fuck are you doing here?"

"Saving you."

"From?"

I gesture to Reginald with my gun barrel. "Him and his guards."

Ruby looks exaggeratedly around the room. "Right. What *would* I do without you?"

"Well, I—"

"No, no, no. Don't say anything." She sighs. "You thought I needed to be rescued? I had a plan, Adrian, and you're ruining it by causing pandemonium out there! I'm assuming the fire alarm was your idea?"

I shrug. "Yeah."

"Nice going, jackass."

I tuck my gun into my waistband. "Hey, hold on a minute, *Gloria Steinem*. You said you had an idea, then this prick and his guards marched you away to his private room. It looked a lot like your grand plan had turned to shit, so I came over here to save you. Are you seriously getting pissy with me about it?"

Ruby turns her body toward me, still holding the gun to Reginald's head. Her expression hardens. Her glare intensifies.

"Okay, two things. First, I'm not some helpless maiden who can't handle herself. Letting this slimy little fuck-knuckle take me to his private room, thinking he was in charge and oh-so-smart *was* my grand plan. Sitting at the bar in there, having gotten a feel for the place, I realized a sniper round to his head wasn't going to be as subtle as we first thought. This way, I could take him out quietly, with minimal witnesses. What, did you think I couldn't handle a few low-rent bodyguards?"

I open my mouth to speak.

Adrian, I swear to God, there is nothing you can say that wouldn't make this worse. Do yourself a favor and stay quiet.

Josh is right. I say nothing.

"Secondly..." Her hard stare softens. Her eyes light up. A smile creeps onto her lips. "You thought I was in danger and came for me?"

Huh?

I shrug. "Of course."

"You just ran in here, no hesitation, and beat a path to me because you thought I was in trouble?"

"Well, yeah. Obviously."

Ruby giggles. "You're the absolute cutest!"

I roll my eyes. She was playing me.

"Okay, can we just... y'know..." I gesture to the room. "Get this over with?"

She looks over at the card table. "You three. Leave."

They stare for a moment. I step to the side and place a hand on the edge of the open door.

"Hey." They turn to me. I point out into the main room. "*Je m'appelle* fuck off."

The three of them scramble to their feet and bolt from the room. I look at Ruby, who's laughing.

"Do you even know what you just said?" she asks.

I shake my head. "Don't know. Don't care. It sounded French, and it made them leave."

She rolls her eyes and turns her attention to Reginald, whose fear has been replaced by a look of bewilderment. A mixture of wide eyes, a raised eyebrow, and a frown contorts his face.

"Who... who are you people?" he asks. His broken English is barely intelligible due to his strong French accent.

I walk over to him. "Your social standing doesn't make you immune to the wrath of the bad people you owe a lot of money to, numbnuts."

"You... you are here for money?"

Ruby shakes her head. "No. We're here to do a job."

She pulls the trigger. Reginald collapses heavily to the side. She crouches beside him and uses his suit jacket to wipe her fingerprints from the gun. I'm assuming she acquired it from one of the guards. She then tosses it down next to him.

She stands, moves over to me, and kisses my cheek. "You're right. This was easy. Let's go."

She walks past me, toward the door. I smile to myself as I turn and head after her.

We reach the main area of the upper floor and join the final group of guests rushing down the stairs. We leave through the main entrance and make our way across the courtyard, camouflaged in the crowds of people lingering outside, anxiously looking back at the museum to see if there really was a fire.

We head out of the main entrance and take a left. A minute later, we're lost in the streets of a typical spring evening in Paris.

20

I'm lying on the bed in our discreet, crappy hotel room above the vape shop. My arms are crossed behind my head, and I'm staring at the cracks in the ceiling. Beside me, Ruby's lying on her front, legs bent up behind her as she studies her phone.

After leaving the museum, we called Corbeau and told him Reginald was dead. He asked how we did it, so we told him the abridged version—which, frankly, sounded more professional.

He thanked us for taking the job off his hands and said he would e-mail us the information we wanted about Holt's assassin bodyguard. That's what Ruby's currently reading.

I just hope it was worth it.

She sighs. "Okay. It says here the guy we're looking for is called Armen Falikov. A Russian national who has spent the last ten years traveling Europe and North America, working contracts primarily supplied by Fortin."

I nod. "The name sounds familiar, although I couldn't have picked him out of a line-up until now. He has a decent rep."

"Fortin's name keeps coming up, I notice..."

"I'm not concerned about him. He's a controller, and he runs one of biggest safe houses in Europe. He's a prick, but I don't think he has an agenda outside of self-preservation."

"Fair. So, Holt hired Falikov through Fortin for a job in Berlin about three months ago."

"Who was the target?"

"I'm just looking now." She scrolls down the screen for a moment. "Okay. It was a known arms dealer called Hans... um... Hans..."

I cross my fingers and mutter, "Please say Gruber. Please say Gruber."

Ruby glares at me. "Do you mind? That's not even a good movie."

My jaw hangs open. "You take that back. You take that back right now."

She rolls her eyes and ignores me. "Anyway, Hans the German arms dealer got real dead, and Holt swooped in to stake his claim."

"Right. So, Holt was simply wiping out the competition?"

"Sounds like it. Word has it he was so impressed with Falikov's work, he paid for exclusivity."

"Not uncommon."

Ruby looks up from the screen. "You ever get offered an exclusive gig?"

I nod. "A couple of times, yeah. Not my thing. Staying independent meant I could charge more and work less. Also meant I didn't have to work contracts I didn't like. What about you?"

"Yeah. Once. It was when I was just starting out. This old businessman had a lot of corporate enemies. His pitch was that he wanted to wipe out his competition one at a time and wanted to use someone he trusted."

"How did that turn out?"

She pushes herself upright and sits cross-legged facing me. "Turns out, he wasn't so much interested in giving me targets as he was suggesting which outfits he wanted to see me in."

"Ah. Right. So, what happened?"

She shrugs. "I did a little preemptive pro bono work and left."

I smile. "Sounds about right."

She goes back to scrolling through the e-mail.

"What else does Corbeau say?" I ask.

She sighs again. "Honestly? Not a whole lot."

I sit upright against the wall. There's no headboard.

"That's it? Falikov was in Berlin three months ago. That's all we have to go on?"

She tosses the phone aside. "Looks like it."

"Jesus. After everything we went through to do that fucking job..."

"Hey, it's not nothing. We now know Holt has been conquering the black-market arms game across Europe for a while. Maybe the team has found something out from his Serbian buyers that connects some dots for us?"

My phone starts ringing. It's vibrating and sliding across the table opposite the bed. I push myself off the bed and walk over to it. I glance at the screen.

"Speak of the devils." I answer and put it on speaker. "Adam, it's Adrian. You're on with me and Ruby."

"Hey, Boss," he says, sounding a little flustered. "You're on with all of us here."

"Tell me you have some good news."

"We have news," says Link. "Not sure I'd call it good."

Ruby and I exchange raised eyebrows of concern.

"Tell me," I say.

Rayne clears his throat. "No one else showed, so we made the approach like we had planned. It worked perfectly. We secured five of the six buyers and interrogated the last one. He was pretty keen to tell us what we wanted to know."

"Did you believe him?" asks Ruby.

"I did, yeah."

"So, what did he say?" I ask.

"Here's the kicker. They weren't buying. They were selling."

Ruby and I look at each other, more confused than anything else.

"Are you sure?" I ask.

"Positive," replies Rayne. "Those crates, Holt was buying them from the Serbians."

"I thought *he* was the gun-running entrepreneur," says Ruby. "What would he need to buy?"

"It was experimental tech," says Jessie. "Proprietary propulsion engines, top of the line satellite navigation and targeting equipment, guidance systems..."

"Jessie, that means nothing to me," I say. "You're gonna have to dumb that *way* down."

She doesn't skip a beat. "Holt just bought all the parts of a next-gen stealth attack drone. It's a prototype we think matches up with one that was stolen from a military base in Kuala Lumpur about three weeks ago."

"How bad is this?"

My question is met with silence, which is never a good sign.

"Guys. Talk to me. How bad is this?"

"Well," says Jessie, "if he can assemble it, he will have control of the most advanced UAV out there. Its stealth technology makes it virtually undetectable, and its near-unlimited range means he could, in theory, take out any target from anywhere in the world."

"Right. So, it's pretty bad, then?" I pace along the side of the bed for a moment. "Okay. We have to assume Holt can actually build this thing. No point in buying it otherwise. But why would he buy it at all?"

"The guy we spoke to didn't know," says Link. "But he seemed pretty scared of Holt."

"Yeah. The way I see it, there are three possibilities. One, he's buying it to sell it on for a profit. That's the best-case scenario. Two, he's buying it on behalf of someone who wants to use it, which would be bad. If Holt's just a middle-man, that means we're not even close to stopping the real threat."

"That is bad," agrees Rayne. "What's the third?"

"That's the worst-case. Third, Holt's buying it to use it himself."

"Is that worse?" asks Jessie. "If he's going to sell it to some militia group or a country looking to establish dominance somewhere, we have a potential terrorist threat to deal with."

I sit beside Ruby on the bed. "No, that would actually be preferable. If Holt has a buyer lined up for it, the chances are they have an agenda, whether that's political or religious. People with agendas are predictable. They have a specific goal in mind. You know what they want, you can figure out how they aim to get it and stop them. Agendas are easy."

"Surely, the same applies to Holt?" asks Link.

"That's the thing," I say. "I'm not sure someone like Holt would have an agenda. An opportunistic arms dealer like him... imagine someone in his position whose only motivation was to watch the world burn. Him buying this drone for himself is the nightmare scenario here."

The line falls silent. Beside me, Ruby places a hand on my leg and squeezes gently. I let the gravity of my words sink in. This is a learning experience for them all. Another lesson in having the right mindset. To fight in this new war like Schultz wants, they need to understand the enemy. They need to see that people like Holt exist. That some people thrive on chaos for the sake of something to do. The world is rebuilding. Part of it is stronger than it's ever been. Much of it is still in turmoil. If we suffer another 4/17 now, there won't be any coming back from it. Not again.

"Did he say anything else to you?" I ask finally.

"Nothing of any use," says Rayne. "Although, he did say Holt's bodyguard always addressed him by a nickname, which confused them when they first met."

"What was the nickname?"

"I couldn't understand what he was saying in Serbian, but we think it roughly translates as *horizon*."

I feel my eyes pop wide. My jaw hangs open. My surroundings fade away from my periphery.

Horizon.

It can't be...

That has to be a coincidence.

Except we know they don't exist. Not in our world.

My mind flashes back to my faked execution. To my life in Dubai. To Josh.

If this means what I think it does, then the nightmare scenario just got a whole lot worse.

I can't believe it.

Holt is...

Oh my God.

"Hello?" says Rayne. "You still there, Boss?"

Ruby looks at me, concerned. I'm aware of her reaching for the phone. I sit down heavily on the edge of the bed, staring blankly ahead.

"Thanks, everyone," she says. "You've done good work. Clean up there and get yourselves back to London. Don't kill anyone you don't have to along the way. We'll meet you in the penthouse tomorrow."

She ends the call and places the phone on the desk. She stands, then crouches in front of me, resting her arms on my thighs. She takes my hands in hers.

"Adrian, I know what you're thinking," she says. "But this doesn't necessarily mean anything. The Order is gone. You saw to that, remember? This could be a simple case of lost in translation, or..."

She stops as she sees my expression harden. My eyes re-focus.

"Yeah." She sighs. "If this means what we think it does, what's the move?"

I push her aside and stand, picking up my phone again.

"I need to make a call," I say absently as I pace away. "I need to speak to Schultz. I have to warn him that Holt is a much bigger threat than anyone realizes." I turn back to her. "Pack up our things and get ready to leave. We don't have a lot of time."

I dial a number and hold the phone to my ear, preparing for the hardest conversation of my life.

21

I'm standing in the penthouse in London, resting against the island in the kitchen. My arms are folded across my chest. I'm staring at the floor, vision blurred, lost in my own head.

In front of me, spread out across the large sofa, is the team. On the other side of the counter behind me, leaning forward, is Ruby.

Everyone's burned out. It's been a long couple of days for us all, with little sleep and a lot of traveling. Any disillusion Ruby or I might have felt after what proved to be a largely unsuccessful trip to Paris is overshadowed by what the team discovered in Serbia.

Now I need to tell them why.

Ruby understands the threat here. She knows what it means to go up against someone like Holt. I fear the team might not, and therein lies the problem. If they view this as just another step, just another obstacle, just another enemy... they'll die.

Link gets to his feet and begins pacing back and forth next to the sofa. His light brown skin glistens in the daylight shining through the large windows. He's wearing a muscle shirt and jogging pants. He probably went for a run or a workout after landing early this morning. The guy's a unit.

The others watch me patiently. I can feel their eyes on me. I can sense the concern and confusion.

"So, what's the deal?" asks Link. "You went all quiet and weird on the phone last night. Kinda like you have now. What's going on?"

I don't look up. "I'm trying to figure out the best way of explaining it to you. You just need to give me a minute."

He idles away, flinging his arms in the arm with frustration.

"This is bullshit, man," he mutters.

"Hey," says Jessie. "Take a breath, Link. We're all tired, okay? Let the man think."

I pull myself out of the trance and stare at the room. First, I glance back at Ruby. She seems fixated on the kitchen counter. That's fair. She knows what's really going on here.

Then I look out at the team. Jessie looks tired. She has dark rings around her eyes, and she's leaning forward against the back of the sofa, resting on her arms. Link is... Link. Easily frustrated and lacking in patience. He just wants to know what's going on. Wants to know what comes next. I get that. Rayne is sitting quietly. He's watching me intently. Studying me. He doesn't look tired. He doesn't look frustrated. I reckon he knows something's wrong. He'll know it was something he said because of my reaction at the time. He'll be curious more than anything.

I nod, mostly to myself. "Okay. Adam, you said the Serbians heard Falikov refer to Holt as Horizon, right?"

He shrugs. "Yeah. Translation was a little rough around the edges, but it seemed like he thought it was a nickname. I know that's what freaked you out, Boss. You gonna tell us why?"

"It's not a nickname. It's a title."

Link sits back down next to Rayne. Jessie sits up, suddenly awake with interest piqued. Ruby doesn't move.

"Any of you heard of The Order of Sabbah?" I ask.

They stare blankly at me.

"I figured." I take a deep breath. "The Order was a secret society of assassins, likely hundreds of years old, who shaped the progress of society by ensuring the wrong people didn't end up in positions of power."

Jessie frowns. "Are you being serious?"

I nod. "Yes. The underworld of... *contractors* Ruby and I were a part of never believed they existed. Everyone thought they were just a twisted fairytale. A campfire story for killers. Including me."

"Were they not?" asks Rayne.

I shake my head. "No. Turns out, they were real. They recruited me shortly after I killed President Cunningham a few years ago. Not long after I joined their ranks, I made them somewhat less clandestine than they would've liked."

Link huffs. "Go figure."

"This underworld you two are a part of," says Jessie, gesturing to Ruby and me, "is that not the same thing as The Order?"

I shake my head again. "The underworld and the Order were like... Protestants and Catholics. Two sides of the same coin. Same goals, just vastly different opinions on how to reach them."

Link rubs his eyes and sighs. "So, what... was there some

kind of civil war of assassins the world just didn't fucking notice?"

"It never got to that stage."

"What happened, then?" asks Rayne. "You keep referring to The Order in the past tense. Are they not around anymore?"

"No, they're not. I took them down before they could execute their endgame."

"What, all of them?"

I nod. "Yes. The Order crumbled and fell when I killed their leader."

"Damn."

"What happened to the people who were involved in it?" asks Jessie. "If they were as big and old as you say, surely, hundreds of people wouldn't just disappear."

"More like thousands," I say, shrugging. "But that's pretty much exactly what happened. The hierarchy fell. All the assassins that worked for them went to ground. Some slipped into our underworld and continued working. But many... I don't know. They went quiet. My guess is they figured that was the safest option. The Order controlled businesses all over the world. They had infiltrated governments, communities... even the Vatican. Ultimately, it became what we thought it was all along—a ghost story."

"What does any of this have to do with Holt and Horizon?" asks Link.

"The Order was a global organization," I explain. "It had chapters on every continent, in every country, in many cities. Dozens of them across the globe. Each of these chapters was managed by one person. They didn't have a name, just a title: Horizon. They were incredibly smart and dangerous people, and their ability to plan ahead and strategize was unparalleled. Think of a chess grandmaster on steroids.

They were responsible for dispatching hundreds of the best killers the world has ever known to carry out hits according to The Order's big plans. I went up against the one who recruited me. He sent half of Europe to kill me. Took me weeks to track him down in the aftermath."

Rayne got to his feet. "Jesus. You're saying Holt is one of these Horizon guys?"

I nod. "I am. Too much of a coincidence. It also makes perfect sense. We know he appeared on the illegal arms scene out of nowhere in the last couple of years. No one's ever gotten close to him. And now a man who makes being ten moves ahead look like you're asleep at the wheel has an undetectable drone capable of waging war, which he can control from anywhere."

Jessie rubs her face, as if stimulating consciousness. "Well, I guess that explains why you went quiet."

"So, what's the move?" asks Link.

"I spoke with President Schultz last night," I say to them. "He understands the gravity of the situation and has said we will have every resource we need made available to us, including NSA satellites and CIA tracking software. The priority is finding Holt before he does something stupid with that drone."

"And once we find him?" asks Jessie. "Is this one of those *any means necessary* situations?"

I nod. "It is. Make no mistake, folks. This is the exact type of mission we were put together for. There's no red tape. No senate confirmations. No Sit Room consultations. No government or military politics. No worrying about a press release or public reactions. We find him and we kill him."

Link shakes his head. "This is fucking insane."

I shrug. "This is the job."

"But we ain't assassins. We're soldiers."

"Is there a difference?"

"Of course, there is!"

I shake my head. "Only difference is that assassins get paid more."

He walks away, across the room. He begins silently pacing back and forth in front of the TV.

Jessie stands. "Link has a point, Adrian. We're supposed to be the good guys. I get that we have to do what needs to be done, but it doesn't feel like we're on the right side of this. It doesn't feel as... I don't know... *legitimate* as it did when I held a rank and wore my camos."

I push myself away from the kitchen counter and walk over to the window. I stare out at the Thames for a moment, then lean on the glass and look back at her.

"This is the job, Jessie. We do what needs to be done. That's why we're here. The old ways of doing things won't get it done against the people we're fighting now. Not anymore. This is a whole new game. I'm here to teach you all how to play it."

"But we're supposed to be the good guys. We're supposed to play by the rules. That's what makes us better than people like Holt."

I shake my head. "That's not true at all. Now, all of you, listen up." I pause until all three of them are looking at me. "If you learn nothing else from me, learn this: good guys don't need rules. They don't need constraints because they have the strength of character to instinctively know what's right and what isn't. It's the bad guys who need rules, and my job here is to make you three understand why I spent the last twenty years living with so many."

Silence falls inside the penthouse. Ruby appears next to me, offering a supportive smile.

I decide to hammer the point home to the team.

"I am capable of carrying out phenomenal acts of violence. But I don't. Not really. I only ever do what's necessary. I have my own rules. My own principles. I also had my old friend, who reined me in when things got too heavy. Now I have Ruby. I've made peace with the fact that I'm a bad guy. On paper, I'm one of the worst. I justify it to myself by saying that all the terrible things I've done were for a good reason. The *right* reason. Fortunately, there are few people who disagree. But that's still who I am, and like it or not, that's who you all need to be."

I look at Jessie.

"The world has no place for good guys and bad guys anymore," I say to her. "Just bad and worse. Not only do we have to play them at their own game, but we have to do it better in order to win."

The gravity of my words echoes in the lingering silence. Beside me, Ruby places a hand on my arm. She knows how hard it is to admit who I really am. She's offering the comfort I haven't yet admitted that I need.

After a moment, Rayne gets to his feet and moves over to the kitchen counter. He leans back against it, as I did minutes earlier.

"Am I the only one worried by how much that makes sense?" he says.

Link shakes his head and smiles.

Jessie starts laughing. "That's a really messed-up way of looking at things. But it's a messed-up world out there, I guess." She looks at me. "I can see why you got the job."

I smile back. "Thanks."

"So, really... what's the next move?" asks Link. "We need to take the fight to Holt, right?"

I nod. "We do. The president's gonna call me with the

details of someone we can liaise with at the CIA. From there, we'll try and track Holt's movements since his original appearance in Serbia and see if we can—"

Ruby wanders in front of me, toward to the window. The expression of confusion and her furrowed brow distract me.

"Guys," she says, pointing outside. "What's that?"

I turn to look out the window. Rayne appears next to me. Link and Jessie move to Ruby's side. Collectively, we all stare out, following Ruby's finger.

The area of London we're in is expensive. Not too many people around. Nice cars on the road. Across the street from our building is the River Thames, which threads around the city. Over the water, facing the apartment, is a large white building. It looks like a warehouse. Maybe a dock or something industrial. It stretches the full width of our view. Over to the right is one of the many bridges in London, linking to another district of the city.

The sky is bright and cloudy. The sun is high but not too warm. Ruby's pointing out between the building opposite and the bridge, where something dark is silhouetted against the daylight.

I narrow my eyes, squinting to make out any detail.

"Yeah, what *is* that?" echoes Jessie.

The five of us stand in a line and gaze silently out, watching the dark shape grow larger as it gets closer.

It doesn't take many moments to take form.

"You're shitting me," I mutter.

Weaving across the sky is a helicopter gunship. The noise of its blades grows louder as it gets nearer. It hovers above the edge of the water in front of our building. The thing is enormous!

It turns to the side, revealing a man standing behind a

mounted chain gun. From this distance, we can all clearly see his face.

Armen Falikov.

He's smiling and pointing the multiple barrels of his gun directly at our apartment.

At us.

No one says anything. No one moves. Like five deer caught in headlights, we stand and stare as death descends upon us.

Oh, shit...

22

"Get down!" I yell as my brain reactivates.

We all scatter and seek cover as the thunderous roar of automatic gunfire rips through the air. The explosion of glass is immediately drowned out by the unsuppressed hail of bullets from outside.

Ruby and I scramble toward the kitchen, seeking refuge behind the center island. Link slides across the floor and stops next to us a heartbeat later, resting his back against the partitioning wall that separates the kitchen from the hallway. I risk a peek over the counter and see Jessie and Rayne crouched behind the wall, near the door.

What now feels like a chasm between us is being torn apart like paper. The floor and the sofas are being shredded. The rate of fire on that railgun is so high, the bullets just form a line like a laser. Holes are relentlessly punched into the walls. This kitchen counter isn't going to last much longer, either.

Fuck.

"How the hell did he find us?" shouts Ruby.

I don't answer. How he found us is irrelevant. The fact is, he found us, and if we don't do something soon, we're all dead.

I reach behind me and draw my Raptor. I check the mag to make sure it's full. Beside me, Ruby has drawn hers too. I nod to it.

"Give that to me," I say.

She looks at me, eyes narrowed with confusion. "Why?"

"Because I'm going to draw his fire while you get out of here."

"What? Don't—"

"I ain't asking, Ruby. I need to get you and the rest of the team out of here. Give me the gun."

I feel my face harden. My gaze ices over. My jaw is set.

She hands me the gun without another word. She's seen my game face enough times to know not to argue with me when I'm wearing it.

I turn to Link. "On three, you get her and the others out of this building. No matter what."

He holds my gaze and nods.

Ruby shuffles around behind me, to Link's side. They both push up onto one knee, preparing to run.

The stream of gunfire is fanning back and forth across the apartment. It chips and splinters the counter above my head. I grip both Raptors tightly, fingers inside the trigger guard, waiting.

After what feels like a lifetime, Falikov strafes his gun back over toward Jessie and Rayne.

I pop up. "Three!"

I unload both mags at the helicopter. I'm not trying to hit

anything. I just need to distract Falikov long enough for Ruby and Link to get clear.

I let out a guttural roar as the chopper rocks back and forth outside, turning itself slightly to shield the fuel tank.

Both hammers slam down on an empty chamber just as Falikov stops firing. I look over and see Ruby and the others huddled in the doorway, beckoning me across. I quickly tuck both guns into my waistband—one in front, one behind. I make it halfway across the decimated apartment when I see the helicopter turning again. I look out to see it leveling out parallel to the building. There's no sign of Falikov. The machine gun is hanging loose on its mount.

My eyes go wide as I see the man standing there instead, holding a rocket launcher.

He's aiming to his right, lining up a shot at the door.

At the team.

I look over in horror and begin waving them away, urging them to turn and run.

"RPG!" I shout as I sprint for the door.

My legs feel heavy, like I'm trying to run in wet cement. I make it to the hallway as the *whoosh!* of the rocket fills the air behind me.

I open my mouth to shout, but the explosion erupts behind me. A cloud of dust and brick bursts out into the hallway, knocking all five of us to the floor.

...

...

...

A high-pitched whine drowns out all other sound. I'm lying face-down over by the railing next to the stairs, pushed up against the wall. I try to stand, but my movements are sluggish and uncoordinated. I manage to turn my head to look sideways.

Where is everyone?

I see the entrance to the apartment is twice the size it used to be. The door's lying flat out here. I think someone's underneath it. I see an arm sticking out from under it. I hope to God that's still attached to someone.

Ahead of me, further along the hall, I see people strewn across the floor. I see Jessie and Ruby. I think that's Link with them too. I can only make out the soles of his boots, which isn't much to go on.

As the ringing in my ears begins to fade, the sound of the chopper outside rises back to prominence. The crackling of fire is audible too.

Thunk!

Thunk!

Thunk!

What the...

I look over at the top of the stairs. I see...

Shit.

I see gas. Lots of gas.

I immediately start coughing.

Through the thick mist, shadows emerge. Five of them. No, six. Maybe more. I don't know. Figures dressed in black. I see guns.

Come on, legs. You need to start working.

The men in black swarm around us all. One of them bends down to grab me. I see a logo on his arm.

Sonofabitch.

Then he disappears. I look up to see Rayne spear him to the floor. The rest of them smother him. He's going down fighting, but ultimately, he's going down. He's thrown backward, out of my line of sight.

The effort to keep my eyes open is too great. The coughing starts to pain my chest.

This gas, it's—

??:??

What happened?

I look around me. I'm sitting up against the wall on the floor outside what's left of the apartment.

Where is everyone?

The hallway is empty. The gas has cleared.

I cough heavily.

Jesus.

I think half of that shit went into my goddamn lungs.

I take a deep breath, which is more painful than it should be.

There's movement to my left.

I try to push myself upright, but I'm too dizzy to do it properly. I make it halfway before falling against the railing overlooking the stairs. I drop to one knee to recover. I feel a hand on my arm. I snap around to see—

"Adam." I let out a sigh of relief. "Christ. What the hell happened? Where is everyone?"

He hoists me to my feet. I lean back against the wall as he steps away.

Man, he looks like shit. Dust and blood cover his face. Some of his clothing is torn. His eyes look half-glazed.

"They took them," he says. "Dragged them away like they were trash."

"How come we're still here?"

"The door hit me as it was blown off its goddamn hinges in the blast. I was pinned under it at first. Must've shielded me a little from the gas... bought me some valuable seconds. I held my breath and started swinging."

I nod. "Yeah, I saw."

"The rest of them took the guys away. Guess they thought they only needed two for me and you. I saw you go out. I was fading fast. Managed to floor one of them, grab his gun, and shoot the other in the leg as I fell. That's the last thing I remember. I woke up about three minutes before you did."

"Fuck. How long were we out?"

Rayne checks his watch. "About twenty minutes."

I listen intently, straining just to get my ears to work again. The chopper's clearly gone. I can hear commotion from the street outside.

"The cops will be here any minute, if they're not already," I say. "Probably why they left us here. Would've taken too much time to come back for us."

"Who were those guys? They came out of nowhere."

I look at him. "They were Tristar Security."

He frowns. "Are you fucking serious?"

"Saw the logo on their uniform."

"So, Holt hired Tristar for protection, as well as someone from your world? He ain't playing."

"No, he's not." I flick my head toward the apartment. "Let's see if we can salvage anything before we get out of here. We should put some distance between us and this place."

We both stagger inside.

Jesus, this place is a mess. The wind is strong, tearing through the large opening where the windows used to be. It whips around the apartment, blowing chunks of loose-hanging brickwork with it.

"Grab whatever weapons and ammo you can find in the bedrooms," I say to Rayne. "We need to leave town."

He nods. "You got it."

As he heads along what's left of the hallway, I take a look around. The sofas are destroyed. The kitchen looks like Swiss cheese. The TV is more like a jigsaw. The table is miraculously still standing, although it's chipped and...

And has a cell phone on it.

"Is that yours?" I shout.

Rayne reappears, holding a bag, and looks over.

He shakes his head. "No. Mine's in my pocket."

I frown. "Huh. It isn't mine. Looks new. Can't be one of the team's, either. No way it would've survived that onslaught."

He walks over to me. As we both stand, bewildered, the phone starts ringing. We exchange a glance and shrug. I reach for it and answer, placing it on speaker and holding it up between us.

I don't say anything.

"Adrian Hell," says a voice on the other end. Strong. Confident. American.

"Hello, Holt," I reply.

"This is your only warning. Stay the fuck out of my business."

I take a deep breath. "Well, we both know that's not happening. Where's the rest of my team?"

"They're safe—for now. They're a little insurance policy. I have a job to do, and I can't have you or your new friends interfering. So, here's how this is going to work. You're going to forget all about me, and when I'm done, I'll release your team unharmed. I get so much as a sniff of you before then, I will broadcast the slow deaths of all three of your friends on the internet, just for you." He pauses. "I know how much you like online torture porn."

I can hear him grinning. Arrogant prick.

Focus.

"I need a guarantee they're safe," I say. "Proof they're not already dead."

"They're not. You have my word."

"Which is worth... what, exactly?"

Holt laughs down the line. "You've probably figured out who I am by now. Or, should I say, who I was. You know how we operate, Adrian. Better than most, as I recall. Leverage is everything. I know what you're capable of. Your involvement in this is unfortunate but not completely unexpected, given your tendency to stick your guns where they don't belong. I don't have time to deal with you. Keeping them alive is an easy way to make sure you do as you're told without wasting any more manpower."

"I swear to God, Holt, you hurt them and I'll—"

"We're done talking. You've had your only warning. You interfere in my affairs again, I turn on my webcam. Now fuck off."

The line clicks dead.

"Holy shit," says Rayne. His voice is little more than a whisper. "What are we going to do now?"

I stare at the phone in my hand for a moment, then launch it out the window with a scream of fury.

I look around at him. He takes a step back as he stares into my eyes. The color drains from his face. I know what he's seeing. I know what's looking back at him. I can feel it, alive and free for the first time in a long time.

Behind my blue eyes, my Inner Satan burns with a rage unlike anything I've felt in recent memory.

My breathing is deep and fast, trying to balance the rush of adrenaline surging through me, numbing any pain and fueling my anger. My teeth are gritted together so hard, my jaw is aching.

"We're gonna go get our team back."

23

This is a goddamn nightmare. I'm so... just... fucking *angry*. I don't know which way to turn. I don't know what to do with myself. I feel like I'm in a maze without walls. The way Holt just attacked me and took my team from me like I'm nothing. Who the fuck does he think he is?

I can feel Rayne watching me pace in front of the desk. His look of concern and apprehension hasn't left his face since we left the apartment building. I don't think he knows what to make of my current state of mind.

You and me both.

We boosted a car parked a couple of blocks from the penthouse and drove here, to the abandoned RAF base where we all first met last year. It was the safest place we could think of to go.

Rayne clears his throat. "Um, Adrian? Maybe you should try to relax. This isn't helping."

I stop and shoot him a glance that would've turned a lesser man to dust.

"You want me to relax?" I ask.

I turn to the desk and proceed to hammer both fists down onto its surface. The impact echoes around the near-empty room. With each blow, a frustrated snarl escapes through gritted teeth. It takes five for me to split the desk vertically down the middle. The loud crack as the frail wood splinters makes Rayne twitch with surprise.

I turn back to him, hands throbbing. "I am relaxed!"

I reach for the nearest chair, scoop it up, and launch it across the room. It clatters into the back wall, causing more noise to ring out at an uncomfortable volume.

"This is me at my most fucking serene!" I yell.

He holds his hands up, pressing the air toward me with his palms. "Okay. Okay."

"I'm gonna kill him, Adam. I swear to Christ, I'm gonna find him, wrap my hands around his throat, and squeeze him until he fucking dies. Then I'm gonna stomp his head into a fucking puddle. Then I'm gonna—"

"Okay, man. I get it. Holt's a dead man. I'm with you. One hundred percent. But you're not gonna be able to annihilate the sonofabitch if you have a fucking aneurism before we find him."

I'm breathing heavily. In through the mouth, out through the nose. It stores more oxygen in the body that way. Helps you regulate your heartbeat more quickly.

My cell phone starts ringing in my pocket. Rayne and I stare at each other for a long moment. He doesn't blink. He doesn't look away. He just nods once, letting me know he understands.

Finally, I reach for the phone and answer it.

"Yeah?"

"What in the blue hell happened over there, son?" asks President Schultz. "Do you have any idea how much shit you've caused?"

I take a deep breath. And another. I close my eyes, summoning every ounce of patience I've ever had.

"Good to hear from you, sir," I say begrudgingly. "I need your help."

"You need to get your ass home! This is unacceptable, Adrian. You're all over every goddamn news channel in the country. You're—"

"Ryan?" He stops talking. "Sense the tone here."

He sighs heavily down the line. "Adrian, what happened?"

"Holt happened. The assassin Ruby and I were tracking, Falikov, rocked up in a gunship and destroyed the building. We tried to escape, but a team of Holt's men stormed in and took the team."

"Took them? Where?"

"I don't know. Rayne fought them off and stopped them from getting me and him. But the others are gone. We don't know where."

"Jesus..."

"He left a phone for us to find. He called and said if we come for him again, the team are dead. I need your help, Ryan. We need the resources to track this sonofabitch and get the team back. Get Ruby back."

"Adrian, I... I'll give you the resources I promised you, but this is a whole new problem now."

"You think I don't know that?" I pause, collecting myself. "There's something else too. The men who took the team. They were Tristar."

I hear Schultz catch his breath. "Are you sure?"

"I am. Why would someone like Holt hire a piss-ant company like Tristar to do his dirty work?"

"I... I don't know, son."

"Ryan, tell me right now—does this have anything to do with what happened at their offices in New York a few days ago? Does this have anything to do with what's got you and Buchanan so worked up? If there's anything you're not telling me... now isn't the time for any *need-to-know* bullshit."

He lets out a taut breath. Impatient yet understanding. "Adrian, I promise you I'm not hiding anything about Holt from you. Yes, Tristar have a connection to the people we're investigating, but I don't think that has anything to do with Holt."

"Are you sure? I told you who he used to be."

"I know that. But I'm sure. Tristar remain an active security contractor. We know their clients can be... less than reputable, shall we say. He's likely just hired them for the manpower. It's a coincidence. That's all."

I really hate that word.

I roll my eyes. "Fine. Adam and I are going to get our team back. I need your help to do it. I need people you can trust in the NSA and CIA to help track the helicopter that attacked us. Wherever it went is likely the same place the team's being held."

"Not a chance, son. I want you and your boy on a plane to D.C. *now*. You'll debrief me personally, and I'll decide how to move forward. But you—"

"Ryan, let me rephrase: I'm going to get my team back. You can either help me, or you can get the fuck out of my way. Those are your options."

"You will do the job you were hired to do, son. And you will not question my orders."

"I *am* doing the job I was hired to do! You brought me in to recruit and train a team capable of doing the jobs no one else can. To do what needs to be done without the burden of rules and regulations and politics. That's exactly what this is. You try and make this all official, my team will die, along with countless other innocent people when Holt gets around to using that fancy new drone of his."

I start pacing, trying to subdue the rising anger inside me. I cast a glance over at Rayne, who's watching my side of this conversation with something akin to admiration.

I continue. "The mission is Holt. I know that. But he came at me. He attacked me and mine, and he made it personal. That's a door you don't ever knock on, Ryan. You know that. I will not let this stand."

The line goes silent. Seconds tick by.

I place a hand over the mic and look at Rayne. "I think I'm on hold."

He shakes his head, smiling with disbelief. "How do you talk to the president like that?"

I shrug. "What's he gonna do?"

Rayne laughs and paces away to the back of the room. He picks up the pieces of the chair I threw over there and rests them on top of a filing cabinet in the corner.

"Well, son," says Schultz, "I've known you long enough to know when you're in this frame of mind, it's unwise to get in your way."

I let slip a small smile to myself.

"If I can't stop you... Hell, I may as well help you."

"I appreciate that, Mr. President," I say. "Thank you."

"You're right, Adrian. Blackstar was made for situations exactly like this one. I guess when the theory becomes the reality, it takes a little getting used to."

"It does. But that's why I was your only choice. You know

I'm already used to it, so I can get the job done while you're wrestling with your moral compass."

"Hmph. I guess you're right. Tell me, son, how did you get used to it?"

"Easy. I got rid of the compass."

He sighs. "Jesus Christ. You better not make me regret this, you crazy sonofabitch. Give me an hour. I'll find out where your helicopter went."

"Thank you again, sir. And don't worry. The only person who's gonna regret this is Holt."

I end the call. Rayne looks over at me.

"Well?" he asks. "What did he say?"

"He says he needs an hour. So, we give him an hour." I pocket the phone and head for the door. "Come on. Let's get a coffee."

He follows me out the door. "Okay, Boss. But the last thing you need right now is more caffeine. Goddamn."

18:22 BST

It was a ten-minute drive into town. Another ten minutes to find a café that was still open. Ten minutes back. Most of it passed in silence. We're now standing outside the entrance to the base, leaning against the fencing, sipping our coffee and killing time.

"You okay?" asks Rayne.

I stare ahead. "Mm-hmm."

He looks at me. "I've been a fighter my whole life. Even as a kid, I was always getting into scrapes. Never could stand to see other kids getting picked on. I would always step in, even if it meant catching an ass-whooping sometimes. It just felt right. So, when I got older, nothing else made sense to me except joining the Navy. I love my country, and I've fought for it all over the world."

I turn to him, tap my neck, and then point to his. "That why you have your eagle tattoo? Because you're a patriot?"

He smiles. "I'd love to say it is. Honest to God, I don't even remember getting it. I was still at Annapolis. I know that much. So, we're going back a few years. I had a couple of days' furlough. Went out with the guys one night. Woke up the next morning with it."

I sip my coffee. "Well, I'd stick with the patriot story if I were you."

"Yeah. My point is, in all my time in the Navy, then the SEALs... in all my travels... on all the battlefields... I have *never* in my life seen passion and rage like I saw in you earlier. It wasn't human."

I momentarily clench my jaw muscles, making them pulse beneath the skin. "That's what happens after you live a life like mine. It changes you. I'm not always proud of who I am, but I won't ever deny it."

Rayne gulps a mouthful of his own coffee. "So, what are you? My ghost of Christmas future? Now that I'm a part of Blackstar, is that shit what I have to look forward to?"

I shrug. "That's up to you, I guess. I'm not a role model. I'll give you the knowledge I think you need to be the best. To win the wars to come. What you do with that knowledge and how it affects you... that's up to you."

"This is crazy..."

"This is what it is."

"But even you have to admit, the way things have gone since 4/17... it's hard to process how we've ended up here."

I finish my coffee and rest the empty cup on the wall behind me.

"Honestly? In hindsight, I think this was inevitable." I stand, take a few paces, then turn back to look at Rayne. "I was there, you know? When 4/17 happened. I was in the room when General Matthews hit the button. When he started it all because he was drunk on Cunningham's Kool-Aid."

His eyebrows arch. His mouth hangs open. "Holy shit..."

I nod. "I knew then that the world would be changed forever. But like everyone else, I got so distracted by how well we all did in the aftermath, I didn't stop to notice the adverse effects. Nothing really changes. Humans are predictable. The world might update around us, but the shit that happens every day stays the same."

"What do you mean?"

"For years... decades... we've fought different wars for the same goddamn reasons. World War II, the Cold War, Vietnam, Cuba, the Middle East—all different battlefields, each one more advanced than the last. Different enemies too, obviously. But the reasons that brought us to the brink of war? They never change. 4/17 wiped the slate clean. It reset half the world back to zero. We've been rebuilding ever since and doing a good job of it. But we're humans, and we will forever be our own worst enemy. Conflict is in our nature.

"Out of the ashes, a new battlefield has emerged, more advanced than the last, just like always. The enemy has changed again too, just like always. Yet, despite the unprecedented global tragedy that put us here, we're still on the cusp of warfare because the reasons why we fight haven't changed and never will. I should've seen that coming. I should've been more prepared for this."

I think for a moment, back to Paris, back to what Ruby and I spoke about.

Maybe Josh *was* more prepared for this than I was. Maybe he *did* see something on the horizon.

Rayne stands. "Well, that's a grim way of looking at things, Boss. But the sad thing is, you're probably right."

I nod. "And that's why this feels different to you. To all of you. Jessie, Link... you've all struggled with the shift in perspective. With coming to terms with having no rules anymore. I get that. Honestly, I do. But you either get used to it fast, or you die along with the old world. If the shit Holt pulled isn't evidence enough of that, I don't know what is."

"Yeah."

The conversation fades away. I sit back down beside him, and we watch the sun slowly descend in the sky. Streaks of pink and deep orange signal the oncoming dusk. It's peaceful.

My phone starts ringing.

Well, it *was* peaceful.

I take it from my pocket, answer it, and put it on speaker.

"You took your time," I say.

"Watch that tone, son," replies Schultz. "I've been working my ass off to help you."

"What have you found?"

A heavy breath wheezes down the line. "We were able to track your helicopter after the attack. It flew a mile and a half east and landed on a construction site. Images show two black vans showed up minutes later. It looks like people were taken from the van and put into the chopper."

Rayne and I exchange a glance of concern.

"That must be the team," I say. "Tristar moved them in the vans to rendezvous with Falikov."

"That's how it looks," says Schultz.

"So, where did the chopper go from there?"

Schultz sighs. "They, ah... they took off and flew south-east. Son... they landed in Rome about twenty minutes ago."

I stare blankly ahead as his words sink in.

Rome.

I feel the color drain from my face. My mind is flooded with images from a thousand nightmares.

Gunfire. Blood. Screaming.

Josh.

"What's wrong?" asks Rayne.

His question pulls me out of my trance.

"I don't like Rome," I say.

"Why?"

"Nothing good ever comes from me being there." I look at the phone. "Sir, do we know why they would've gone there? Is that where Holt is?"

"We don't know for certain, son, but we think so. Satellite images show them landing at a private airfield not far from the airport. There's been a lot of movement in the last few days, including deliveries of large, wooden crates. We think that's where Holt is, and we think he has the drone with him. Makes sense he would take your team there."

"But why Rome?"

"We have no idea, but I have the entire intelligence community working to find out. This sonofabitch is good. There's no chatter, no sightings—nothing. Whatever he's doing in Rome, he's managed to keep it hidden from everyone."

I walk inside the grounds of the base and head for the car. Rayne quickly follows.

"How quickly can you get me to Rome?" I ask him.

"The U.K. government are gonna arrange military transportation for that," says Schultz. "But Adrian... you know what Holt said. He sees you coming, your team are dead.

And there's no way he won't see you coming. You have to think about this."

"I have, sir. The mission is to stop Holt from using that drone. I haven't forgotten that. But I'm going to get my team back. Adam and I will figure it out on the flight over there."

I stop beside the passenger door of our vehicle. Rayne leans on the roof opposite me and looks over expectantly.

"Godspeed to you both," says Schultz, then he ends the call.

I nod to Rayne. "Looks like we're going to Rome."

We climb inside the car and drive away, putting the RAF base in our rearview. I gaze silently out the window as Rayne navigates the traffic.

Rome.

The slideshow of horror begins playing in my head again.

I close my eyes, willing it away.

I'm honestly not sure I can do this.

24

"You okay?" asks Rayne. He gestures to his own face, then points at mine. "You look a little... pale."

I smile at him. Not in a pleasant way. Imagine if you could make a middle finger using just your mouth.

Like that.

"I'm fine," I reply. "I just don't like flying in these things."

"What, planes?"

I shake my head. "Not just planes. *Big fucking* planes."

We're sitting in the back of a C-130, resting against some cargo netting. The hold is mostly empty, apart from the three British soldiers who are sitting across from us, minding their own business. Schultz's idea of the U.K. doing us a favor was them allowing us to hitchhike to Italy on an RAF training mission.

I look over at three soldiers. Well, I say soldiers... they look like kids. All three of them—fresh-faced, a week out of puberty, not a facial hair between them. They look terrified.

One of them catches me staring. I nod courteously. He returns the gesture.

"Why don't you like planes?" asks Rayne. "You scared of heights?"

I shrug. "Scared is a strong word."

He smiles. "So, yes..."

I look at him. "So, shut your mouth."

"Hey, nothing wrong with being scared of heights. Perfectly common phobia. For me, it's clowns. Clowns and Playboy Bunnies."

I raise an eyebrow. "Playboy Bunnies?"

"Yeah. The way I see it, if I'm ever captured and tortured, and they want to expose me to my biggest fear to break me, or if I die and go to Hell and have to spend an eternity surrounded by my all-time greatest phobias, I can truthfully tell people I'm terrified of Playboy Bunnies. That way, the whole thing ain't so bad, y'know?"

I regard him for a moment before a smile escapes across my face.

"You remind me of an old friend," I say. "You two would've gotten on great."

"Was he scared of Playboy Bunnies?"

"No, but he was just as fucking crazy to think that would make sense."

He laughs.

"Anyway, fear isn't a bad thing," I say. "Fear keeps you human. Keeps you grounded. Keeps you focused. Fear is a good motivator as long as you control it. I'm not scared of heights. I don't like them, and I acknowledge how dangerous they can be, but I deal with them when I have to."

Rayne nods. "That makes sense. So, why don't you like planes?"

I sigh. "Because I'm rarely in one that I don't get thrown or blown out of."

"Oh."

I gesture around us. "Last time I was in one of these things, The Order pushed me out the back of it as we were flying over a forest in Vietnam."

"Jesus." He stares through wide eyes at the floor. "You had a parachute on, right?"

I roll my eyes. "No, I just bounced off the fucking trees..."

"There's no need to be sarcastic."

"There's *always* a need to be sarcastic."

I am so proud of you right now.

I smile to myself as I imagine Josh's reaction to that.

After a few moments of silence, Rayne looks over at me again.

"Hey, can I ask you something?"

I shrug. "Go for it."

"Before, back at the base, you said nothing good comes from you being in Rome. What did you mean?"

I lean back and glance at the roof, resting my head against the netting. I let out a long sigh.

I hate this story.

"Back when I went up against The Order, it was in Rome," I begin. "The leader of it was the Camerlengo of the Vatican."

He frowns. "The what?"

"Basically, the Pope's accountant."

"Ah, okay. Wait a minute... a few years back, during that 4/17 remembrance service... the attempted assassination of the Pope..."

"Is that what they called it? Huh. Yeah, that was me. I didn't *attempt* anything. I shot the guy standing next to His Holiness, just like I wanted to."

"Holy shit..."

"That's probably what the Pope said. Anyway, while I was in Rome, dealing with all that, my best friend was killed right in front of me."

There's a moment's silence as the words hang in the air.

"Damn," mutters Rayne. "I'm sorry, man. Was that Josh? The guy who ran GlobaTech for a while?"

I nod. "Yeah. I knew him most of my life. We were brothers, and I spent our last moment together covered in his blood. So, yeah, I don't like Rome much."

"Yeah. Understandable." He taps my shoulder with the outside of his fist. A universal gesture of sympathy from a brother-in-arms. "Sorry."

"Thanks."

"Do you think that's why Holt's there? Some kind of weird-ass ironic revenge against you?"

I shake my head. "He didn't know about my involvement until Ruby and I started poking around in Paris. If Rome's his endgame, he will have been planning it for a while. That's how people like him work. I just don't understand why. There are no significant targets there. Right now, the biggest and most obvious thing to hit would be GlobaTech's headquarters, and with that drone he's got, he could do that from anywhere. So, why Rome?"

We fall silent again. I begin running everything through my head. I've beaten one Horizon before. I can do it again. I just need to work out what he has planned.

I don't think it's about money. He'll have plenty of that, and if he was with The Order long enough to earn his Horizon title, he was with them long enough to buy into their sales pitch. It was never about money with them. It was about power.

So, Holt wants power. Or does he? Power over what? The

only powerful nations left are all friends now. An assault on one would incur the wrath of the others. He doesn't have enough drones to fight off the world. The only obvious target is GlobaTech, but he's given no indication that they're on his radar. So, what's he playing at?

I rub my forehead with frustration. I'm too angry and have had too little sleep to figure this out, but I have to think of something, or Ruby and the team are as good as dead. Not to mention whoever Holt decides to hurt along the way.

I glance at Rayne beside me. He's staring at the floor. His lips are moving slightly, like he's talking to himself without volume. I can see his eyes moving back and forth.

I smile.

I can almost hear the cogs turning inside his head, racking his brain over the same problem I am.

He suddenly jerks in his seat and turns to me. "Wait a minute."

"Talk to me, Adam. What have you got?"

"One sec."

He uses his finger to point at the air next to his head, as if he's typing on an invisible keyboard as he finishes his thought.

Then he claps his hands. "Okay. You taught us to think outside the box, right?"

"Yeah."

"In fact, you taught us there is no box. That's how the enemy works nowadays. They use psychology and influence to fight in ways that simply weren't viable before 4/17."

"Exactly."

"So, Holt was in The Order. He was a big deal. One of these Horizon characters, yeah? He clearly survived and did well after you stopped them. Maybe he's just pissed."

"Go on…"

"Okay. What did The Order want?"

"Mostly, they wanted to shape the world to their own design. They wanted it to run the way they felt was best."

"So, they wanted control... power?"

"Yeah."

"Well, that didn't work out all that well, did it? What if he's pissed at the fact this new world we're all coming to terms with is so different than what his old boss had planned, and he just wants to tear it down? Like the ex-girlfriend who broke up with you but still gets mad when you meet someone else."

I can't help but smile at the analogy.

"It's a good theory," I say. "In fact, I wouldn't be surprised if you were dead-on. It makes a lot of sense. But it doesn't explain why he's in Rome."

"Maybe it does. The Order used conflict to control things. They sent... people like you to take out certain targets. Nothing too big. Just a little kill here, a little kill there... gently nudging things in the direction they wanted. But in order for that tactic to work, there needed to be conflict. There needed to be something play on. Like, it only takes a spark to start a fire, but you need the kindling first."

I nod along. I think I'm starting to see where he's going with this.

"You think he's going to use the drone to trigger a fresh conflict," I say. "Which he can then manipulate to essentially kickstart the second coming of the world before 4/17."

He nods. "Exactly. Hitting a big ol' reset button."

"And what's the biggest catalyst for conflict in human history?"

"Religion. It's one of the biggest things that's brought people together over the last couple of years. And where's the home of the most popular religious faith in the world?"

"Rome!"

"Exactly!" He holds up a hand, which I gladly high-five. "Holt's going to use the drone to blow up the Vatican!"

That's it. We figured it out. That has to be it! It's the only thing that makes any sense.

We start laughing. I hate not knowing the game I'm playing. I imagine Rayne is the same. The relief in finally understanding what's happening is overwhelming. It means we can start thinking about how to stop him. It means we can figure out a way to get our team back. It means we might stand a chance of winning. It means...

As we look at each other, our laughter dies down. Our smiles fade. Our eyes widen as reality sets in and the gravity of the situation hits home.

"Holy shit," says Rayne somberly. "Holt's going to blow up the Vatican."

"Yeah..."

Rayne sighs. "Is he, though? You just said the guy who used to run The Order was a Vatican official. They were some ancient religious organization. Would Holt destroy the one thing The Order served just to prove a point?"

I nod. "Absolutely. The thing was, The Order was full of shit. Yes, they were a religious cult originally. But that was a long time ago. When the Camerlengo found reference to them in the Vatican archives, he resurrected the name to serve his own purpose. The version of the Order I fought hadn't been around for centuries. It had been around for six years. Sure, they played on the religious thing to motivate the people involved. Some of the higher-ups really bought into the idea of a greater purpose. But it was all bullshit. Nothing but an excuse to make people believe in what they were doing."

"So, they were essentially brainwashing everyone involved?"

I shrug. "Pretty much. It didn't work on me, and that's where the problems began."

"If that's the case, then Holt targeting the Vatican makes even more sense. He's not precious about it because The Order was never about a religious mission."

"Exactly."

"Goddamn. This is bad."

I stare blankly ahead, gazing at the bare metal floor of the plane until my vision blurs.

Yes. This is really bad.

23:55 CEST

We touched down on the runway of a military base in Vincenza, a city in the northeast of Italy, about fifteen minutes ago. After a brief conversation with the pilot to thank him for the lift, we climbed into the waiting Range Rover and set off on the five-hour drive to Rome.

There's no time to waste.

After getting over the initial shock of having figured out Holt's plan, we came up with the beginnings of our own to stop him.

Rayne's driving. I'm studying a folder full of intel that was waiting for us with the car, on top of two bags of weapons that took up the entire back seat. I had to smile when I saw them.

You can take Schultz out of GlobaTech...

"Where does it say Falikov's chopper landed?" asks Rayne.

"At an industrial complex just off the A12," I say, still buried in the file. "Just north of LDV airport on the outskirts of the city."

He expertly weaves through some freeway traffic at high speed. "You think Holt's holding the guys there?"

I look up at the sudden swaying of the vehicle and stare at the road. "Get us there in one piece, will you? And yes, I think that's where Holt and his drone is, and I think he has the team with him."

"I dunno," Rayne says, absently shaking his head. "Having a drone that close to public airspace is risky. That thing might be undetectable via radar but not line of sight. The people in the control tower at the airport will see it out their window."

I nod. "You're not wrong, but I honestly don't think Holt's concerned about being caught. He probably believes he *can't* be caught. Not after taking us out so effectively. Scary thing is, he might be right."

I begin sifting through the printouts of satellite images taken of the area over the last twenty-four hours. They show the helicopter arriving. They show people emptying out of it and moving inside. Looking at the timestamps, about a half-hour later, a smaller group reappears and gets into a vehicle. I search the printouts for the ones that track the vehicle after it leaves...

Got them.

I follow its journey until it finally stops at an address in the city. It looks like a bunch of storage units. The vehicle is parked at the rear. It doesn't appear to have moved since. The most recent photo was taken an hour ago. Schultz must have arranged for someone to gather the intel on-site for when we landed.

I tap the image of the building. "Falikov and a group of

Tristar mercs left Holt's base and traveled here. That's where we start. We find out everything we can from them, then we take them out."

Rayne nods, remaining focused on the road ahead. "Then we go for Holt?"

"Goddamn right, we do."

I put the papers back in the file and toss it on the back seat. There's nothing more to be said. We're both fried. We're both running on pure adrenaline. We both know what needs to be done.

I stare out the window and watch as the lights of the city stream past us.

I'm coming for you, Ruby. Just hang tight.

I'm coming.

25

_____

What I wouldn't do for some coffee right now.

It was a long drive from Vincenza. I took over the driving halfway to give Rayne a break. He scanned the intel Schultz had arranged for us while I had the wheel. We discussed our theory about what Holt's planning. We dissected it over and again, questioning everything. We kept arriving at the same conclusion.

Holt has to be planning to use the drone to attack the Vatican.

When we made peace with that, we turned our attention to the more immediate task at hand.

We're sitting in the Range Rover now, parked in a wide alley between two buildings, cloaked in what remains of the shadows of night. In front of us, a road expands across. It's more like an alleyway. It links together two main strips of road running parallel to one another at each end. Vehicles

234

are parked along it, leaving little space for another vehicle to travel down it.

Ahead of us is a row of three buildings. Even in the low light of dawn, I can see the sickly pastel colors used to paint the cracking plaster on the outside. They look like they have jaundice.

Of the three, the two on either side are both two stories tall. The one in the middle, covered in illegible graffiti, is just a single story. That's the one we know Falikov and his merry band of Tristar assholes came to after leaving Holt's base. Their vehicle is one of the ones lined up outside.

"How do you want to play this?" asks Rayne, nodding toward the building. "Do we wait for them to come out? Hit them before they can drive away?"

I shake my head. "No. We go in. Good chance they're still sleeping, so we might get the drop on them."

Rayne points to the metal shutter that's fastened down over the single entry point. "What do we do about that? Gonna make a hell of a noise getting inside."

"If we move quickly, it shouldn't matter." I look at the left side of the building, at the low gate linking it to the next building along. "You head around back and find a way up onto the roof. It's flat, and there's a skylight that should be big enough for you to drop through. On my signal, we go in together."

"And your signal will be..."

I reach behind me, into one of the weapons bags, and take out the long breaching charge and detonator.

I smile at him. "Obvious."

We gather what we need and climb out of the vehicle. I rest the breaching charge on the hood as I holster my twin Raptors behind me. I haven't used this back holster in a long time. The weight of it presses against my lower back, causing a dull ache that never used to be a problem. But despite the discomfort, I can't help feeling comforted by its presence. It's even nostalgic, in a way.

Just like old times.

Unfortunately, I find myself in a situation that requires the old times, so the trip down memory lane is marred somewhat. But when the shit hits the fan, I instinctively revert back to what I know... to what's safe, to get me through it. For me, it's this.

I look over at Rayne and watch him load up spare magazines into his tactical harness. He adjusts the grip of the assault rifle he selected from the small armory we've been given.

"You ready?" I ask.

"Always," he replies.

We both place comms units in our ears and test the connection.

I grab the charge. "Let's go."

We move quickly and quietly toward the building. Rayne scans a full three-sixty for signs of life. There aren't any. Most of the surrounding buildings appear to be businesses—small offices or produce markets—so they're all closed at this ungodly hour.

He heads around back as I rest against the wall beside the door. The shutter that's covering it seems thin and rusted.

I hear Rayne grunting with exertion over the comms.

"You good?" I whisper.

"Yeah, I... *gah!*" He sighs. "Yeah, I'm fine. I'm on the roof now and in position."

"Okay. Give me a minute."

I set to work with the charge. It's what's called a Breacher's Boot. There are three clumps of C4 attached together by a cord. Each one is encased in thin plastic, with a strip of double-sided adhesive on one side. I peel away the covering strip and gently attach each one to the shutter in a straight line, running top to bottom, ensuring the cord is taut between each one to maximum coverage. I then take out the primers—three thin, metal rods with wiring attached that are inserted into the C4. The wiring is then tied together and clipped to the detonator. When I press the button, an electrical charge will travel along the wire and down into each rod. They'll conduct the electricity and send a shock-wave into the plastic explosive, triggering the detonation.

Then... no more door.

I finish configuring it all and walk a few paces away, toward the side gate, putting a good ten to fifteen feet between me and the door. The wire trails along the ground. I flip the cover up on the detonator with my thumb, revealing the button.

"I'm ready," I say.

"Likewise," replies Rayne.

"On three."

"Count it."

I pause. "Three."

I press the button, triggering the detonation. The noise of the blast is instantly deafening but fades after just a few seconds. The explosion is contained by the design of the charge, resulting in little outward damage. The tearing and warping of the metal shutter continues to ring out as it's blown inward, removing the door behind it from its hinges in the process.

I hear the faint sound of glass breaking from above as Rayne drops down. I quickly draw one of my Raptors and move inside, waving my arm through the cloud of dust billowing out through the doorway.

The building is a simple, large box—probably one open space, retrospectively segmented with drywall. There are no doors, just spaces leading into the small rooms.

The smoke begins to clear, revealing more of the interior to me as I quickly navigate the makeshift hallways. Rotting floorboards creak beneath my weight. I tread carefully, gun aimed and ready. I sweep through the first two rooms I come across. Both are empty. Patches of wallpaper, faded with time, hang off the walls. A single lightbulb hangs from the ceiling, swaying back and forth in the aftermath of the blast, causing the shadows to dance around me.

I head around to the back and meet up with Rayne as he steps out of one of the rooms.

"Anything?" I ask.

He shakes his head. "Nothing. This place is empty. Looks like it's been abandoned for a long time."

"I agree. Which begs the question... where the fuck is everybody? Their vehicle's still outside. Why drive here in the middle of the night, only to leave again within a couple of hours but not take your car?"

Rayne shrugs but says nothing.

"Where did you drop into?" I ask.

"Back here," he replies.

He walks away. I follow him into one of the rooms, nestled into the back-right corner of the building. It's the same as the others. There's glass scattered across the floor—a result of Rayne's entrance. The only thing that's different in this room is the fireplace resting against the outside wall. It's cast-iron, with a grill plate built into a small door. It looks weathered and well-used but not as decrepit as the rest of the building.

"That's odd," I say absently.

Rayne looks up at me. "Hmm?"

"That fireplace. Bit out of place in this shithole, wouldn't you say?"

He shrugs. "I dunno. Never been big on interior design."

I crouch in front of it. The floor has visible scuff marks on it. Fresh lines in old dust, as if something's been moved recently.

"Wait a second..."

I stand and tuck the gun behind me, then grab one end of the fireplace and pull. It moves easily away from the wall, following the path of the lines on the floor. Rayne turns to look.

"Sonofabitch," he mutters.

Revealed behind it is a large hole in the wall. It's small enough to be completely covered by it but large enough for a grown man to crawl through.

I sigh. "I think we know how Falikov and his men left without being seen."

Rayne shakes his head. "Goddammit. There were some old wooden pallets stacked against the back wall out there. Didn't think anything of them. They must've been put there to cover that."

"Why have an escape route from a place like this? Why come here and—"

The words catch in my throat as my brain puts pieces of the puzzle together for me.

I stare at Rayne, who looks confused by my blank look of confusion and dread. My vision glazes over as I concentrate.

There's only one thing that makes sense here. One reason for everything we've seen inside this building.

What if Holt anticipated us having some kind of intel saying where he is? He knows he's safe with his drone, so it wouldn't be a smart move for us to attack him there head-on.

That's why we didn't.

We saw Falikov and a team of Tristar operatives leaving there to come here. The obvious move would be to go after Falikov separately and use him to gain access to Holt.

That's exactly what we did.

We did the only thing that made sense with the information we had. If Holt bet on us doing that, then he could've easily...

I refocus to see Rayne studying my face. His eyes dart back and forth, as if watching his own cogs turning. I see him arrive at the same conclusion I have.

"This is a set-up, isn't it?" he says.

I nod. "I reckon so. Question is: for what? Why would Falikov lure us here specifically?"

Rayne begins looking around, seeing the building through eyes fresh with a new perspective.

He leaves the room. I remain staring at the fireplace, desperately trying to fill in the last couple of blanks.

If Falikov were going to hit us, he would've done it already. As soon as we breached the building, he would've followed us inside and popped us both in the back of the head while our hearing was still impaired by the blast. So, no, this wasn't done so that Falikov could take us out.

So, why?

Why would Holt want us—

My eyes pop wide as the realization hits me.

I sprint out of the room, past Rayne, and head outside. He quickly follows.

"What is it?" he asks.

I turn in a circle, searching the early morning skies, hoping I'm wrong. The buildings around us aren't more than three or four stories high, but they're close together, restricting my view.

I run to the end of the alley and step out into the middle of the road, looking up again with a clearer view.

Please be wrong. Please be wrong. Please be wrong…

I stop turning. My gaze locks onto an ominous shape silhouetted against the pink and orange slivers of dawn.

Shit.

I run back toward the car. Rayne is standing outside the building. I wave him toward the car.

"We need to go!" I shout. "Now!"

He shakes his head as I approach him at pace. "I don't understand. What's wrong?"

I slide to a stop in front of our vehicle and look back as the demonic shape of Holt's drone turns into view, beginning its descent. It looks like an arrowhead. It's too high and too far away to make out any significant detail, but the frightening plethora of weaponry stuck to it is clearly visible, even from this distance.

What's also clear is the fact that it's aiming straight for us.

I point to it. "*That's* what's wrong."

He lowers his weapon and begins to backpedal toward me.

"Yeah, okay. We should probably go."

I climb in behind the wheel and start the engine. A moment later, he dives in next to me. Tires screech as I accelerate away before he's had the chance to close his door. I turn left and thread between the lines of parked cars.

Rayne shifts in his seat and looks back out the window. "That's the drone."

"It is," I reply, checking my rearview to see exactly where it is. "We need to get away from anywhere residential in case whoever's flying that thing decides to start shooting at us."

Rayne looks at me. "Can we even outrun it long enough to draw it away?"

I grip the wheel tightly, draining the color from my knuckles. My eyes are fixed on the road. My jaw is set.

I glance in the rearview again. "Let's find out."

26

I'm doing sixty along a road barely wide enough for the Range Rover to fit down. Rayne's leaning out of his window, looking back at the sky, trying to keep a visual on the drone.

I take a sharp left, then an immediate right, putting us on Via Casilina. Porta Maggiore is up ahead, a few hundred meters away. The lanes are getting wider, which makes them easier to navigate. But traffic is getting busier as people start their journeys to work, which brings with it a new set of problems.

I check the mirror and see nothing.

"Adam, talk to me," I say. "Where is it?"

He ducks back inside and looks at me. "It's almost directly above us. No way we're outrunning that thing."

He might be right about that. But maybe we can outmaneuver it.

I see the arches of Porta Maggiore in front of us, on the

243

right, where the intersection forks. I have almost no idea where we are and no time to consult a GPS.

"Which way?" I ask Rayne.

He looks ahead and shrugs. "Don't you always say, *when in doubt, go left*?"

"I do."

I accelerate and thread through a gap in the oncoming traffic beside us, moving into the other lane to miss the changing lights in front of us. I move back across and follow the dogleg to the left, putting the arches behind us.

Via Labicana.

"Adam, I need you find us a route out of the city." I quickly point to the center console of the Range Rover, which has a built-in touchscreen. "See if you can get that to work."

Without a word, Rayne leans forward and begins pressing the screen. Within seconds, a map of Rome flashes up; a blue dot displays our location.

"Let me see here..." he mutters.

"If it helps, we're heading toward the Colosseum."

"I thought you didn't know where we were going?"

I tap his shoulder, so he looks up at me, then point out through the windshield. He sits up and looks, quickly seeing the mammoth structure of the famous Roman arena looming over the road ahead.

"Oh." He shrugs. "That helps. Thanks."

I weave around some slow-moving traffic in front of us, accelerating as I cross into the opposite lane to get around them. Horns blare as I cut back across, narrowly avoiding an oncoming car.

I check the rearview. The drone just dipped back into my eyeline. It's a lot closer now. It must be capable of incredible speeds, which means it's likely hanging back for a reason. It rocks and sways in the air, seemingly fighting to stay level in the turbulence it's generating.

I look ahead. The sidewalks are almost deserted. Too early for people still. The roads aren't getting any easier, though. Another minute, and we'll be alongside the Colosseum.

This isn't good.

"Adam, you gotta work faster," I say urgently. "This road's too straight, but every turn we pass looks like it leads to a more built-up area. We're sitting ducks here."

I'm met with silence.

"Adam, what are you—"

"Take a right!"

"What?"

We shoot past the last right turn before drawing level with the Colosseum.

He sits up and quickly looks outside.

"Okay. Never mind," he says, then lowers himself back to the console.

I roll my eyes. "Yeah, maybe a little more notice next time."

Whoosh!

…

…

…

Oh, no!

I yank the wheel left, almost rolling the Range Rover as I swerve to avoid the explosion three feet to our right.

Rayne is jerked upright. He places a hand on the dash and another flat against the roof, bracing himself.

"What the fuck was that?" he yells.

My teeth are gritted tightly together. My jaw aches as I try to wrestle us out of this fishtail without getting hit.

"I think... that was a missile from the drone. Get us out of here already, will you?"

Whoosh!

...

...

...

Oh, come on!

A thick cloud of dust and rubble erupts in the middle of the road directly in front of us.

"Shit!"

I swerve again, mounting the curb on the right. I drive over the wide sidewalk and plow through a stack of guardrails, presumably used to organize the lines of visitors during the day. They clatter and bang as they're strewn in all directions.

Screw this. We're going to get slaughtered if we stay here.

I slam the brakes on and watch as the drone goes flying past us overhead. I take the next left I see, which leads us along Corso Vittorio Emanuele II. The street is momentarily cobbled, which tests the suspension of an already battle-worn vehicle.

"Can you see it?" I ask.

Rayne looks out, checking the skies.

"Nothing," he says after a moment. "Lot of tall buildings here, though, all bunched together. Makes our visibility limited, but that works both ways, right?"

Ahead, the road meets another running across us. Beyond it is a single, low building that stretches the full width of our scope of view. I vaguely recognize it, but I'm not sure where from.

I slow, preparing to turn left, which I think will lead us—

"Fuck! Get down!"

The drone flies in from the left and hovers over the

building in front of us. It has a multi-barreled machine gun mounted on its nose and one more under each wing.

I'm momentarily blinded by the unfathomable muzzle flash. I instinctively turn right and stamp down on the gas.

The noise from all three guns is a near constant whine. The rate of fire is so high that the stuttering is audibly blurred. The road is torn up by a stream of laser-like bullets behind us.

"Where the hell did that come from?" shouts Rayne.

"I guess we know its stealth capabilities work pretty goddamn well. Oh, shit!" I slam the brakes on and turn sharply, mounting the curb and driving along the sidewalk to avoid an oncoming car.

Rayne looks at me. "Wrong way?"

"Wrong way." My gaze is so narrowed and focused that I'm giving myself a headache. "Ah, shit. Move! Fuck."

I bounce us back onto the road and slide left, almost losing control of the back end and spinning out. I speed away, using the acceleration to pull us straight.

"Where are we?" I call out.

Rayne turns his attention to the screen again.

"Coming up on the Pantheon," he says. "Take this left!"

I do, bouncing over the corner of the curb at high speed. Sparks fly up off the fender.

The cobbled street bridges over a river and drops back down into a large courtyard. There's a water fountain in the center, with buildings surrounding it on all sides. On the right, the Pantheon yawns into view.

"Which way? Which way!"

He points to his two o'clock. "Straight over and right."

I brake and turn, sliding the rear out clockwise, lining us up with the road that will hopefully lead us out of here.

To our right, one of the pillars that makes up the lavish, ancient entrance to the Pantheon explodes.

"Shit! It's found us," shouts Rayne.

I grunt as bricks fly into the side of the Range Rover. "You think!"

I steer to correct the impact and accelerate away, down the side and out onto a main street. Traffic is heavy and slow, likely distracted by the flying war machine plaguing the skies.

The Tiber River's on our right. A few people are strolling along the bridges that stretch over it.

"Adam, talk to me..."

"I'm looking. I'm looking." He leans out of the window. "I can't see it."

There's a large intersection coming up. The lights are red. Lines of traffic are at a standstill. I know I'm going to have to go around them and run the light. Vehicles are coming from the left, but I should be able to avoid them and make it across if I—

I slam the brakes on, screeching to a stop.

Rayne lurches forward. His ribs collide with the dash.

"What's wrong?" he asks, wincing.

I nod to the road ahead. "I found the drone."

He follows my gaze to the intersection. The drone is hovering over it, silent and ominous. This is the first time I've had a proper chance to look at it.

It's impressive. It's fucking big. It has missiles lined up beneath the wings and spaces where the three it's fired at us used to be. I have to admit, seeing an aircraft that's trying to kill us up close is intimidating. Puts things into perspective a little.

I suddenly feel really small.

"Adam?"

He glances at me, seemingly not wanting to take his eyes off the drone.

"Hmm?"

"Grab the bags."

"Yeah."

"Like... now."

We both reach behind, scoop up a bag each, and throw ourselves out of the Range Rover. Rayne hurries around the trunk to join me just as—

Whoosh!

We set off running for the nearest side street. Three quick steps later, a wave of hot air knocks us from our feet as the Range Rover goes up in a fireball.

We both use the momentum of the blast to roll away and back to our feet.

"Run!" I yell.

We sprint along the narrow street. I have no idea where we are, yet this, too, looks oddly familiar.

Side by side, we run as fast as our bodies will allow. We turn in any direction that keeps the buildings high around us, reducing the chance of the drone being able to follow.

All around us, people are screaming. Tires screech, horns blare... chaos reigns in the immediate aftermath of the drone attack.

"This way," says Rayne, panting from the exertion.

I follow him to the right, along an alleyway between two narrow buildings. He's maybe a second ahead of me.

I jump over a pile of trash bags and stumble out into the street. Rayne is standing motionless, staring up. We watch the drone fly away, disappearing behind the trees that line the street opposite.

I look around. The road is littered with abandoned vehicles, standing with open doors. The intersection in front of us, where the drone was hovering a few minutes ago, is the same.

Where did it go?

I walk slowly to the end of the street. Rayne appears next to me.

"Is it coming around for a second pass?" he asks.

I hear him, but I don't answer. My mind has locked me out. My brain is no longer functioning. I turn a slow circle on the wide street corner, taking in my surroundings. The Tiber is in front of me. Beyond that is the Piazza dei Tribunali.

It can't be...

I look to my right. To the building next to me. To the café not yet open for business.

I stare at the ground beneath my feet, focusing on the grit until my vision blurs. Without looking, I know the Castel Sant'Angelo is behind me, over my left shoulder. I know that because I've been here before. That's why certain places have looked familiar to me. It makes sense now.

I've been here before. On this street corner. Outside this café. Almost three years ago.

The world fades away, taking all noise with it. I have no sense of time. I'm surrounded by a true absence of... anything.

I feel the bag fall from my grip.

I lower myself to one knee, place my hand flat on the ground, and close my eyes.

I feel the blood running over my fingers as if it were yesterday. The echo of a distant gunshot fills my head. A single tear escapes down my cheek.

This is exactly where I was standing when Josh died.

27

I feel the wind on my face, carrying with it an unearthly silence I know cannot exist. I swallow, tasting the air of that day, which feels so long ago and yet could have easily happened yesterday.

Images flash into my mind like bolts of lightning. Vivid memories of blood and pain and darkness. Thinking back, in that terrible moment, I genuinely had no idea what had happened. I couldn't see. I couldn't feel anything.

I thought I had died.

When I first focused on the horrified faces of Josh and Ruby standing before me, I wished I had. I knew right then that I had lost one of them. I sensed the sudden absence of life. I was alive, which meant someone close to me wasn't.

I remember the pain on Ruby's face. The shock. The fear. I was convinced it was her. But I realized the moment Josh fell that she wasn't in pain. The shock and fear she felt was because she knew what I didn't. She knew Josh was gone before I did.

I rub my palm on the ground, feeling the grit and dust bite at my skin. In the distance, I hear movement. I hear voices.

I close my eyes.

It was my fault.

It really wasn't.

It was. You're dead because of me.

And yet, I'm still here, talking to you.

You're just in my head. You're my brain giving a voice to my own sanity. You're not really here.

Brother, if I'm the voice of your sanity, you're screwed.

I'm sorry.

For what? You didn't pull the trigger, and you punished the man who did. And the guy who told him to. We're good.

But you're not here, and that's because of me.

Look, just because bodies die doesn't mean the person does. As long as you remember me, I'm never truly gone. I'm stuck inside your head with no one but your pet Satan for company. And let me tell you... I had no idea how troubled that fella was until I met him.

I've never forgiven myself.

Well, you should. I had enough of your pity party when I was alive. Adrian, you were never to blame for any of the bad shit that happened in your life. That's what I spent my last years trying to make you understand. I'm just glad you have Ruby— someone to carry the torch for us poor bastards whose job it is to keep you alive.

It's not the same. Nothing is.

I know it's not. Ruby is way hotter than I was. Plus, you're also getting laid way more often now. Good for you. I bet she's—

All right—eyes front, soldier.

Sorry. I don't know where the line is until I cross it.

I'll put a bullet in my head right now just to shut you up.

Please don't. Now look, I know this is hard. I know how upsetting this must be. But I need you to do me a favor now, okay?

What?

I need you to focus, Adrian. I need you to snap out of this and focus. Remember where you are. Remember who you're with. Remember what's happening.

Why should I? I don't want to remember. I don't want to see this world anymore.

Shut the fuck up and focus! Come on, Adrian.

"Come on, Adrian!"

Get up.

"Get up!"

We need to move.

"We need to move!"

I open my eyes. My brow furrows as I stare the ground, adjusting to the daylight.

Josh sounds a lot like Rayne.

I look up and stare into Rayne's wide eyes. He's screaming at me, but the words aren't quite audible yet. He's gesturing wildly with his arms—at me and at the world around us.

My surroundings are rushing back to me, as if everything's being played in reverse, pulling me back to where I was a minute ago. The noises are close by. Cars screech to a stop. Doors open. Heavy footfalls.

I narrow my eyes, trying to zoom in on Rayne's mouth.

What the hell's he saying?

"Come on, Adrian! Get up. We need to move!"

We need to move.

That's what Josh said.

Did I?

Yes. You just...

Oh. I see. That wasn't you, was it?

It really wasn't.

Ah, crap.

What's going on?

I slowly stand and turn to look behind me. Rayne's protests have fallen quiet. I look over at the intersection. Among the sea of cars abandoned by panicked drivers are two that don't belong. They aren't trying to leave, fearful they might be the next victim of the drone's superior fury. No, these two just arrived. Men are standing around them, holding guns. Seven in total. Six are wearing the same matching black outfits worn by the guys who attacked us in London and took the team.

Tristar Security.

Well... *those* guys are dead.

The seventh is standing next to the hood of one of the cars, resting a short-barrel shotgun over his shoulder. He's much bigger than the rest, and he's smiling at me like a man who knows something I don't.

I hate that.

I step toward the group. Rayne reaches out for my arm to stop me.

"Adrian, what the fuck are you doing?" he asks.

I don't reply. I stare at him through deadened eyes until he removes his hand, then I look back at the group and take another step toward them. I stop in the middle of the street, maybe fifteen feet away, and gesture to the big guy with a flick of my head.

"Hello, Falikov," I say.

He responds in Russian.

I roll my eyes. "Hey, we're in Italy, dipshit. Speak English."

He laughs, his voice booming. "Good to see you again, Comrade."

"Is it? First time we met, you kinda shot at me. A lot."

He moves his hand back and forth between us. "This is how we understand, yes? How we show respect in our world."

"I mean... it fucking *isn't*, man. Say hello, buy me a beer... don't destroy my home and kidnap my friends. That, by the way, was a really stupid thing to do."

Falikov laughs again. "It was necessary. Horizon sends regards."

"Horizon, Holt... whatever you want to call him. He's on borrowed time."

"Now, now, Adrian." He lowers his shotgun, loosely aiming at me from the hip. "I understand you are angry, but please, this is not fight you win."

"Oh, I'm not angry." I look back at Rayne. "Do I look angry to you?"

He raises his eyebrows. "You look bat-shit crazy to me, Boss."

I smile and turn back to Falikov. "No, I'm not angry, *comrade*. I'm so far beyond angry, I've come all the way back around. I'm actually quite calm, all things considered."

The Tristar men snap their weapons up in unison, aiming at Rayne and myself.

Our bags are a few feet away from us. I have my Raptors at my back. I don't know if Rayne is armed. It doesn't matter. He can sit this one out. Save his ammunition.

I've got this.

Falikov continues laughing. "Good. Positive outlook makes dying easier."

"Then I hope you're feeling positive today, asshole."

My hands disappear behind me. Time slows to a crawl. The Tristar guards are spread out in front of me, forming a wide semicircle. Falikov's in the middle of them. I grab my Raptors and bring my arms back around. I start shooting almost instantly. My aim follows the shape of the semicircle. I fan the bullets back and forth as I first cross my arms, then move them back out to the sides.

Both hammers slam down on empty chambers. I throw the Raptors behind me for Rayne to catch and reload. Time resumes as I sprint toward Falikov. In my periphery, I watch all six men drop to the ground, their faces and torsos riddled with bullets.

Falikov has no time to react. I reach him and immediately step across him, deflecting the shotgun away from me before he fires. I deliver a forearm to his throat as the shot goes off. He staggers back, stumbling over the hood of the car. I brush the weapon from his grip and throw two more punches in quick succession—one to the sternum and the other to his jaw. He slides to the ground, wheezing.

I step away, kicking the discarded shotgun farther out of his reach. Then I bend down and hoist him up to his feet by handfuls of clothing. I push him back against the car.

Three more blows to the head.

He glances to his side and spits out blood.

"How many more men does Holt have with him?" I ask. "Tell me!"

Falikov turns his head slowly toward me and smiles. His teeth are stained with crimson.

Oh, shit.

He plants his feet, places two giant hands on my chest, and launches me backward. I easily clear six feet, then land awkwardly on my back with a heavy grunt.

Considering this guy's size, he moves like a college athlete.

No sooner have I cleared the cobwebs, he's on me, raining blow after blow into my body. He's got fists like bowling balls. I turtle up for a moment, weathering the storm, then thrust my legs out and kick him away. I roll back and up onto my feet in time to see him sprinting toward me again.

He drops his shoulder, preparing to spear tackle me. I quickly shuffle to the side and lash my foot out, as if kicking a field goal. I catch him flush on his jaw. Gravity takes over, and he plummets to the ground. His head bounces off the hard blacktop.

I lean forward, resting my hands on my knees to catch my breath. I watch him for any signs of movement, but there aren't any. I think he might be out.

I hear groaning. His arms start to move, trying to push his massive frame back upright.

Okay, maybe not...

"Come here, you giant prick."

I grab the back of his jacket and drag him over to one of the cars. The passenger door is open. I'm breathing heavily through gritted teeth, snarling at the exertion my body isn't quite strong enough to deal with. I pull him and drop him, resting his head on the bottom of the doorframe so that it's pushed against the side of the seat.

He tries to move, but I jab him in the ribs to subdue him.

I grab the edge of the open door with one hand. I use it for leverage as I push myself back to a vertical base.

"Last chance," I say, gasping for breath. "How many men does Holt have with him?"

He spits out more blood. "Fuck... you."

I sigh. "Fine. Have it your way."

I place my other hand on the door. With every ounce of strength I have left in my body, I slam it closed. His body jolts as the door collides with his head. I pull it open, then do it again.

And again.

And again.

Maybe six times in total. Each time, I slammed it shut as hard as I could.

I heard cracking. I heard squelching. Each time I did it, the door got closer to the car. I kept going until the body stopped twitching on impact.

I stagger away and drop to one knee, resting in the middle of the now-empty intersection. I'm sucking in air so quickly, it hurts. The adrenaline carried me this far, and now that it's subsiding, the pain it was hiding from me is taking over.

I stand and arch my back, staring up at the morning sky as I unleash a primal scream, expelling any rage left inside me.

I look over at Rayne. He's standing on the sidewalk, mouth open, eyes wide, holding both my Raptors.

I walk over to him, and he holds the guns out for me without hesitation. I take them from him and slide them back into their holster behind me.

"You good?" I ask.

"Uh-huh." He shakes his head. "I mean... are you? Jesus."

"I'll be fine once we get our team back. Come on. Only one more house call to make now."

We grab our bags and head over to the nearest of the two vehicles Falikov and the Tristar men arrived in.

"What *was* that back there?" Rayne asks. "On the corner, before these guys showed up, you checked out big time."

I shrug. "Reminiscing, I guess. It's fine. Let's just... get the job done, so we can go home. Schultz is gonna be pissed about all this. Sooner I tell him, the sooner he can get over it."

As we reach the car, I look up, instinctively searching the sky. In the distance, across the river and beyond the Piazza dei Tribunali, I see the drone circling around.

"No time to waste," I say to Rayne. "You're driving. You know where to go."

He sees it and nods. "You got it."

He climbs in and starts the engine. I linger a moment longer, staring at the drone as it bears down on us once again.

"Come and get me, you sonofabitch."

28

Rayne is a much better navigator than I am. Within minutes of leaving the intersection massacre, we're driving along a freeway, putting the center of Rome in our rearview. Buildings flatten and disappear, trees sprout to border the roadside, and traffic is moving fast enough that we can really punch it.

There is a downside, however.

We're completely exposed, with no hope of finding cover, and we're surrounded by innocent people who are unaware of how much danger they're in. Oh, and Holt's heavily armed drone is pursuing us, and it's much faster than we are.

Two streams of orange light tear up the road on either side of us, strafing wildly back and forth. Vehicles panic and swerve, causing accidents all around. Rayne expertly navigates them, weaving around them while managing to evade the drone's assault.

So, yeah… there's that.

"How far is Holt's base of operations?" asks Rayne.

I glance back through the rear windshield, checking the position of the drone.

"About a mile north of the airport," I reply.

He brakes hard, fishtailing around the flaming metal husk of a car in front of us, which was struck by the drone moments ago.

I brace myself against the sudden movements. "Just put your foot down. We have to make it. That thing will pull away when we get close. It won't risk hitting the building Holt's in."

Rayne swerves left again, then back across two lanes to accelerate through a gap in the traffic up ahead.

"Adrian, if we stay on this road, that drone is gonna keep shooting. More people are gonna get hurt. Or worse."

I reach for one of my guns. "Don't you think I know that? But if we don't make it to Holt and stop that thing, thousands more will almost certainly die. Not to mention its impact on the world if the Vatican goes up like the Fourth of July."

He glances at me. "So, we have to choose between endangering the people here and protecting the people back there?"

"We do. Welcome to my life—it sucks."

"Hey, this is my life too."

"Yes, but you're following orders. The buck stops with me. The president will hold me accountable and no one else. I'm just banking on him forgiving a couple of hundred casualties to prevent a couple of thousand deaths."

"Man, I would hate to be you."

"I know I do. Why should you be any different? Now try to keep us steady."

"What for?"

"I'm going to shoot that piece of shit."

I twist in my seat and lean out the window. I hold onto the headrest for balance with my right hand as I aim with the Raptor in my left. If we're doing less than eighty, I'd be surprised. But the wind's pushing at me from behind, which might help the bullets. Plus, now that I'm actually staring out at it, this drone is... really fucking close!

I duck back inside just in time to avoid a fresh stream of gunfire from it.

"So, how did it go?" asks Rayne.

I roll my eyes. "Shut up and drive, will you? I got this."

The shooting stops. I lean back out to try again. This time, I'm able to unload the entire magazine at the drone. I think I saw a spark from impact once. I didn't make a dent. Honestly, I didn't really expect to. I was just hoping to get lucky and hit one of its missiles.

I move back inside and buzz the window up.

Rayne doesn't say anything. He doesn't need to.

"It's better than sitting here doing nothing while you drive," I say.

There's an exit coming up on the right with an image of the airport on it. He speeds across the lanes and takes it, braking to slide around the curve of the road that leads us off the freeway.

He's a damn good driver. I'll give him that.

The drone zooms past us, following the freeway. We watch as it circles right, coming around to line up behind us again. Luckily, the road ahead seems pretty clear, and Rayne puts his foot down accordingly.

I look over my shoulder, out the rear windshield. The drone is leveling off, having now taken position on our tail once again. It's not as close as it was before. It doesn't seem to be looking to get too close, either.

Why's it hanging back?

I look over at Rayne. He's not going any faster than he was before.

"What's it waiting for?" I ask.

Rayne checks his mirror. "I dunno. Maybe it's just lining up its kill shot?"

"A little pessimistic." I see the airport on our left, whizzing past us. "That's why."

"Public airspace..." says Rayne.

"Too risky to fly and engage so close to air traffic control, even for Holt." I look back. The drone peels away. "Yeah, it's gone. We're close to Holt's base now. Good work."

"We got a plan for when we get there?"

I shake my head. "I figure we just drive through the front door and shoot anyone we didn't come to rescue."

He glances at me. "Are all your plans that vague and violent?"

I shrug. "I just stick with what works."

"That shit works? Seriously?"

"I'm still here, aren't I? What do you think I've been doing for the last twenty years?"

He focuses on the road, which is following a gentle curve to the left. The airport's behind us now. Coming up, I can see the one road that's going to lead us right to Holt's front door.

I point to it. "There."

I check that both mags are full in my Raptors, then secure them at my back. Then I reach behind and take an assault rifle from one of the bags.

We turn and speed along the narrow road, which is little

more than a dirt track cutting through an empty field. Awaiting us at the end, having just appeared over the slight rise in the road, is a small industrial complex. It looks exactly like the satellite photos Schultz arranged for us. Two main buildings stand side by side, one bigger than the other. A tarmac runway is behind it, although I can't see it from here.

A chain link fence surrounds the buildings. A rolling gate topped with barbed wire blocks the entrance. Inside, I can see three vehicles parked haphazardly. They all look like black versions of the Range Rover we had.

I rest the assault rifle between the seats.

"That's yours," I say to Rayne. "For the welcoming committee."

"No sign of anyone yet," he muses.

"All those vehicles must've brought someone. Remember: always presume the worse."

"Yeah, yeah. I know—always be paranoid."

I draw one of my Raptors, ready. "Hey, it ain't paranoia if the bastards are really after you."

He nods toward the gate up ahead. "Do you want me to..."

I smile. "I really, really do."

Rayne hits the gas as we approach the entrance.

"Cup your balls, so they don't fall, folks!"

We burst through the gate, flatten it with the impact, then run over it almost immediately. There's a loud bang as the tires are shredded by the barbed wire. Rayne slides us to a stop in front of the door to the larger building.

I'm out and have my second Raptor drawn a second later. I move around our vehicle for cover. Rayne quickly joins me, rifle in hand.

"You ready?" I ask him.

He nods. His lips are pursed with determination. "Let's get our team back."

We stand from cover as men start to pile out of the building. Eight... nine... eleven... fifteen of them in total. They fan out as they clear the door, seeking cover behind vehicles and walls nearby. All are dressed in Tristar black.

How many of these clowns does Holt have? Jesus.

I look over at Rayne. I recognize his hard expression all too well. Narrowed, focused eyes. A snarl held back on his lips. It's the look of a man about to go to war with no way of knowing if this is his last sunrise.

"Hey." He looks at me. "Shoot to kill. No hesitation. This is us or them. You understand?"

He nods. "Way ahead of you, Boss."

Rayne starts firing, aiming at any movement on his side of the building's entrance.

I like him.

I bring both Raptors up and start shooting at my side. I clip three almost straight away.

Sorry... four.

No way Holt didn't know we were coming, but this will definitely let him know we've arrived.

Five.

We can't linger out here too long. It gives him—

Six.

—time to prepare. Time to hurt the team. Time to hurt Ruby.

That can't happen.

Shit!

I duck behind the hood as a burst of gunfire shatters the windshield from my left, almost taking my head off.

I look over at Rayne.

"Reloading!" he shouts.

I roll my eyes. "Thanks for the head's up. How many do you have left?"

"Bullets?"

"Bad guys."

"Oh. Three. You?"

"Two."

More *thunks!* in the aluminum chassis inches above my head.

I glare upward. "That's it..."

I pop up and split my aim, pointing the Raptors at ten and two. I fire two bullets in each direction.

Seven.

Eight.

I duck back down as Rayne stands. He fires three controlled bursts and remains standing.

"Got 'em," he announces. He looks over as I get to my feet. "How many did you take out?"

Without looking, I aim to my two o'clock and fire two more rounds. I hear the thud of a body behind one of the vehicles over there.

"Nine," I say.

"Six. Good work."

"We can compare body counts later, *Fabio*. Let's go."

We reload and head for the entrance. I take a look around as we cross the open space. No sign of life anywhere else out here. No sign of any security cameras. And most importantly, no sign of that goddamn drone.

Rayne takes point, walking in a slight crouch, rifle aimed straight and steady. He moves with precision, checking every angle as we proceed along a corridor. I've holstered one of my Raptors. The other, I'm holding low and ready, measuring each footstep as I follow.

The corridor divides the building down the middle, with

rooms branching off on either side. It kind of resembles a ribcage. Stained, broken tiles hang from the wall. There are a few crates stacked along the sides, which appear empty. Rooms on either side stand empty.

"Where is everyone?" whispers Rayne.

"Gotta be here somewhere," I mutter back.

As we near the opposite side, the corridor branches left, winding around a large room that occupies most of the width of the building. There's a set of double doors just to the right. We follow the corridor around to the left, which brings us into a small vestibule with another set of double doors leading into the same room.

We exchange a nod.

Holt and the team have to be inside.

I silently gesture for Rayne to head back around and cover the other doors. I'll take these. We'll breach at the same time and hit them from both sides.

I signal to him to go on three. He confirms and disappears around the corner. I wait a few moments, then let out a low whistle. He responds.

One.

Two.

Three!

I step back and kick the doors open. I move in with my gun raised. I hear the noise of Rayne's entrance over to my right.

I quickly take in the room and—

Oh, shit.

I hold my hands up. Rayne does the same.

Six more Tristar guards are facing us, automatic weapons aimed at both doors. Three men have me dead to rights. Same for Rayne.

The room is oblong, like a shoebox. Opposite us, built

into the bend of the corner, a large L-shaped console flashes and buzzes. Lights flicker. Screens are bright with information. Three men sit along it, their backs to us.

Over to the left, I see Jessie, Link, and Ruby. All have their wrists bound, hanging from meat hooks affixed to the ceiling. Their feet are barely touching the floor.

In the middle of it all, visible in the gap between the two groups of guards, is Holt. He's wearing a suit with no tie. The jacket's open. His white shirt has bloodstains on it that likely aren't his own. He's standing there, calm and calculated, smiling as he points a gun right at me.

"Adrian Hell," he says. "Right on time."

I sigh with frustration.

Damn it.

29

I glance over at the team, working my way along the line to look at each of them in turn. They've been beaten. My eyes linger on Ruby a second longer. She has blood and bruising on her face and arms. Her clothes are torn in places, revealing the skin beneath.

Someone's going to pay for that.

"Hey, honey," I call over. "Sorry I'm late. Be right with you. Ruby, Jessie... I'll get you down too, okay?"

Ruby manages a weak smile. Jessie doesn't say anything.

Link spits out some blood and sighs. "Jesus Christ..."

Holt's eyes narrow at me. "Do you think you're funny?"

I shrug. "Only when I'm awake."

"Are these really what you want your last words to be? You're going to die here, Adrian. I hope you know that."

"You first."

Holt smiles at me. It's a sickening, wide grin that displays every bad intention he's ever had in one expression. "Put your gun down. Both of you. Slowly."

I do. So does Rayne.

He waves his gun at me. "And the other one?"

I roll my eyes and retrieve the second Raptor from behind me. I place it next to its brother.

"There you go," he says, lowering his and pacing in front of me. "Your president is deluded if he thinks this pathetic collection of military rejects can stop me or what's coming. Blackstar? He would've had more luck if he'd just sent you."

I frown. "Wow. There's a lot to unpack there. First of all, he's your president too, dumbass."

Holt shakes his head. "I don't recognize the authority of an overweight hillbilly from a state that no longer exists. He was never elected."

I think for a moment. "Okay, that's a surprisingly fair point. But you think we're rejects?"

"Just them. I know you better than that. I've seen your file."

"Which file?"

"The one The Order kept on you. It's far more detailed than anything that's still hanging around in the Pentagon's basement."

"Ah, yes. The Order. I forgot you were a survivor of that. How's your boss? Oh, wait..."

His smile drops for a split-second, but he recovers without skipping a beat.

"You may have stopped Martinez three years ago, but you didn't destroy The Order. We simply disbanded and went our separate ways. Now I can continue his work. Continue our mission to bring order to the world."

I shake my head. "Except that wasn't your mission, was it? See, you people were brainwashed. Given a shit-ton of expensive Kool-Aid. The Order began centuries ago as a religious sect. Assassins who believed they were doing God's work. Like The Blues Brothers with sniper rifles. But they died out long ago. Their history was little more than a footnote in the Vatican archives until your boss found them and decided to resurrect the idea. I've spent the last six months training these *rejects* to understand and fight a new type of enemy at a new type of war. Well, all that started with The Order, who were nothing more than thugs and killers in Armani suits, using corporate espionage and media campaigns instead of sending troops into battle. Frighteningly effective but ultimately a lost cause."

"Such a shallow and ignorant assessment of our history," says Holt. "If you mattered to me at all, I would be offended."

I shrug. "Give me a minute. I'll offend you whether I matter or not. Now I'm curious—how did you know about Blackstar?"

Holt laughs. "You were right, Adrian. I'm offended you would feel the need to even ask that. I'm Horizon. We have resources that allow us access to all kinds of information. Do you honestly think I don't know every word spoken in the Oval Office?"

I fall silent. That's worrying. There's no reason for him to lie. It explains a lot, like how he's been able to move and conduct business almost unseen. He isn't psychic. He doesn't have next-level foresight. He just knew which direction people were looking in.

"Yes..." he says, staring at me. "The realization. The defeat. It's written all over your face, Adrian. Tell me, how did you think this would play out? Honestly. That you would waltz in here and arrest me? Charge me with war crimes?"

"Why not?" I look over at Ruby. "The beatings you guys took—were you hanging there when you took them?"

She nods. "Yeah."

I look back at Holt and tut loudly. "There's that pesky Geneva Convention that keeps getting in the way. If you went to The Hague, you would be locked away forever."

He holds his hands out to me, pressing them together at the wrist. "Then arrest me. You're a company man now, Adrian. Do your job."

I shake my head. "I didn't come here to arrest you."

He grins. "Well, what else are you gonna do? Look around, assassin. I have control of the drone, I have your team captive, and I have you at gunpoint, dead to rights. I'd say you've lost, but doing so would suggest that this was a game you ever stood a chance of winning in the first place."

I need to stall him, so I can think of something. Only thing I hate worse than an arrogant bad guy is an arrogant bad guy who makes a good point.

I crack my neck. "So, let me guess... you're gonna make us all watch you level the Vatican with your new toy before shooting us and disappearing?"

He tilts his head, narrowing his eyes. He's still smiling, but I think it's more bemusement and confusion now.

"What?" I shrug. "You thought your grand plan was impossible to figure out?"

He shakes his head. "Not really. I'm just surprised *you* were smart enough to do it."

I nod toward Rayne. "To be fair, he figured it out. I just shot everybody."

Rayne frowns. "Hey, you didn't shoot *everybody*. I took out six back there. You only got three more than me."

"And what about the six at the intersection? And Falikov?"

"Oh, yeah..."

I turn to Holt. "You should see your boy Falikov now. I tenderized his head with a car door so badly, even dental records wouldn't identify him."

Holt shrugs. "I know. My drone has cameras. I wasn't impressed. All I saw was a man who wasn't in control. A man who is reckless and, ultimately, predictable. You've done everything I expected you to. Even when you and your girlfriend were running around Paris. You're exactly like my old colleagues said you were."

"Considering I'm so reckless and predictable, I still managed to stop you guys three years ago. I also managed to kill quite a few of you, including one of your Horizon buddies. Number seven. What number were you?"

"Four."

"Right. Well, it'll be nice to add another to my collection. Maybe I'll get around to completing the whole set one day."

"Unlikely. Now, if you'll excuse me, I have a world to change."

He turns his back to me and walks over to the three men at the console. I look at the men in front of me, holding their guns at me with unwavering precision. Same with the ones guarding Rayne. I flick my gaze behind him, to the team. All three of them are staring at me with expressions of hope and concern.

Truth is, my plan went to shit the moment we kicked the doors in. I know what we need to do. I'm just not sure how we're going to do it.

Unless...

It'll get you killed.

Will it?

Almost certainly.

Almost is good. Almost means there's a chance it won't.

A really small chance.

But a chance, nevertheless.

You're insane.

Probably.

Do it!

See? Satan's on board.

He's also insane.

Oh, for sure. But that's why he's the fun one.

Silence.

My devils have spoken. If today's the day when my book is written, at least I'll have a big finale.

"Hey, Adam," I call over. He turns to me. "Remember the intersection?"

He nods. "Yeah."

"You wanna try it?"

He furrows his brow for a moment, then smiles.

We move in unison. No warning. No countdown. No wind up.

I lunge forward, thrusting my forehead into the nose of the guy standing directly in front of me. I quickly turn and kick the guy to his left in the balls, as hard as I can. The impact with his pelvic bone stings the top of my foot through my boot. I shuffle around him, putting his body between me and the third guy, on the right. I reach around and grab this guy's hand, controlling it to aim his weapon in front of him, and pull the trigger. A short burst rips into the torso of the third guy. I then deliver a swift elbow to this guy's temple, dropping him like a stone.

I slide into a crouch and scoop up my Raptors. I put two bullets in the guy I headbutted, then one for luck in each of the other two.

By the time Holt's reacted and turned around, I have both guns aiming at him. Over to the right, Rayne is holding one of the assault rifles, having dispatched the three Tristar operatives guarding him. He's also aiming at Holt.

"Drop it," I shout over. "Now."

Holt alternates his aim between me and Rayne. I don't think he's properly panicking yet, but he's certainly more concerned than he was a moment ago. Reluctantly, he tosses his gun away.

"Didn't see that coming, did you?" I glance at Rayne. "Go and free the team. I've got this guy."

He dashes across the room without a word and begins unhooking them.

"You're just like the other Horizon was," I say to Holt. "Blinded by your own arrogance. Now call off your drone."

"No." He looks back at the three men working the console. "You know what to do."

Before I can react, there's a flurry of activity. Hands move with speed and precision over the various keyboards.

"Hey!" I shout over. "Step away from there right now!"

But I'm too late. All the screens flash red. Holt starts laughing.

"You were saying?" he says.

I move toward him and place a gun barrel against the side of his head. "What did you just do?"

"The drone is locked onto its target. I'd say you have about twenty minutes."

"Then stop it."

An evil grin creeps across his face. "I can't."

"Bullshit. Stop it right now."

He shrugs. "It can't be stopped. And even if it could be, I wouldn't."

The team appear around me. They look broken and tired, but they're alert and focused. There's plenty of time to recover once this is over.

"What's he done?" asks Ruby.

"He's going to use the drone to destroy the Vatican."

"Are you fucking serious?" says Link. "Why?"

I stare into Holt's eyes. "Because he's the bargain basement version of his old employer. He thinks blowing up the religious center of the new world will plunge it back into chaos. Kickstart a whole new wave of conflict across the globe."

He nods. "And from that chaos, a new order will rise, Adrian. A new Order that will finally fulfill the vision Martinez had for us all. And there's *nothing* you can do to stop it."

I jab the butt of the gun into his nose, then turn to Rayne. "Watch that piece of shit."

The team step away, giving me space. I move toward the console and aim both guns at the three men sitting behind it.

"On your feet, all of you."

They stand, holding their hands up slightly without prompting. They don't look like soldiers or mercenaries. They're technicians.

"Which one of you pilots that thing?" I ask them.

The two on either side glance at the one in the middle.

I nod. "Okay."

I adjust my aim, so the Raptors line up with the faces of the men standing on either side of the recently outed pilot.

Then I pull the triggers.

Both men fall hard and fast to the floor, showering the pilot with clouds of blood as they go down.

He twitches and screams from the shock. I aim both barrels at him.

"Take the drone off whatever autopilot setting you just activated and divert it away from the city. Do it now."

He's shaking. The color drains from his face. His pale skin shines against the contrast of blood covering it.

"I... I can't," he says. "It l-locks the system once activated. T-there's no stopping it."

"He's telling the truth," says Holt behind me. "It's the ultimate failsafe."

I turn to see him smiling at me over Rayne's shoulder.

"Always planning ahead," he says.

His hand disappears inside his pocket. He pulls out a trigger and presses it, holding the button down.

"Hey, drop it!" yells Rayne. But he's too late.

The five of us turn to face Holt, forming a semicircle in front of him, backing him into a corner. He waves the trigger at us frantically to keep us at bay.

"This is a dead man switch," he says. "If I let go, we all die."

I gesture to the team to hang back and give him space.

"You're not going to do that," I say to him.

"You think?" he replies, waving it at me again.

"You've been planning this for months. All the work you've put in... no way you don't want to be around to see it play out."

He shrugs. "I'd prefer not to die, of course, but I'm prepared to. Are you?"

He's bluffing. I'm sure of it. Almost sure of it.

Pretty sure of it.

I think he's bluffing.

Is he?

Shit.

I look around the control room, scanning the surfaces of desks for something... anything that might spark some inspiration.

Bingo!

"Keep your gun on him," I say to Rayne.

I walk between Ruby and Jessie, toward a table near the far wall, where the team were hanging.

There's a roll of duct tape.

I holster one of my Raptors and grab it, then walk back. I hand the gun to Ruby, who immediately aims it at Holt. I then grab the pilot and shove him over to where Holt's standing.

"Put your hand over his," I say to him.

"Get away from me!" yells Holt.

I point to him. "You—shut the fuck up. I think you're full of shit. I believe that's a dead man switch. I believe it's linked to a boatload of explosives. I don't believe you're willing to die for your cause. And I'm going to prove it."

Knowing Rayne and Ruby have him covered, I grab the pilot's hand and place it around the trigger, clamping Holt's hand in place. I then wrap them both in duct tape, binding them together.

"What are you doing?" screams Holt.

"Proving a point," I reply. "If you were prepared to blow us all sky high, you wouldn't have let me do that. Now be quiet."

I rush over to the console and stand behind a chair, holding the back of it. "Jessie, you're up. Get over here and stop this thing."

She sits down in front of me and gets to work. Link moves beside her.

She presses something that changes the display on one of the monitors to a countdown. It says twenty minutes.

"Can you stop it?" I ask her.

She shakes her head as she desperately navigates the systems. "I don't think so. I'm locked out, and there's not enough time to hack something this sophisticated."

"Can we call somebody?" asks Link. "Get an air strike to shoot it down?"

Jessie shakes her head. "That wouldn't work. No radar can detect this thing. There's not enough time for them to scramble jets and eyeball it."

"Not enough time for them..." I say.

Jessie looks up at me. "What do you mean?"

"We have your pet drone in the car outside in one of our goodie bags. Can you eyeball it? Use your toy to kamikaze that thing?"

She sighs heavily. "I mean... maybe? I don't know."

"Good enough for me." I move to Ruby's side and address the team. "You three, take one of the cars outside. Get Jessie line of sight on that thing, so she can blow the fuck out of it."

Jessie and Link run for the door. Rayne follows them but pauses beside me.

"You good?" he asks.

I nod. "We're right behind you. Now go."

He runs after the others, leaving Ruby and I alone. I take out my other Raptor and place it against Holt's temple.

"You and I have some things to discuss," I say.

He laughs nervously. "Like what?"

"Like the fact that you beat my girlfriend while she was strung up and defenseless. Like the fact that you used your drone to destroy half of Rome in an effort to kill me. Oh, speaking of which..." I turn and aim at the pilot. "Were you controlling that thing the whole time?"

After a moment of hesitation, he nods.

I pull the trigger. A crimson mist lingers and fades where his head used to be. He slumps to the floor, dragging Holt down with him, still taped together.

I crouch beside Holt, who has no choice but to huddle over his deceased pilot.

"I'm one of the good guys now," I say. "I answer to the president, which means there are certain things I have to do by the book."

Fear has set in on his face. He's no longer calm and calculated. He's staring up at me with eyes that now see what his colleague saw three years ago—the face of a man who doesn't deserve to be underestimated as often as he is.

"So, you're going to arrest me?" he asks.

"No."

"You're going to kill me?"

I pause. "No."

"Then what happens now?"

I stand, holster my gun, and take Ruby's hand. "Now we're gonna go try to save innocent people from being killed. Because that's what matters."

"What about me? You can't just leave me here!"

I shrug. "You have a free hand. Use it."

Ruby steps in front of me, raises her Raptor, and puts a bullet in Holt's left hand. He screams in pain, unable to comfort the wound. He can only stare at the space where three of his fingers used to be.

"Huh. Maybe not." I look at Ruby. "You good, baby?"

She nods and smiles. "I am."

"See you around, Holt."

We turn and run from the room, along the corridor, and out into the open. We squint as our eyes adjust to the influx of daylight. I look around. The vehicle Rayne and I arrived in is gone. One of our weapons bags is resting on the ground where it was parked.

"Come on," I say to Ruby.

I scoop up the bag and head toward one of the cars the

Tristar guards used as cover. I climb in behind the wheel and toss the bag on the back seat. Ruby slides in next to me. I gun the engine, perform a quick J-turn, then speed away from the building, along the road that brought me here.

Ruby places a hand on my arm. "Are you okay?"

A thunderous explosion erupts behind us. I watch in the rearview as both buildings disappear in a mushroom cloud of flames.

I smile. "I am now. What about you?"

"I'll be fine. What's the plan? Where are we going?"

"We need to get to the Vatican. Start evacuating people from the streets."

"Don't you think Jessie and the others will be able to stop the drone?"

"I think Jessie wasn't sure, and she's the expert. We gotta do something."

I slide around a bend and merge onto the freeway. I reckon we're ten minutes out. This will be close.

30

We both scan the skies as I drive, looking for any sign of the drone. I'm navigating the still-chaotic roads from short-term memory. I feel calm and almost Zen-like after putting an end to Holt. After everything he put me and my team through, he was ultimately just like everyone else. He was just a guy. Nothing special. He died easily and with little fanfare, and that was all he deserved.

Now we just have to stop his legacy from becoming part of history in the way he couldn't.

"You look like shit," says Ruby.

I glance over to see her staring at me.

I frown. "Speak for yourself, Princess."

"Hey, I was strung up like cattle in a slaughterhouse and beaten for sixteen hours. What's your excuse?"

I gesture to the world around us. Pillars of smoke rise from small craters in the roads. Fire dances from the husks of abandoned cars and buildings too tall to avoid the drone's indiscriminate assault.

"I've been busy tearing this city apart, trying to find you," I say.

She smiles. "I know, and that's really sweet. But that's not what I meant, and I think you know that. Of course, you can bring the fight when you flick your Satan switch. You're tired, but you're still you. But something's happened to you. I can see it in your eyes."

I'm suddenly self-conscious.

"What about my eyes?"

She sighs. "Those ice-cold baby blues aren't just focused on where we're going or what we're doing. I see the struggle to hide something. Some... pain. I know it ain't just about me being taken, so what happened?"

She places a hand on my leg. I see her arm trembling, still suffering the effects of being held the way she was for so long.

I say nothing. I forget sometimes how well she knows me.

"It's being in Rome again, isn't it?" she says.

See?

I nod. "Not just being here. That drone, it was chasing Rayne and me all over the city. Blew up our car. We scrambled and ran. We ended up... we ended up outside the café where... the street corner we were standing on when..."

I suck in a deep breath through pursed lips, pushing back on the emotion trying to escape.

I hear Ruby quietly gasp. She puts a hand to her mouth. I glance over and see a tear on her face.

"Oh my God..." she whispers. "Adrian, I—I'm so sorry."

I shake my head, picturing the carnage strewn across that intersection. "Don't be. I handled it."

"Was that when you caught up with Falikov?"

I nod. "Yeah."

"Well... beats therapy, I guess."

I speed along Piazza Pia, passing under some arches. I swerve around a car in front that was moving too slow, then slam the brakes on and slide around the sharp right turn onto Via della Conciliazione, between the two pillars guarding the entrance. The car spins to a stop, and we leap out. Ahead of us, across the intersection and along the plaza, stands St. Peter's Basilica.

Last time I saw this place in person was through a scope.

We spin in slow, concentric circles, taking in the surroundings. It's still early, but the day has begun. There are a lot of people around, and it's only going to get busier.

Then I see it. I think Ruby did a second before me. It's in the distance and gaining fast, screaming over the Tiber toward us.

Holt's drone.

Locked onto its course by terminal autopilot.

There's nothing to plan. Nothing to discuss. I think some people around us have seen it. Many haven't. Why would they? It's not something they would be looking for.

"Everybody move!" I yell.

"You need to run, now!" adds Ruby.

We start waving our hands back toward the Piazza Pia, trying to usher people as if we're directing aircraft to land. They're staring at us. A couple are even filming on us on their phones.

Christ.

"I know you all know English," I shout. "Put your phones down and fucking run!"

I take out my Raptor and fire it into the air.

Shouting and screaming and panic ensues.

"That worked," says Ruby.

I continue shouting. "Go, now! *Correre! Correre!*"

I think that means run. I hope it does. If I've just started yelling *cheese* or something, that isn't going to help.

We set off running toward the entrance to the Vatican, continuing our campaign, shouting and gesturing for people to run away. I have no idea what kind of payload that thing is carrying. If it's going to nosedive into St. Peter's Square, it could flatten everything within a square mile for all I know. But we have to do something.

We have to try.

We reach the gates of the Vatican. I turn around and fire more bullets into the air, adding more incentive to the people who are still hesitating nearby.

Side by side, Ruby and I stare up at the drone, watching it get closer. It's getting lower too. I don't know if we've done enough. I don't know if—

"Look!" shouts Ruby, pointing to the sky.

A small black object has appeared to the right, moving fast.

"Is that Jessie's drone?" I ask.

"It has to be."

A moment later, the object collides with the drone, detonating on impact. A brilliant white flash fills the sky for a spilt-second, followed almost immediately by the thunderclap of the explosion. A visible shockwave bursts outward, almost knocking everyone—including us—off their feet.

We stagger backward, staring in disbelief.

They did it.

Ruby and I turn to each other.

"They did it!" she shouts. "Holy shit, they did it!"

Her brief period of celebration fades when she sees the look on my face.

"What is it?" she asks. "What's wrong?"

I set off running. She follows, calling after me.

"Adrian, what is it?"

I point to the sky as I look back at her. "The debris. It's falling, and we've just told people to run toward where it's all gonna land!"

"Oh, shit!"

I'm sprinting as fast as my body will allow. The air burns in my lungs. My chest is ravaged by a thousand knives from each breath.

"Get inside!" I shout, gesturing to the rows of stores along each side of the plaza. "Take cover!"

The first chunks of debris begin to hit. Large plumes of smoke and dust spew up from the points of impact. Craters appear in the streets. Bricks fall from the sky as buildings are pummeled. Cars driving across Piazza Pia up ahead swerve to avoid the falling remnants of the drone. Some manage to. Some aren't so fortunate.

People are screaming and diving for cover. Some are helping others. Some are just running. Some lie injured on the ground. Some lie dead.

Over to my right, I see a mother and a little girl standing still in fear. A large shadow expands around them. I don't look up. I don't hesitate. I divert toward them, opening my arms. I dive and grab them both, turning to pull them on top of me as I land hard on my back.

As the air is driven from my lungs, the deafening crash of impact fills the world around us. A large sheet of twisted and torn metal lands flat on the street, only a couple of feet away from us, exactly where the mother and child were standing.

I relinquish my grip on them both, letting them roll

away to the sides. Without pausing for breath, they grab each other's hand and run away, screaming.

I take a valuable second to lie here and breathe.

Man, that hurt.

As I get to my feet, Ruby appears next to me.

"Come on," she says. "We've done all we can. We have to get clear."

We stumble and stagger away, staying close to the buildings along the right side as we join the thinning crowd of people making a run for it. We head right along Piazza Pia. Behind us, the violent rain of debris slows and stops. The silence that follows is eerily total.

We stop on the sidewalk to catch our breath. People are still running past us, but a few have lingered, perhaps realizing the worst is over.

Tires screech behind us. We both turn to see the borrowed Tristar vehicle sliding to a stop, having come the wrong way along the one-way street. Doors open in unison, and our team step out and run toward us, looking strained.

"Is everyone okay?" asks Rayne as they approach us.

I shrug. "There are a few casualties and some property damage, but we're mostly fine."

Jessie steps past me, a shaking hand covering her mouth. "Oh my God... what have I done?"

Ruby moves to her side and puts an arm around her shoulder. "You, madam, just saved thousands of lives. What you did was incredible."

Jessie turns to her. "But at what cost? Look at this place. The fallout. I... I didn't think. I didn't even—"

"Hey, Jessie, look at me," I say. She turns. "You did your job. You did something few people could've done. Neither you nor I were sure it was even *possible*. But you did it, and like Ruby said, you saved thousands of lives. If that drone had done what Holt intended for it to do, you would be standing in a mile-wide crater right now, looking for my body. And tomorrow... the world would've gone to war as it tried to process the death of religion. Ruby and I sent hundreds of people running into the path of the falling debris without realizing it. All those people who are hurt or worse... we couldn't have accounted for that. We had a job to do, and we did it. All of us."

She nods, sniffing back understandable emotion.

Link and Rayne move to my side.

"You should've seen her," says Rayne. "Link held her legs while she leaned out the window, piloting that little drone of hers by line of sight while I was doing almost ninety."

I smile and look at Jessie. "And that's extra impressive, given I've seen this guy's driving."

She rolls her eyes and smiles. The smile turns into laughter. Ruby joins her. So does Link. Eventually, so does Rayne.

I smile and watch as my team celebrate. The relief on their faces is clear to see. They've impressed me every step of the way. At no point did I ever doubt my decision to pick these three. Even Link, who's a miserable bastard and probably hates me. He's the backbone of the group. The devil's advocate. The voice of reason. A necessity for a team that's run by me.

Jessie clearly has no issue working under extreme stress. I think she and Ruby will grow closer. The badass big sisters to their three reprobate little brothers.

And then there's Rayne. I got to work closely with him. He's a leader. He's talented and fearless. He's the future.

Ruby catches my eye and smiles. Her resilience never ceases to amaze me. It was hard to think of her as just a member of the team this whole time. She's obviously more than that. Way more than that. But I knew I couldn't let my emotions affect my decision-making. There was too much at stake.

"Come on," I say to them all. "We should get out of here. I'll call Schultz—get him to put in a call to the Italian government and smooth things over."

The five of us walk away, heading over the road and along a walkway that leads down the side of the river.

"This is actually a nice city," says Link. "You know, when it's not being blown up."

"Yeah... it's something, all right," I reply absently.

I feel Ruby's hand slide into mine. I turn to her and she smiles. It's the kind of smile that feels like home. It makes me certain that everything will be okay. After the last few days, it's just what I needed to see.

Jessie points across the river. "What's the building over there?"

I look over and smile. "That... that's Castel Sant'Angelo. Looks like it survived unscathed."

"Yeah, it looks nice."

I nod. "It is. Great view of St. Peter's Square from the roof."

31

I knock on the door of the suite and wait. There are sounds of movement from within. A moment later, it opens. Link is standing in front of me, shirtless, wearing shorts and running shoes. His impressive torso is shimmering with sweat.

"Put some clothes on, would you? I've just eaten," I say, smiling.

He laughs and holds out his fist, which I bump courteously as I walk past him.

I'm carrying four coffees in a cardboard tray, with a fifth balanced on top, which I set down on the kitchen counter.

"Come and get them," I call out.

Rayne and Jessie appear like dogs who sense their owner is cutting steak. He's dressed for the beach, in a fitted Tee with shorts and flip-flops. Jessie is wearing a thin, oversized top that's hanging off one shoulder. It's long enough to cover whatever shorts she's wearing.

Finally, Ruby appears. She came straight here while I diverted for coffee. She's wearing a red crop top that hangs off both shoulders. Her bare midriff is toned and tanned. Her white shorts match her sandals.

She's a vision.

As everyone gathers around the counter, I look at each of them in turn. They seem happy and relaxed. They look rested, which I'm glad of. They needed it.

I debriefed Schultz shortly after we left Rome. I told him everything that happened. I left nothing out. It was a courtesy. He knows who I am and what I do. It's why he hired me to train this lot. But I also wanted to show that I wouldn't hide anything from him, in the hope that he would continue to reciprocate. So far, there's been no cloak and dagger bullshit from him, and I'm grateful for that.

He explained to me everything he would do to smooth things over with the Italian government, then started to tell me about the next mission he had for us.

I cut him off pretty quick.

I said the team needed a break. They needed some furlough to recover from what was a true shit-show of a mission for all concerned. He was reluctant at first, but I politely explained that I wasn't asking, which seemed to solve that little issue.

The twenty-four hours after Rome were rough on everyone. Ruby explained to me everything she, Jessie, and Link had endured while in Holt's custody. They were all beaten pretty bad. Physically, they recovered and moved on. Mentally... well, that took a little longer.

Ruby is tough. It wasn't her first rodeo, and she dealt with it. But it's still an ordeal no one can prepare for. She likened it to what she assumed I went through with Miley, back in Tokyo. She said she didn't know how I could do everything I've done after going through what I did.

Link actually suffered the least. Holt was a real piece of shit. He saw how physically strong Link was. How much he could likely endure. So, he made him watch as his men beat on Ruby and Jessie. He found that harder to deal with than if he had been beaten himself. He felt guilty, and even being consoled by Ruby did little to alleviate that.

But it was Jessie who struggled the most. Her reaction to it was probably the most... human. She has a brilliant mind and is one hell of a pilot. But she saw little combat up close in her time with the Air Force. Her body and her life have never been on the line. The torture, the pain, the helplessness... it broke her. Coupled with the guilt she felt over the damage she caused by taking out Holt's drone with her own, she was a wreck for few days. The team rallied around her and helped her realize the struggle is natural. That it wasn't a sign of weakness. She struggled, but she's getting there.

So, on my own dime, I put the three of them up in the executive suite of a hotel in Las Vegas for two weeks. I told them to enjoy themselves and take a well-earned vacation.

This place is nice too. Top floor. Large windows offer a view of the city. Uninterrupted sunlight streams through them. It's a massive room, decorated with marble and mahogany. Three large sofas. Two bathrooms. Four bedrooms. A kitchen. A bar.

No wonder it's costing me seven grand a night. Damn.

Naturally, Ruby didn't want to be left out, so she and I are in another resort a little further along the strip. We've enjoyed our time together, and we've given the team some space to unwind.

"So, how are you guys enjoying your break?" I ask.

"Have you ever been to Nevada at this time of year?" asks

Rayne. "The suite is beautiful, but it's hotter than hell out there."

I smile. "Last time I was this far west was about eight years ago. It was August and much hotter."

"Where did you stay?"

"About eighty miles north of here."

"Heaven's Valley?"

I nod.

He smirks. "Man, that place is crazy. Seen its fair share of shit too. Remember that big explosion? When was that?"

I grin. "About eight years ago."

He laughs, but it quickly fades when he sees my expression.

"Wait, was that... was that you?" he asks.

I just smile.

He shakes his head. "Holy shit..."

"What have you guys been up to?" Jessie asks me.

I nod toward Ruby. "She's been enjoying the pool at the hotel."

"What about you?"

"I've been—"

"He's been restless," says Ruby. "And annoying as hell."

I shrug. "I don't like doing nothing."

"Speaking of doing nothing," says Link. "What brings you here now? This just a courtesy call, or is the vacation over?"

"I'm not sure yet. I had a message from the president last night to say I should expect a call today. Didn't say from who, but I have a hunch. Thought it best I take it with all of you here, just in case, so I diverted my cell to the phone in your suite."

Jessie leans back against the counter and sips her coffee. I notice Ruby has moved to her side. Those two have really bonded since Blackstar began and even more so since Rome. It's done them both some good, I think. Ruby doesn't really have girlfriends, and I know she'd love to hang out with someone who isn't me for a change. And Jessie has always been straight-laced and professional, so she's needed someone like Ruby to loosen her up a bit.

"Must be weird having the president of the United States send you texts," she says to me.

I take a sip of my own drink. "The novelty wears off quicker than you'd think."

Idle small talk and banter take over, which I'm happy to observe. Ruby catches me looking at the group like a proud father and pulls a face at me. I roll my eyes and smile at her. Truth be told, I am proud of them. They're a hell of a team, and I reckon we're ready for whatever—

The phone in the suite starts ringing.

Speaking of which...

The conversation dies down. I wander over to the phone, which is sitting on the desk in the opposite corner. I perch on the end as I answer.

"It's me," says a voice I recognize immediately. "I need to call in one of those favors you owe me."

Moses Buchanan.

I smile. "I was wondering when you were gonna call. What do you need?"

"Can't a guy just check in on an old friend?"

"I guess. Is that what we are now? Old friends?"

"I sure as hell hope so, Adrian."

"Josh trusted you, so I will until I'm given a reason not to. How's life treating you?"

"Like a baby treats a diaper. You? I'm hearing good things about the new team."

"We're all doing okay. Rough time of it in Rome a week

or so back, but we got the job done."

"I understand you had a run-in with some folks from Tristar."

I nod. "We did. Our target had hired them for protection. Not that it did the piece of shit much good in the end. Is this where you tell me my thing had something to do with that clusterfuck in New York a couple of weeks back?"

"Thankfully, no. We're pretty sure those two events are unrelated. Sadly, Tristar's involvement in both of them is no coincidence. Since the somewhat public closing of their head office in New York, their CEO has disappeared. That's left a lot of mercenaries with questionable ethics to their own devices."

"You're worried they're going rogue?"

"I think the job some of them took for your guy, Holt, was simply a minority trying to make some legitimate money. But more and more of these minority groups have been popping up..."

"And you think there's someone else pulling the strings now?"

"Honestly? No. I think their CEO is pulling the strings as he always has. We just don't know where he is."

"So, you want my team to find him?"

"No. I've got somebody else working on that. I need your team to find the assassin who works for him."

I sigh. "I just got done doing that. I'm happy to send a couple of the guys over to help, but this isn't gonna need the whole—"

"It is. Adrian, this woman is dangerous. She took out Julie and Ray on her own. Another asset I'm trying to recruit has also had a run-in with her. More than once. He's a capable man, Adrian, and he barely survived the encounters."

I raise my eyebrows. Buchanan sounds almost afraid of this woman.

"She sounds like a real piece of work," I say.

"She is. She fights with an almost uncontrollable violence. Like nothing we've come up against before."

"I see. So, she's the kind of enemy my team were brought together to fight?"

"I believe she is. How quickly can you and your team get to California?"

I pause. "Give me three days."

"Seriously? You're in Vegas. That's, like, six hours away."

"I know. But my team are on vacation for another two days, and I'll need to see someone before I start working with you. So, give me three days."

There's a moment's silence, then a heavy sigh.

"Fine. I'll see you in three days. Thanks, Adrian."

"No problem." I go to hang up, then think of something I should probably ask. "Hey, does Jericho know you've invited me to the party?"

Buchanan chuckles. "I told him before placing the call."

"How did he take it?"

"Oh, he'll come around, I'm sure."

"Right." I smile. "Take it easy, Moses."

I hang up and look over at the team, who are all staring at me with curiosity.

"Well?" asks Link.

I shrug. "You have two days of vacation left. Then it's time to go to work."

"What's the mission?" asks Rayne.

I stand and crack my neck, releasing some of the tension. I look at each of them in turn and smile.

"The mission is a favor for GlobaTech," I say. "They want us to go catch an assassin."

THE END

EPILOGUE

I stride across the floor of the casino. My Raptors hang in their shoulder holsters beneath my brown leather jacket and bounce against my ribs with each step. I ignore the looks from people as I walk by. The place is busy and alive, but it's as if I'm dragging a wall of silence behind me, muting the world as I pass it.

I head to the VIP area at the back. I breeze past the security guards standing there, who simply stepped aside and removed the velvet rope blocking my path. I climb the few steps and head around the corner, stopping in front of a booth shielded by frosted glass.

Bathed in neon and surrounded by women, Remy Fortin stares up at me blankly. I stand and smile. Waiting.

He quickly recovers from the shock of seeing me and gestures to the chair opposite him.

"*Monsieur* Adrian, a pleasure as always," he says. "Please, join us. We have just ordered some champagne."

I shake my head. "I'm good, thanks. This is just a quick visit."

He nods. "What can I do for you?"

"I'm gonna need you to call off the dogs," I say, holding his gaze.

He laughs nervously. "*Monsieur* Adrian, I... I do not know what you mean. Sure, of course, I heard some of our brothers and sisters had... how you say... *capitalized* on an opportunity the last time you graced this city with your presence, but that was not me. That was not—"

I hold up a hand, cutting him off. I then reach inside my jacket and retrieve one of my guns, which I aim squarely at Fortin's head. The women shriek and tense.

"Nothing happens in Paris in our world that you don't know about or authorize," I say matter-of-factly. "You're also the first one to talk about honor and tradition and reputation. How we don't go after our own."

He shuffles in his seat. More nervous chuckling. "*Monsieur* Adrian, all due respect, but... you are not one of us anymore. You are retired. You know the target you have on your back now. This I cannot control. You know this."

I shake my head. "What I know, Remy, is that I was in Paris and found it difficult to do what I needed to with swarms of assassins trying to kill me at every turn. That needs to stop. I've got shit to do, and I don't need to be looking over my shoulder the entire time I'm trying to do it. Am I clear?"

Fortin nods hurriedly. "Of course, but as I say, I cannot control what our people do in their spare time."

"Right. Well, maybe you should remind people of that honor and tradition you're so fond of."

"But that only applies to..." His eyes go wide. Then he smiles with a mixture of nerves and excitement. "*Monsieur* Adrian, are you saying you are coming out of retirement?"

I hold his gaze and keep my gun aimed at his head, unwavering. I say nothing. I let the moments pass, embracing the uneasy silence. Then I slowly put my gun away. I smile. Then I turn and walk away.

"*Monsieur*," he calls out. "Are you saying..."

I stop and adjust the collar of my jacket. I don't look back at him.

"Yeah, Remy." I smile to myself. "I'm back."

A MESSAGE

Dear Reader,

Thank you for purchasing my book. If you enjoyed reading it, it would mean a lot to me if you could spare thirty seconds to leave an honest review. For independent authors like me, one review makes a world of difference!

If you want to get in touch, please visit my website, where you can contact me directly, either via e-mail or social media.

Until next time...

James P. Sumner

CLAIM YOUR FREE GIFT!

By subscribing to James P. Sumner's mailing list, you can get your hands on a free and exclusive reading companion, not available anywhere else.

It contains an extended preview of Book 1 in each thriller series from the author, as well as character bios, and official reading orders that will enhance your overall experience.

If you wish to claim your free gift, just visit the website below:

linktr.ee/jamespsumner

You will receive infrequent, spam-free emails from the author, containing exclusive news about his books. You can unsubscribe at any time.

ACKNOWLEDGMENTS

And so, we reach the end of my twentieth book in eight years. This has been a real landmark for me, and something I'm incredibly proud to have reached.

This book went from a blank page to a full novel in a little over six weeks, which is a personal best in terms of writing.

I want to take a moment to thank my incredible team for all their hard work in getting this book ready for the world. There's a reason I offer their services to other authors!

As always, my editor and significant other, Coral, has done an incredible job of polishing and fine-tuning the vision I had for this story. She's on the same wavelength as me in so many ways, which makes working together so much more rewarding.

I also want to thank Daniel, my designer, who worked really hard to bring the new branding for my Adrian Hell series to life. The work he's done is first class, and the impact this has had on the series as a whole is already evident.

Finally, I want to thank my readers. I started this journey back in 2013, and many of you have been with me since then. Your continued support makes this the most rewarding job in the world, and I wouldn't change it for anything.

Here's to another twenty books!

Made in the USA
Columbia, SC
15 August 2023

21693020R00188